*The Parody Murder Case*

# THE PARODY MURDER CASE

Cornelia Bonsack

**VANTAGE PRESS**
New York / Atlanta
Los Angeles / Chicago

This book is a work of fiction. Any resemblance to any person, living or dead, is purely coincidental.

FIRST EDITION

All rights reserved, including the right of reproduction in whole or in part in any form.

Copyright © 1987 by Cornelia Bonsack

Published by Vantage Press, Inc.
516 West 34th Street, New York, New York 10001

Manufactured in the United States of America
ISBN: 0-533-07279-4

Library of Congress Catalog Card No.: 86-90352

To my brother, John Heisler

# Contents

1. Beaulinia, Gem of the Ocean.................. 1
2. Life in Beaulinia, Death in Keene Valley........ 10
3. Family Reunion............................. 17
4. The Parody Inquest......................... 28
5. A Blessing in Disguise....................... 38
6. A Black Eye and a Blue Brooch............... 43
7. The Unhinging of Horace.................... 51
8. Unexpected Departures and Arrivals........... 58
9. Upsets and Questions........................ 68
10. Two Funerals............................... 75
11. Fran Amber Arrives.......................... 81
12. Two in a Row, One to Go..................... 90
13. A Chase and Photo Finish.................... 97
14. Grave Situations............................ 105
15. The Root of All Pain........................ 112
16. The Muddler's Theory....................... 123
17. Overdose .................................. 131
18. Departmental Doings........................ 142
19. Back to Square One......................... 148
20. Bohner Comings and Goings.................. 152
21. Beaulinian Idyll............................. 158
22. The Flight of the Humble Bs.................. 165
23. Flag Day at the Embassy..................... 172
24. A Benign Caper in a Pickle................... 186
25. "Libation Day"............................. 193
26. Just Blew In................................ 197
27. The Cope and Dope Specialists............... 203
28. Awareness and a Warehouse.................. 208
29. Up a Tree.................................. 218
30. Going to the Dogs.......................... 224
31. Breeding, Instinct, and Training.............. 230
32. Torpedoed ................................. 233

*The Parody Murder Case*

## Chapter 1

## Beaulinia, Gem of the Ocean

The American ambassador sat waiting in his limousine for the arrival of the plane from Miami, thinking grimly, *It's ironic; my first ambassadorship and it has to be in this wretched, out-of-the-way island, with its wretched heat, wretched sunshine, wretched language—Creole—that's not even a language, that's a dish; and wretched bananas, repugnant fruit.*

This was Dr. Eric Bohner, a distinguished-looking, soft-spoken man, who had spent almost thirty years in the Foreign Service. Tall, still slim, with graying hair and moustache, he wore old-fashioned gold-rimmed spectacles, which lent a scholarly air to his appearance. Through the years while serving as a third or second secretary, he had been respected as an outstanding linguist and was always in demand as a translator and interpreter. Parties and politics bored him. He preferred continuing his linguistic research and writing occasional scholarly papers on the Basque language and legends, in which field he had received a doctorate.

He leaned back and sighed, "It's fate! No, it's all due to Carlos as president of this Franglais-speaking republic. I thought he'd have been jailed as a con man or shot as a soldier of fortune by this time. Well, back in our school days he was just plain Carlton Drexel Hill; kind of wild then but decent enough. Wouldn't you know he'd have the luck to marry an heiress, Charlotte Wood from Bryn Mawr. He must have used her money to buy this island. Beaulinia! What a name! It doesn't actually mean anything linguistically, but perhaps 'beautiful shape' is intended." The ambassador had a habit of analyzing names.

"How long have Candace and I been here? Almost ten months? We arrived around the first of last October from Washington, where I had been waiting for her while she helped Aunt Nittie close up the house in Keene Valley after Aunt Dottie's death. It was pretty quiet at first. But then the flood of visitors started. How many times since then have I waited here for a planeload of officials: Pentagon brass, bankers unlimited, defense contractors, even a vice-president on the loose; and now some junketing congressmen with a clutter of wives and aides. And all because Carlos has the world beating a path to his door to buy his 'better mousetrap' or more appropriately, 'mantrap,' his 'secret weapon.'" Eric snorted. "Some awful, lethal one, I guess. And all in the name of world peace, of course!"

Then he smiled slightly. "So he demands that the State Department send me, his 'old and dearest friend'—Carlos does like to exaggerate—as a full-ranking ambassador, to 'smooth the path of negotiations,' he said. Why, I'd hardly gone beyond second secretaryship. That did upset the chief. Shook up the entire department. But this is only an insignificant island in the Caribbean. He doesn't need me, though it was a nice gesture to help pave the way for a more comfortable retirement. Quite a character!

"Thank goodness, Candace is on this flight too. She never stays put long. Insisted on going to England three weeks ago to watch some tennis at Wimbledon, of all things. At least she'll be back now to help entertain the jolly junketeers."

Fred, his aide and driver, interrupted his thoughts.

"Excuse me, sir, President Carlos has arrived and they are rolling out the red carpet."

The ambassador stepped out on the tarmac to greet Carlos and Charlotte and watch the BAA (Beaulinia Air Atlantic) touch down. Eric groaned, "Of course, there's Candace first out the door and at the top of the steps, waving like a celebrity, smiling and laughing. Even as an ambassador's wife she never takes these ceremonies seriously. Now she's calling too. Surely she doesn't expect me to respond in public! Well, let's pray she doesn't trip down those steep steps with that weak ankle of hers. She is one for making a scene." Eric clenched his teeth as she dashed over to him.

"Oh, Eric, what a trip!" She kissed him on the cheek.

"Welcome back, Candace." He brightened up and relaxed a little.

The ceremony began. While congressmen and entourage clumped down the aircraft stairs to meet President and Mme. Carlos Hill (pronounced "Heel" in French-speaking Beaulinia), the band played a stirring rendition of *Beaulinia, the Gem of the Ocean*. A small military escort, wearing U.S. army surplus combat uniforms with matching guns, stood at attention.

After these brief formalities, Eric was compelled to make conversation with their leading visitor: "Ah, Congressman Brasher, I hope your flight was comfortable?"

"Well, Ambassador, it was uh . . . unusual. Being served banana bread, banana wine, and something frighteningly spectacular called banana flambée was a trifle much."

"Oh, President Carlos likes to have his little joke, reminding visitors that his island has a banana economy and single export."

Thus Congressman Sam Brasher and his oversight committee were given a taste of Beaulinia. More was to come. They were herded into a dilapidated bus for the drive to their hotel in downtown Bulim, the capital and only city on the tiny island.

After seeing them off, the ambassador turned in amazement to watch his wife's twenty-three scruffy bags, bulging cartons, and torn packages (he counted them) being carted from the plane to be piled up near the limousine.

"Really, Candace, you did all that shopping in England?"

"Now, Eric, it's mostly food I bought in Miami. We don't want to serve bananas to our guests. Why, Fred, it's good to see you. I didn't recognize you in a chauffeur's cap. You look very dashing."

Fred smiled and thought how much she livened things up at the embassy.

"Oh, and I did find those two books in London you wanted, Eric."

"Quite. Let's not dawdle. Get in, Candace. And, Fred, you can return with Jack in the station wagon to collect all this stuff."

Candace, eyeing the old limousine, remarked, "So you got the old Packard to run again."

"It was good of your aunts to give it to us. Much more dignified for the embassy than that battered old station wagon State supplied. Pity they don't make automobiles like this anymore. I don't get my head cut off on entering; I can sit without slumping and can step out in a trice."

Candace, being shorter, hadn't suffered from that problem. In fact, she looked as if she never suffered; just pleasant and wholesome and putting on weight which didn't seem to bother her. Her clothes were bought "off the rack" and hung that way. That didn't bother her either.

As they drove through the embassy gates, two guards in gaudy and plumed attire saluted them. "Haven't you gotten rid of them yet?" asked Candy. "I mean their uniforms."

Eric sighed. "What can I do? They were donated by the White House. Someone thought them appropriate for here."

"You mean someone did not dare throw them away

after all that talk of economizing. They must be leftovers from Nixon's whimsical 'Student Prince' days, which at the time provided the whole nation with a good laugh."

"Well, the last laugh's on us, Candy. By the way, how are the children?"

Before she could answer, the Packard pulled up to the embassy door. Candy was pleased to see Jack, all smiles, come bounding down the verandah steps. He was now her social secretary, as Fred was Eric's private one. The rest of the official staff were "just staff." But Fred Nearim and Jack Farnon were special. "Near and Far," Eric called them. Candy thought. *Why, they're the best thing that happened to us in Foreign Service. Arrived by ship in January, wasn't it? The Navy, in passing, had just dumped them here; cast them adrift, so to speak, from the SS Sinclair as additional embassy staff. Both young medical corpsmen and good looking in their smart white uniforms. I couldn't tell them apart at first with their reddish hair and bright blue eyes. But no problem later when Fred tanned and Jack freckled. Of course we didn't need medical attention, what with Dr. Duval down the road; but how typical of Washington! I'm glad Eric thought to make them aides: 'First Aide and Band Aide,' he said. Well, they've been wonderful. Fred's such a help and really a companion to Eric, knowing spelling and typing, not to mention driving and repairing motors. And I couldn't do without Jack. He's such a good mixer—both with drinks and people.*

Candy was happy to be back. She loved Beaulinia with the warm Caribbean on one side and the rolling Atlantic on the other. The embassy terrace faced the Atlantic. The rambling structure had been built at the turn of the century by an American millionaire, Harry Snow. Older natives called the place "La Maison-Neige," or Snow House. He had selected the site on top of a grassy knoll overlooking Hangman's Bay, where he could dock his yacht and climb up a path through hundreds of red poinsettia bushes. The house with its pointed shingled roof and broad verandah across the front looked like any one of those gray-green, weather-beaten, wooden hotels found in old mountain resorts. It was large, spacious, high-ceilinged, and cool. The grounds were pleasantly arranged, containing a small swimming pool for the staff, a grass tennis court for Candy, and a rifle range which Eric used occasionally. One had to be on the lookout for stray balls and bullets. Farther afield could be found a shady pasture for a cow to supply the ambassador with fresh cream for his coffee and ice cream for his dessert. A run-down stable now housing the rejuvenated shiny black Packard and the government-issued Ford, and a few other out-buildings, hidden in the tall trees beyond, completed the embassy domain. The house had no air conditioning, the plumbing was antiquated, the furniture old-fashioned and frayed. All this pleasantly recalled to the Bohners the comfortable and more leisurely and gracious way of living they had enjoyed in their childhood.

As Candy entered, half a dozen clocks, one after the other, chimed the hour. The ambassador collected fine clocks and watches. He was always punctual, in fact preferred being early.

And so he and Candy were that evening, for the reception at the President's Palace, La Casa Blanca, so named by Carlos who spoke Spanish better than French. As he explained once, Maison Blanche sounds like a dessert, not intriguing enough. It was a dazzling white, three-story building, a former governor's palace in fact, done in rococo stucco with gleaming floor-length arched windows, wrought-iron balconies, two surprising bell towers, and a broad, paved terrace in front and old prison quarters in the rear. Carlos and Charlotte were waiting for them at the top of the broad terrace steps. They looked like any respectable middle-aged, well-to-do couple. What was once an athletic, swashbuckling young man, nicknamed "the Pirate," with bristling moustachios and gleaming black eyes, one of which he occasionally covered with a black patch for effect, had now become a paunchy but astute businessman (his island was his business) with clipped mustache and beaming eyes. His wife was friendly, gracious, putting on weight, but still handsome and extremely well liked.

Carlos spoke first: "Eric, my friend, come in and let me show you my latest 'toy'!" To Eric that meant either a new invention or an unusual weapon—or both.

Charlotte led Candy to a small reception room near the entrance to hear all about Candy's latest trip. "How was Wimbledon?"

"Charlotte, it was thrilling. So many tennis upsets. I was invited to sit in the royal box."

"Did you see your son Konrad?"

"Oh, I stayed with him in his tiny flat near the Gloucester Road underground station; so easy to catch the train there for Wimbledon, just twenty minutes away. Of course he was studying for his examinations while I was enjoying the tennis. But he'll be home soon with a master's degree in economics, looking for a job in Washington."

"Tell him to apply here. Carlos could use a chief banana counter. But now tell me how you joined the elite in the royal box. Did you meet the queen?"

"Not exactly. But I ran into some old friends from Washington, Johann and Margery Harper. Oh, you met them, Charlotte, when they visited here at Easter."

"Hanno and Margy? They were delightful. She's so bright and modern and he's so charmingly old-worldly. I loved listening to his stories. He seemed to know everybody."

"Wait until you hear this one, Charlotte. The first day my seat on center court was way up in the rafters sheltered and with a good view of the players through binoculars, but uncomfortable and crowded. On scanning the royal box, I was surprised to see Hanno and Margy enter it. I had no idea they were that well connected and currently in London. Their seats, armchairs, actually, looked so comfortable and so close to the court. After the first match was over, I dashed out and managed to locate an official to deliver a message to them. It helped to address it to Doctor Harper. He's a doctor of law, you know, but the official of course was thinking 'medical and emergency.' They appeared shortly."

"They didn't know you were in London."

"Oh, no; they'd been traveling all over Europe for some time. But Hanno was surprised at my plight, because he thought surely an ambassador's wife would know someone in the London embassy to help. Well, Charlotte, it had never occurred to me! On asking them how they acquired an invitation, Margy explained succinctly, 'Connections, Candy. My Congressman telephoned his good friend the ambassador here.'"

"But of course. Really, Candy," laughed Charlotte, "you've got to learn to assume your position in life. Throw a little weight around."

"I've got the weight for it now, and I'm learning. But let me tell you Hanno's fuller explanation, because you'll love this one. Now, how does it go? I hope I have the names correct. He began, 'You see, back in my university days in Vienna, I lunched infrequently but pleasantly with another young law student, Arpad Halevy, whose sister Elena became an opera singer of no renown in Munich. She first married a cellist in the Salzburg String Quartet. I believe he was stabbed to death in Rome. She soon acquired a second husband—she was still a beautiful woman—an American from Cleveland, Philip Marsh—no, Philip Mallow.' He did not give me a chance to joke about a slip of the tongue, but went right on: 'He died a year and a half ago in an automobile accident near Cologne. Elene was with him, or perhaps not. Their son—they had two daughters and a son, Stefan is his name—became cultural attaché at the American embassy in Geneva—or is that a consulate? Until last year when he was sent to London. He recently married a very charming English girl from a very good family, Pamela Partridge, who is a close friend of . . . how do you call them, Margy?'

" 'Royals.'

" 'Ah, yes. Young Royals, who is a tennis enthusiast.'

"Well, Charlotte, by that time, I had almost forgotten what the subject of our discussion was. But I did get the connection, and an invitation very soon, thanks to Hanno."

"You're coming up in the world," joked Charlotte.

"It was really very pleasant. I met Pamela Partridge Mallow and her aunt, a Mrs. Parradine, I think her name was, but forgot to ask her for her address."

Just then a commotion was heard in the great hall. Charlotte went to the door to greet the arriving band members. Candy peeked out and asked, "Is that a marimba band? Are we expected to dance?"

"Don't worry. Not you and Eric. Only those who want to." Charlotte was thinking how Eric couldn't lead and Candy couldn't follow. "We like to have you and Eric keep the conversation going."

The guests soon arrived. The old dusty bus pulled up with its congressional load from the Bulim Bon Hotel, followed by various ambassadors in their limousines; first and foremost British Ambassador and Mrs. Austin Healey; then the "new boys," whom Carlos, forgetting their ambassadorial names, referred to as Boris Nyet, Herr Gerber, Pierre Bonjour, and Franco Bello. This was a gala occasion.

The reception broke up early, due to jet lag, undigested bananas, or perhaps because the band packed up and departed at ten-thirty.

## Chapter 2

# Life in Beaulinia, Death in Keene Valley

The next morning the telephone was heard to ring while the ambassador was tapping and decapitating his boiled egg at the breakfast table. He looked up, irritated. "Candace, if that's the Austin Healeys calling to arrange another shut-the-door-and-battling-cocks, tell them . . ."

"It's battledore and shuttlecock."

"Quite. I am not going over again to whack another silly 'flimsy' with a paddle."

Fred entered carrying the telephone trailing its long cord from the hall. "Excuse me, Mrs. Bohner, there's a Judge Wackman from Keene Valley calling."

"Why, Eric, what on earth could he want?" and then taking the phone: "Hello!"

"Aunt Candy? Horace here. We've just found Cousin Peregrine."

"Found Perry? How? Where?"

"In the icehouse. Frozen stiff."

"After all these months! Can you thaw him out?"

"Throw him out?" Horace had a poor connection.

"No, thaw him out." Candy raised her voice.

"Wouldn't do much good. He's dead, you see. Frozen stiff."

"How can you be sure? I mean with Cousin Peregrine." Candy was a bit flustered, and added. "He did seem a little off."

"Well, he went off too far this time. Look here, Aunt Candy, do you think you could make it to the preliminary inquest next Thursday? In Elizabethtown. You were the last person in the family to see him alive."

"Surely you're not conducting an inquest? Really, Horace, you just got yourself appointed a judge and now you want to . . . The next thing you'll tell me is that you suspect foul play."

"I can't hear you too well. But I suspect foul play."

"Now, Horace, don't lose your head over Peregrine."

"That's right, he did."

"He did what?"

"He lost his head. It's in a block of ice."

"Where's the rest of him?"

"In another one."

"That must be a huge block. My word! He weighed three hundred pounds at least. You know, he was a spy. Is that what is meant by being out in the cold? Poor Perry!"

"Well, can you come? We need you to identify him officially. No one else in the family except for Aunt Nittie, who's semi-comatose, knows what he looked like, for certain. The coroner, Col. Abel Smythe, says your presence is important."

"Yes, Horace, we'll probably both come. I'll call you back later."

The ambassador, having finished his breakfast, asked, "What was all that about?"

"Horace said they found Cousin Peregrine in the icehouse. He must have been there since—well, since he's been missing. Although I didn't realize he was considered missing. They suspect foul play and want me to identify him. I believe he's a first cousin once removed."

"Quite. But really, Candace, your family does dramatize everything so. And this means another distasteful explanation to the State Department will be required. Let's keep this quiet for now. I must be off. What time is dinner tonight for the Junketeers?" Without waiting for a reply, he was out the door and into the Packard to attend to the visitors in town.

While Eric and the congressional committee were meeting with President Carlos at the palace, the congressional ladies were boarding a bus for a sightseeing tour to be conducted by Jack, Mrs. Bohner's right-hand man and social secretary. He thought he'd have a little fun assuming the role of a local tour guide by changing his appearance and adding a bushy red mustache, dark glasses and a beret. As he jumped aboard the bus he announced in an exaggerated French accent: *"Bonjour, mesdames.* I am zee tour gueede, Jacques. Yes, vee have no bananas today. Vee see other Beaulinia. Vee begeen here at Guillotine Park, now call Sandbag Square. *Voilà,* no more bootiful trees, no more guillotine, no more statoo of Général De Gaulle. We cut off hees head. Now we just pile up zee sandbags in honor of noo president and current owner, Carlos. Saves zee time and trouble for next revolootion." Jack was enjoying making it all up as he went along.

"On zee right, zat pink building in progress ees to be zee Hinkley-Pilkington. Noo, I should say the pinky Hiltington Hotel. We expect many lovely ladies like yourselves to veeseet. We move on to colorful bazaar and—how you say—flea market. Only no fleas for sale. They geeve them away. Beyond are warehouses to let for bananas, our beeg export, and contraband, and docks loading and unloading used cars and nonsuch.

"As we drive along the coast we see blue Atlantic halfway 'round the island and green Caribbean the rest. Notice windmills, originally built by French prisoners. They are our energy plant today; eez cheaper than noocular, *n'est-ce pas?* We call that progresso. Up on plateau ees president's palace where you party last night. An old prison fort you see too. *Oui?* Thees island belong to France once where well-to-do white collar creeminals sent. They had comfy cells and run of the island. Many natives now descended from these naughty aristocrats. Later, island become haven for rum runners. They naughty too. Now make naughty tax haven today. The mansions we pass were built with rummy money. Now make rummy embassies."

They wound their way around the island stopping at a beach here, a lookout there, and banana trees everywhere while Jacques talked away. "Zee *montagne* in zee center ees volcanic perhaps, Mont Dieu Merci, a landmark for sailors. That name mean 'Thank God,' which ees what shipwreck sailor say bobbing in wavy water. We go now up for gorgeous view near top where admiral bird situate."

At the bird monument "Jacques" continued, "We debark to take pictures of lovely poinsettias and bird's eye view of harbor. Thees eez our nationale bird, the Giant Gnatcatcher. It soars thirty feet high and fabricated from blocks of tufa. It's a beakern for sheeps at sea."

Mrs. Brasher remarked. "That's an awfully big gnatcatcher."

To which "Jacques" replied, "You outta see the gnats!" Mrs. Brasher admitted with a smile that the gnats did seem that big when biting.

Eventually the tour bus returned to the city encountering little traffic, to stop before an old French church. "Reformed," "Jacques" explained, "into the Bank of Beaulinia. Noteece the one tower standing, called Tower of Strength. The sign read '*Force avec* Dollars,' which mean 'Strength through Dollars.' The people call it 'La Blanchisserie,' meaning 'The Laundry.' You see, the bank clean up dirty money. Casino on other side of park clean up money too. On your left is Greene Park."

Jack was asked, "What is that funny-looking thing over there in the park? It looks like part of a giant vacuum cleaner; you know, the floor-brush attachment."

"We debark here to take a look." Jack needed time to think up a story, since he hadn't the fuzziest idea. It was actually the damaged roof of an abandoned air-raid shelter.

"Ah," he continued brightly, "Zat ees monument to *Le Vendeur d'Havane,* which mean 'Our Salesman in Havana.'"

"How extraordinary," exclaimed Mrs. Brasher. "But what's that got to do with . . ."

Jack proceeded recklessly. "Thees man, Henri Hoover of Beaulinia, sold vacoom cleaners. One day he decide to clean up in Cuba, so he open branch office there and do very well with installment plan by selling parts of cleaner separately. He begin advertising on television. *Mais, alors,* Castro went crazee mad over loud commercials on Tee Vee; say he sound like used-car salesman and had him thrown in preeson for capitalistic activities, wheech eez capital crime in Cuba. Rumor say he was vacuumed to death. Zee punishment feets zee crime, *n'est-ce pas?*"

The ladies loved Jack's tour. On being deposited back at their hotel, they tipped him lavishly. He hoped that they would not recognize him at the party that evening.

Meanwhile, back at the embassy. Candy was unpacking, repacking, talking on the telephone to her daughter Claudia, who lived at home and worked in Washington; to Konrad, still in London for another week; to her brother John in Syracuse; to her sisters, Honey and Peaches, in St. Petersburg; to inform them all of Cousin Peregrine's mysterious demise and icy grave. John was later to refer to it as "freezing in hell." Also of the upcoming inquest on Thursday, which she and Eric would attend. It was pleasant to look forward to a family reunion in Keene Valley, even though it was due to rather bizarre circumstances. Then she turned her attention to arranging the evening party for the junketeers. "Buffet would be easier," she told herself. "Arrange some flowers; lay out the food in the dining room; tell Jack to set up a bar in the drawing room; and then we'll open all the doors to the verandah and terrace to let the guests wander at will. Later, those who wish may visit the casino."

That evening while Fred showed those junketeers who were interested around the embassy grounds, the ambassador and Congressman Brasher were conversing on the terrace and enjoying the view of Hangman's Bay and of a cruise ship silently passing by far out on the ocean.

"Someday, Carlos expects those ships to stop here," began Eric.

"Good for the economy, of course," added Brasher.

"Yes, but it will spoil the tranquility and simplicity."

"Well, that's progress. I noticed much activity on the docks. An awful lot of bananas were being loaded and some strange nuts, too."

"Those nuts are what the natives call *elus;* not very edible but they make a fine grade of oil."

"Those warehouses appear full of all kinds of goods and equipment."

"I believe Carlos brings in extra revenue by leasing them to outsiders. They must have been fine-looking buildings a century ago. Built by French prisoners, who appreciated fine surroundings."

"You know, I'd forgotten about this place and its quaint history until the emergence of Carlos. I understand your friendship with him goes way back."

"We were good friends back in school. But after the war we went our separate ways and rarely saw one another. He'd always look me up when I was sent to a new posting. He was always on the go."

"Those warehouses interest me. You say he leases them to foreign traders. Rather a nice, quiet place to store contraband, I'd guess."

There was a pause, then Brasher continued: "Is this Carlos on the level? I mean, can he be trusted? He's so cagey about that secret weapon he has for sale. Acts as if he doesn't trust us. I can't say we've gotten any more information by coming here than we got from those hot shots in the Pentagon, who wouldn't know a water pistol from a pop gun except by the price. If it costs a lot, it must be okay, is their thinking."

"You can trust Carlos, but I don't think he trusts the

current administration. 'A bunch of pirates,' he calls them and then jokes that it takes one to know one."

Brasher changed the subject. Looking around, he commented, "This is a fine old house. I visited it with my father many years ago. He was a friend of the owner, Harry Snow. He was a rum one. Everything looks just the same. I even remember some of the furniture."

Just then, Brasher's aide, William Riddle, appeared on the terrace bringing cocktails for the two men. Eric declined and excused himself to see to his other guests. He noticed Mrs. Brasher approaching Candy in the reception hall, so he ducked into the drawing room, as Mrs. Brasher began: "Oh, Mrs. Bohner, I hear you'll be going to Keene Valley, I had no idea you had a place there. We spend a month every summer close by at the Ausable Club." This statement surprised Candy. Mrs. Brasher continued, "So sad, though, to be attending a family funeral."

This too surprised Candy that Mrs. Brasher should know. Ah, yes, the telephone has ears, she realized. She calmly replied, "Well, it's just for a first cousin once removed."

"When was he removed?" Oh, I mean, when did he—er—pass away?"

"About nine months ago, I believe."

"And he's just being buried?"

"Well, he's been on ice all that time."

"How extraordinary," remarked Mrs. Brasher. She moved on.

As Candy turned, she noticed Brasher's aide open the door to the library, normally off-limits to visitors because it was used as a family sitting room. He slipped in quietly. Candy walked over and stood in the doorway watching him poke around for a minute. Not liking what she saw, she asked him rather sharply, "Mr. Riddle, are you looking for something?"

Bill Riddle turned around in surprise and then proceeded to explain in a most charming manner that he was just admiring all the fine books. Candy smiled, thinking, *He does cut such a dashing figure; it's that Latin look: shiny black hair, romantic eyes, slender build. I wonder if he plays tennis.* She asked him. He did. A match to include the Brashers was arranged for the following morning. She and Riddle thrashed the Brashers in the first set, and tactfully lost the second.

## Chapter 3

## Family Reunion

Tuesday came all too soon or not soon enough. The Bohners and junketeers departed Beaulinia via BAA to Miami. Fortunately for Eric and Candy the "fasten seatbelt" sign remained lit for the entire turbulent flight over the Atlantic. This gave them a breather from the "Jovial Junketeers" as Eric was now calling them. Candy turned her head to make some trivial comment to Eric, but when she saw his head back and eyes closed, she remained silent.

Eric wasn't asleep, though. He was wondering why he should find himself in one predicament after another. *That's what comes of marrying into a large and eccentric family*, he sighed to himself. *That Peregrine, never met him: odd sort. The family never bothered to mention him. How could three hundred pounds of human flesh just disappear? Went on a diet? No, that's something silly Candace would say. Always joking; what can she always find so funny? In any case, he's encased in ice. There I go again! Candy's way of thinking must be contagious. It's so un-*

*dignified. But she seems well-liked. That family of hers, though! Her mother's family, the Ambers. I don't believe her mother spoke more than two words to me. And her Amber aunts, two little old ladies with plenty of money. I never knew the family had money until after we were married when Candy took me to Keene Valley. That's quite an impressive property; a large and unusual house built by Stanford White; wonderful old leather furniture, oriental rugs worth a fortune; a fireplace large enough for a dozen men to stand in, even if they're the size of Peregrine. And Peregrine; what his last name? Amber? No, it's something odd. Parody, that's it! Originally "Paradis," Candy said. French, of course, which some ignoramus couldn't spell correctly when Perry's grandfather landed on Ellis Island. Well, Perry was a paradox. The whole family is, in a way. What an argumentative bunch; always blathering! Ah, here come the drinks. I could use one today.*

Candy spoke then. "I hope they don't think I had anything to do with Peregrine's death. Horace said the coroner thought it highly important that I be at the inquest, since I was the last person to see Perry alive. Well, I couldn't have been."

"Candace, stop fretting. No one suspects you, unless you hit him with a wild tennis ball."

"I never . . ."

"Quite. You never could have cut off his head. You can't even carve a chicken. But let's not discuss this here. You do have the package, don't you?"

*Oh, the packet Perry gave me,* thought Candy. *Thank goodness Eric found it in the safe. I'd forgotten all about it. Perry was going to pick it up when he came to Beaulinia. He had written such an odd message on it: "To be opened only at my death by my attorney, Casper Swain, Esq., of New York City." Why didn't Perry leave it with him? He must have suspected some trouble brewing. Perhaps that's why he came to Keene Valley—to hide out. It was just shortly after Aunt Dottie had died. Eric didn't want* **me** to stay on in K.V., since he had to report to Beaulinia. But there was no else available to help Aunt Nittie close up the big house. And it was so cozy staying in the Gate House. It was the first time I had been there in the fall to see the glorious foliage. Probably the last time, too. Then Perry appeared suddenly, asking Aunt Nittie to put him up for a couple of weeks. No one in the family had seen him for years. Lived in England since the war. And fancy, being a spy; well, now a retired one. At least that's what he told me one evening sitting by the fire and watching television. When a spy retires does he become a spire? And when he dies, has he ex-spired? Candy smiled. *There now, I'm becoming a linguist like Eric.*

After the plane landed at Miami, Candy and Eric caught the next flight to New York, where her brother John Hassel and his wife, Pattee, met them. At Candy's earlier request John had managed to locate Peregrine's lawyer, Casper Swain, that morning, or rather, his former office. Old Mr. Swain had died recently and it was believed that his files had been destroyed. They thus decided to avoid going into New York City and settled for the Happy Hours Motel just off the Taconic Parkway heading north, they hoped. John hadn't driven in that area for years, and found it all changed. "And just try to find a free road map these days!" exclaimed Pattee.

John got along well with Eric and even resembled him in height, blue eyes, and mustache, but he had been a businessman. He had settled in Syracuse after the war to work for a toy manufacturer, creating interesting toys and games, and earning a comfortable living. Eventually, he became president of the firm. But he found himself always outsmarted by the big companies. His "Sorority Dolls," Ginnie, Winnie, Connie had sold well until the Barbie doll came along. So had his Death Valley Guns until Death Varder Zap-Phasers appeared. His board game "Know It All" was popular, but just a forerunner of Trivial Pursuit. Finally he invented the Gizmo, a small plastic gorilla that could be transformed into the Empire State Building. *Alas,* it too became a has-been when more updated robot transformers began selling like hotcakes. He retired then to become active in civil affairs.

John's wife, Pattee, like the Hassels and Ambers, was also from Albany. She was the vivacious one with titian hair, smiling brown eyes, and flamboyant clothing. They made a handsome couple. She enjoyed sewing and had made cloth dolls for her grandchildren. John began calling her Madame Poupée and suggested she make a life-size bridge dummy because she frequently found herself to be one at her weekly bridge party. Thus was Loretta born, full-grown. When not at the bridge table, Loretta spent her time sitting on the living room sofa. The children all loved her. And what a conversation piece! Pattee had a great sense of humor.

So the Bohners and Hassels left the Happy Hours Motel early the next morning, discussing the odd couples they had glimpsed and wondering which hour would be considered happiest in that "den of sin." Eric thought it was while "paying the bill—cheap; and checking out—with relief." John was at the wheel, Eric beside him, and Mme. Poupée and Mme. Ambassador in the rear surrounded by odds and ends of small luggage. It was a hot July day as the foursome rolled past Poughkeepsie, past Albany—"but it looks so different now," they agreed—past Saratoga and Lake George, on to Warrensburg, where they knew of a pleasant place to have a good lunch.

They resumed their drive after eating and strolling around the attractive town, chatting continuously and catching up on family news. Johnny Hassel had started his own law practice with a close friend in Syracuse. Rick, his brother, liked teaching and hoped to get a book of humorous verse published soon. Both had lovely wives and lively children. Claudia Bohner, "Our budding botanist" as Candy called her, was in Keene Valley by now on vacation from her museum job. It had been arranged for Chester, Horace's brother, to meet his cousin Konrad at Kennedy Airport in a few days, and drive him to Keene Valley.

Pattee asked, "Are Klara and her husband, David, coming from New Mexico?"

"No, they are taking a holiday in the Alps to climb Mont Blanc or Monte Rosa," replied Candy. "I'm not sure which color mountain, white or pink. Take your pick."

"Let's hope they take their picks, too. That's ice picks, dearie," Pattee added, turning to John.

He answered, "If I were in their boots—that's climbing boots, Pattee—I'd pick a mountain with a cable car and ride up in comfort."

"That's what aging does to one," remarked Pattee. "By the way, what about Fran? Will she be in K.V.?"

Both John and Candy stated, "I hope not!"

"You two never cared for your sister, did you?"

"Too bossy," explained Candy.

"Acts too superior," added John.

"Well it's going to be a houseful with or without Fran," commented Pattee. "And now that Aunt Dottie's gone and Aunt Nittie's in the hospital ill with senility, who's in charge at the house?"

"Probably that old curmudgeon, Martha, the cook," laughingly replied John.

Candy decided she would "supervise" Martha, the Amber cook of many, many years.

"What about Horace and Mary? They're up there already and might not like that arrangement, Candy," persisted Pattee.

"Horace told me they were staying in the Gate House, where the children would be more comfortable."

"Does Mary Wackman still practice law?" asked John.

"Yes, she has her own firm in White Plains, I believe, and is active in the League of American Women Lawyers. She used to handle domestic cases."

"How does she do it with four small children?" asked Pattee.

"Servants, I suppose," was Candy's guess.

"They don't get called that anymore," commented Pattee.

Then John mentioned that he wasn't certain he wanted to return to the Keene Valley house, with all that family bickering, jealousy, and backbiting he remembered. But Candy remarked that she'd been happy there all those summers; the bickering, backbiting, and jealousy never bothered her. She could give as well as take.

Eric spoke up: "The first time I visited there, I dubbed that 'battle camp' 'Fort Amber'."

Pattee laughed at that. "Why not 'Forever Amber'? What is the name of the place, dearie?"

John said, "It doesn't have a name. Some relative called it 'The Poplars' because of all those poplar trees Grandpa had planted along the stone wall. But Dottie and Nittie didn't take to that suggestion. They didn't like being told what to name it. It's just the Amber Place."

Pattee persisted by suggesting "Stonewall" or better still "Stonewalling" and then wondered what names other summer residents gave to their properties.

Soon the conversation got around to Cousin Peregrine Parody. John vaguely remembered seeing him in Albany fifty years ago and wondered if he'd changed much. "But really, Candy is the one to know what he looks like now."

"You mean I'll have to identify him by his decapitated head?"

"Oh, I imagine they've put him back together again by now."

John and Eric tacitly agreed to keep the diverse family personalities and tempers under control, and to prevent their nephew, the newly appointed judge, from dominating their activities. It was a matter of age, experience and pride, in spite of their lack of knowledge concerning murder. But then that wasn't the judge's field, either. He was in probates or some such. Of course there would be a local detective, they expected, though wondering how so small a community as Keene Valley could produce one. Perhaps the State Troopers in Plattsburg or Elizabethtown had an investigator. Little did they expect what they got.

Now they were entering the village of Keene Valley, an unforgettable place surrounded by lovely lush meadows and soft, green mountains, while the shallow, sandy Ausable River flowed pleasantly through. The main street carried traffic north to Lake Placid seventeen miles beyond. Two side streets, Market and Adirondack, were lined with fine old, well-kept, and prettily painted large wooden farmhouses with wraparound porches and outdoor staircases to the second story. The summer residences were unseen off dirt side roads and up wooded hills. The village had its own white and spired church, modest but modern one-story hospital, a picturesque library with diamond-paned windows and brown shingles, a large, functional-looking red brick central school set in a meadow, the necessary hose-and-ladder company, tiny post office, large and busy garage, a small supermarket, hardware store, fully stocked mountaineering and ski shop, a gun shop, a diner especially busy on Sundays for picking up the Sunday papers and staying for breakfast, one or two gift shops, a restaurant and bar, and a small country club offering tennis and swimming. Some of the summer residents had returned to live all year 'round on reaching retirement age, adding a worldly touch to a peaceful, comfortable village.

A half-mile up Adirondack Street brought them to the Amber stone gate and past the Gate House; then around a curve and up the steep, short, dirt road in the woods to the stone front steps of the large house. Judge Horace Wackman emerged to greet them, followed by his large; playful golden retriever called Torpedo. The young judge was another Amber look-alike variation with prematurely graying curly hair, blue eyes, mustache, and glasses to add weight to his court decisions, undoubtedly.

He was in complete charge. "Uncle John, you and Aunt Pattee will have the tower room with bathroom attached. Aunt Candy, you and Uncle Eric will take the room across the hall in front overlooking the fountain and use the first of the three bathrooms in the rear. Claudie is already here and settled. Konrad can use Aunt Nittie's room when he arrives. If Henny and Seth and their two little girls come over from Vermont, they can use the two back rooms. That will still leave enough rooms for Johnny and Ricky and their families, or aren't they coming? And what about Klara and David, Aunt Candy? Chester can stay in the playhouse, if it gets overcrowded. Oh, and your car, Uncle John, should be kept down by the barn, which is locked and we don't know where the key is."

With their marching, billeting, and parking orders issued to them, the new arrivals retreated upstairs for changing, unpacking, and holding a council of war between "General" Hassel and "Admiral" Bohner. It was decided that John and Candy would go right to the hospital to visit Aunt Nittie and receive permission to assume authority.

After they attended to that and returned to the house, Mary and Horace and their children joined them around the living room fireplace to await dinner. Now this had always been a teetotaling Methodist house. And God-fearing, perhaps, except that Aunt Dottie, now in heaven, had probably taken charge up there. She was fearless. So when Horace suggested cocktails before dinner, no one dared accept. It was then agreed that those who felt the need of "spirits" could find them at the Spread Eagle Restaurant and Bar down at the corner on Main Street. "After all," as John so aptly pointed out, "we are faced with a very sober, cold-blooded murder. By the way, Horace, where is Cousin Perry?"

"And where is Claudia?" asked Candy.

No one seemed certain about Claudia. But Peregrine had been taken in his icy shroud to Elizabethtown for an autopsy, Horace informed them, and furthermore the detective in charge, Lieutenant Whistler, would be around later with more details. The inquest was tomorrow. Horace explained about that.

"It's most unusual to have one until there is a definite suspect. But Col. Abel Smythe, the coroner—you remember him, Aunt Candy—he said he used to play tennis with you and Mother and Aunt Franny."

"You mean Buddy Smythe pronounced the same as 'tithe'?"

"Yes. He's of some local importance now that he's retired from the army. He bought Justice Foote's property and settled in Elizabethtown, and got himself elected an Essex County coroner last year after his wife died. She was English; he met her in England, stationed there during the war. A real anglophile, you'll see: riding boots, britches, and I wouldn't be surprised if he sported a monocle tomorrow. Anyway, the preliminary inquest is his idea, because it is done in England."

"He used to be sweet on Franny. But he isn't a doctor, is he, Horace?" asked Candy.

"No, a coroner does not have to be a medical man in Essex County."

"Who does the autopsy, then?"

"He appoints a local doctor or undertaker as medical examiner."

"Who, Dr. Cough?"

"No, he's too old now. A Dr. Graffe from Westport, I believe."

Just then, Claudia appeared with camera, butterfly net, and specimen bottles—the complete botanist. "Lost track of time; so sorry; just wait until you see what I found down by the pond," she explained.

Everyone expecting slimy toads or killer bees chorused, "Oh, no, wait until after dinner."

But Claudia, after greeting her parents, reached into her pocket, saying, "I think this is Aunt Nittie's opal ring," as she held it out for all to see.

"This is a surprise." "How did it get there?" "Why would Nittie . . ." and so on, they chatted. Since it was now the dinner hour, they all trooped out to the porch, down the outside steps and into the dining room to be greeted by Martha with, "Dinner isn't ready yet."

"Well, Martha," said Candy in her Mme. Ambassador voice, which always made Eric wince, "we'll all just pitch in and help." They had agreed not to discuss Nittie's ring at dinner, since Martha frequently came into the dining room, not to serve, but to stand and listen to the conversation. It's no wonder that all of Keene Valley knew what went on in the Amber house.

After dinner, at Mary's suggestion, the men washed the dishes, while she took the children, not feeling well, back to the Gate House. She had given Candy an idea, though. Tomorrow she would hire a kitchen helper or waitress. Although how was anyone's guess, since any available girl in the village refused to work with Martha anymore. *Well*, thought Candy, *let's try a young man.* And she eventually did. It turned out to be her son Konrad, who was to arrive a day earlier than expected. Candy and Eric had reached the age of some forgetfulness involving names, places, and dates. If it wasn't written down, it was forgotten.

Lieutenant Whistler appeared at eight. He was of medium height, with brown hair, brown suit and brown shoes; but he had a pleasant face, matter-of-fact voice, and was most polite. Horace met him at the front door to lead him through the large, square entrance hall into an enormous living room dominated at the far end by a huge tan and pink brick fireplace set in an inglenook. A shabby old moosehead hung on the wall above.

After being introduced to everyone, he took out a little brown notebook and pen and proceeded to ask questions. He was facing the family members seated in a semicircle of overstuffed chairs and a leather settee arranged around the fireplace, and was standing directly under the moose.

Gradually he became aware of his head being dusted with something flaky, and looked up to see that the jaw of the moose had dropped open, sprinkling sawdust on him.

Later, back at headquarters, he reported, "Gave me a turn it did, but no one appeared to notice, so I refrained from commenting. But when an antler came crashing down, its point nicking me on the forehead, I did ask them how old that moth-eaten beast was. The judge apologized, concerned that I was injured, and muttered something about it being an unruly witness he'd have wired back together in the morning. I assured him I was unhurt. Well, I never saw such a serious bunch of people, but so casual about it. You'd think the old moose did that frequently."

However, after Lieutenant Whistler's departure, some spritely remarks were made that the old moose was whetting his whistler, and some wondering how the good lieutenant would explain to his chief his "nick on the noggin" by saying, "It's all in a day's work, sir." Candy suggested that the moose was trying to tell the lieutenant something, while Eric believed it was caused by a poltergeist. John added that maybe Aunt Dottie was sending a message. Pattee had the last word. And the worst. "It's all very a-moosing."

Since serious discussion was useless, they decided to call it a day. They needed to be fresh for their courtroom appearance on the morrow.

Chapter 4

The Parody Inquest

The inquest was scheduled for ten o'clock in Elizabethtown, a twenty-minute drive to the east of Keene Valley. The Essex County Courthouse, distinguished by a white portico and spire, was one of a row of assorted, attached red-brick official buildings, stretching across a broad green, shaded by stately old elms. Shortly before ten, the Bohners, Hassels, and Wackmans, as members of the Amber family, drove up to the curb in front of the green, where state troopers were waiting to escort them through a throng of photographers and curiosity-seekers. On entering the courtroom, Candy, who had never been in one before, found it quite small, windowless, and white walled with a large oil painting of John Brown's Trial on one side and "Pocahontas's Tribulation," as Candy called it, on the other. Beyond the dozen rows of park-like benches for the spectators stood a mahogany railing behind which were placed mahogany chairs and tables, a raised judge's bench, a witness chair, and on the right the jury box. It was dignified and simple, Candy thought, as she walked down the aisle with Eric at her side, smiling at a few old summer friends and village acquaintances.

Eric was annoyed at her behavior and shuddered to see Candace making a spectacle of herself by enjoying such a friendly reception at such a grim event. She was a "star" witness, he believed, and would probably end up a "chief" suspect. He hissed at her, "Now don't make a scene," a frequent remark of his which Candy had long ago learned to smilingly ignore. She'd always tell herself, *Eric is a bit old-fashioned.* They sat down in the front row next to John and Pattee. Horace and Mary were seated directly behind on the aisle.

All rose as the coroner, Col. Abel Smythe, entered from a door on the left and seated himself at a table placed in front of the judge's bench. He smiled at Candy. She hadn't changed much in forty years, he thought. The inquest began.

Detective Lieutenant Whistler was called first to present what facts he knew about Col. Peregrine Talcott Parody's disappearance last September, which was very little since it had not been reported, no one being particularly aware of his presence or absence. Not unusual, if he were an intelligence officer. But on July thirteenth of this year, Judge Wackman of Keene Valley had reported a head and body, separated, encased in two blocks of ice in the Amber ice house. And so on through his preliminary investigation.

Judge Horace Wackman was called to the stand next to describe the surprising reappearance of Colonel Parody. "I had driven my family to Keene Valley from my home in White Plains, arriving the afternoon of July 12, to stay in the Gate House, while the main house was being opened and cleaned. Early the following morning of the thirteenth at approximately four-thirty, my wife and I were awakened by a loud crashing sound coming from the direction of the nearby ice house. I looked out but found it too dark to see anything, and hearing nothing more, decided to wait until daylight, believing it to be the old, disused ice house that collapsed. Of course my guess was correct. It had been in rickety condition for some time. I proceeded to pull apart some boards and lift off pieces of roof to discover blocks of ice beneath in sawdust. Then I noticed a block of ice clearly containing a head. Further examination produced the body in a six-foot-long block. This was most unexpected. I then called the sheriff's office here in Elizabethtown. I also questioned my aunt's caretaker, Ernest Middleton, when he arrived to perform his daily chores. He told me he had nothing to do with the ice house for years and knew nothing of its being used. I could not make an identification at the time since the features were so iced over, nor later when the ice had thawed a bit. But Ernest Middleton said it looked like that Parody fellow, of whom I had never heard. Ernest explained that it was my aunt's cousin, Peregrine Parody from England. The rest you know from Lieutenant Whistler."

"Thank you, Your Honor," spoke the coroner. "Please call Ernest Middleton to the stand."

Ernest repeated his words when asked: "It looked like that Parody fellow. He was staying with Miss Nittie and Mrs. Bohner in the Gate House last September." He was excused.

There was now a slight disturbance when wheezing Dr. Graffe, the medical examiner, hurried in, apologizing for being late due to an emergency at the hospital. A whiff of nonmedicinal but potable alcohol was detected by many as he bustled down the aisle. He immediately took the witness stand and proceeded to hand some eight-by-ten glossy photographs to Col. Abel Smythe, reporting, between coughs, the autopsy findings: "One bullet from a hunting rifle, in the back, piercing the heart, causing instant death. Couldn't say when, exactly, but on a chilly day since the victim was wearing an overcoat. Remarkable state of preservation, for which I have no explanation. Decapitation, though, was performed at a later date. His breakfast had been digested; the contents of the stomach contained pieces of crabapple with the head of a worm, which might place the time of death in mid-September." At least that is what the Bohners and Hassels think they heard. Dr. Graffe did cough and mumble so!

Now it was Candy's turn to take the witness chair. Col. "Bud" Smythe jumped up to shake hands and greet her: "It's so good to see you. How's Fran? We must get together for tennis or cocktails." Eric felt this was a bit out of order, but resigned himself to what would be worse to come.

Colonel Smythe, in his capacity as coroner, then handed Candy the gruesome photographs of the remains of the victim. Could she make a positive identification? Turning a shade of green on viewing such candid shots, Candy pulled herself together to declare that they were of Peregrine Parody, she was certain. Of course the features were slightly blurred, but the shape of the head, the neat goatee, those distinctive ears, and the massive shape of the body were his.

"Now, Mrs. Bohner, would you please describe for us the events taking place September twenty-ninth, when you last saw Colonel Parody alive, in spite of the Medical Examiner's placing his death mid-month."

Candy began: "I was packing up to leave that morning for the long trip to Beaulinia where my husband had recently been appointed ambassador. Miss Amber, my Aunt Nittie, was leaving also; but on Dr. Cough's recommendation, planned to spend a few days in the Keene Valley Hospital before returning to Albany for the winter. She seemed to be suffering from exhaustion, and has been there ever since."

"We're sorry to hear that, Mrs. Bohner. She's a fine woman and with her sister has done so much for Kenne Valley. I remember them so well from the summers I spent there in my youth."

"Thank you, Colonel. Well, my cousin, Peregrine Parody, went out for a walk. It was a cold, crisp day; there had been a frost the night before. He put on his coat and hat and I believe took his cane too. At about eleven o'clock I went looking for him to say good-bye and found him in the meadow overlooking the pond, down by the cow pasture. We both loved that view of the surrounding mountains. We discussed his coming to Beaulinia later in the year. And he added he'd look in on my aunt in the hospital, which of course he was never able to do. I started back to the house, and then, remembering I wanted to use up a roll of film, took some pictures of the view, one of which included Cousin Peregrine sitting near the pond. By that time it was eleven-thirty and Ernest Middleton had arrived to drive my aunt to the hospital and then take me on to the airport in Albany."

"Have you that photograph with you, Mrs. Bohner?"

Candy found it in her handbag and gave it to Colonel Smythe, who, on looking at it, exclaimed, "Why there's a strong resemblance in this backview of him to that of Sir Winston Churchill."

Candy leaned over to look at it again. "Why, so there is! That had never occurred to me before."

"Have you one of his face?"

"No, because I really took it for the view. But now that I think about it, his face looked like Churchill's except for the goatee."

By this time the courtroom was abuzz until brought to order.

"Now, Mrs. Bohner," continued the colonel, "since you have been close to your aunt, Miss Nightingale Amber, perhaps you could explain the words Lieutenant Whistler reported earlier he had jotted down at her bedside in the hospital. 'I am pondering'."

"Well, it means: I am thinking it over."

"Yes, yes, we know that, but have you any idea what she might be pondering?"

"Probably the answer to the lieutenant's question. She said the same thing to me. Her memory is pretty much gone, you see."

"Thank you, Mrs. Bohner. No further questions."

Candy returned to her seat while, to her surprise, Mrs. Emily Melville, an attorney living in Keene Valley, was called to the stand. She then explained that her house was at the turn on Market Street with a good view of the Ambers' stone wall and meadow with woods beyond and up the hill to where the house stood. "I really hadn't given the matter any thought until this week. But I do recall now that it was September the twenty-ninth, because I was returning from the grocery store with provisions for my daughter's birthday party that evening. I noticed an unfamiliar-looking car parked across the street. I didn't recognize the make, but did see that it had license tags from Washington, D.C. And near the old wooden stile over the wall was a man peering through binoculars. I assumed he was a bird-watcher at the time. He was a complete stranger."

"Can you recall the time, Mrs. Melville?"

"I know exactly because the noon siren was blowing. That means two or three past twelve."

"Can you describe this bird-watcher?"

"Not too well, I'm afraid. Dark hair, medium tall, I'd say; wearing a sports jacket and neutral-colored slacks. Oh, yes, he was wearing gloves. Quite handsome, slim, athletic-looking, well dressed, even debonair, and somewhat out of place for us in the village."

"One more question. Did you hear a gunshot?"

"Not that I recall."

Suddenly, Mabel Legler stood up and came forward shouting, "Colonel Smythe, I have something to tell; I've just remembered it." That set off a slight commotion.

"Order! Order! Have you anything more to add, Mrs. Melville? Then you may step down." And looking aghast at Mrs. Legler, who was now being restrained by the bailiff, the coroner announced, "There will be a ten-minute recess. Officer, bring this witness forward so that she may explain herself."

When the inquest resumed, Mabel Legler was called to tell her story. She began: "The back of my house looks out over the Ambers' stone wall and the meadow and the pond, and of course the lane that cuts through down to the end of their property. I was sitting at a window having lunch as usual that same day, and I too noticed the bird-watcher, although wondering at the time what birds he might possibly find. I never saw him before."

"What time was that, Mrs. Legler?"

"I'd say about twelve-fifteen. That's when I usually eat my lunch."

"Please continue. Then you noticed something?"

"Yes, one of those hippies."

"Hippies, Mrs. Legler?"

"I call them that. This one was staying at Stone Wall Cottage. That's Jane and Sarah Wall's place. They take in boarders and had a bedraggled-looking girl staying there. This hippy, draped in some kind of tattered blanket—they do wear such outlandish clothes—bustled up the lane toward the pond. That bird-watcher Mrs. Melville mentioned seemed to turn his attention on her. Then she disappeared from view, where the meadow dips behind a hump, and a few minutes later she bustled back down the lane, only looking different. I realized then that she must have been carrying something under the loose blanket when I first saw her, but had since set it down out of my view and then wrapped the blanket up around herself. She did pause to look at the bird-watcher several times before climbing over the wall back of Sarah Wall's boarding house."

"You're very perceptive, Mrs. Legler. Can you further describe this young woman?"

"Besides bedraggled and wearing a blanket? Well, her hair was dark and long and uncombed. She was skinny—nothing but skin and bones. Oh, and wore sneakers without socks. But I'd misplaced my glasses so I didn't get a very good look."

"Did you see Colonel Parody in the meadow or near the pond?"

"No, I can't see the pond from my kitchen window.

I can from upstairs, but I wasn't up there at the time."

"How long was the bird-watcher there?"

"Well, he disappeared while I went to the stove to pour a cup of coffee."

"One more question," continued the coroner. "Did you hear any gunshots that day?"

"It was close to huntin' season, so I wouldn't have paid attention if I did."

"Thank you, Mrs. Legler. You have been most helpful."

There were no more surprises. The inquest now wound down to its official end, and the spectators filed out, grouping on the green in animated clusters. The sun had disappeared and rain seemed imminent. The Hassels, Bohners, and Wackmans crossed the road to the Deer's Head Inn for a well-earned lunch.

They discussed the bird-watcher, a character in the case new to them.

Eric commented: "I find him appropriate for the occasion since he was watching a Peregrine."

"Oh, a peregrine falcon you mean," replied John, smiling. "I noticed that Bud Smythe was most interested in him. And did you see those tough-looking guys sitting in the back?"

Eric remarked, "Quite. Just typical Washington musclemen of the FBI and CIA, I imagine. Does your family make a habit of this?"

"Of what?" asked John. "Oh; I assure you, Eric, that this is the first time the family's been haled into court. And I hope, the last. Well, there was that trouble over a will some years ago but we'll forget that. This is our first murder. I think it involves espionage. The solution is to be found in Washington." John enjoyed reading spy novels.

On the drive back to Keene Valley after lunch, Candy asked Eric if he thought she had done well in court.

"I—am—pond—er—ing," he replied. "By the way, Candace, when you and John paid your first visit to Nittie, what all did she say?"

35

"Just 'I am pondering.' That's all. She just kept saying that or something like that. Her speech was slurred."

"Ah, just as I suspected," mused Eric, while he continued to ponder.

It began to rain hard, which slowed down the driving. By the time they reached Spruce Hill leading down into the valley, John at the wheel remarked, "There's quite a procession behind us. Horace's car I recognize, but those behind him look mighty suspicious with their antennae. I think we can expect the law and the press for tea. I'll just swerve off at the foot and head toward Keene Center and take the back road home. Shake them up a bit." It did.

By the time they pulled up to the house, it was pouring. And no sign of their tailers. Just a bewildered Horace and Mary Wackman, wondering what they had been up to.

John gleefully explained, "We wanted to head off the posse at the pass." John also liked to read Westerns.

Pattee laughed. "Dearie, do you know what that means?"

"My meaning is clear. Come on, Eric, let's watch some television in the library. Judge Wapner in 'People's Court' will be on soon, I know you enjoy that. Oh, I forgot. I must park the car down by the barn first."

While John and Eric attended to the parking, Pattee and Candy went over to the kitchen to confer with Martha about dinner.

En route, Pattee asked, "What's 'People's Court'?"

"It concerns real small-claims cases in a real courtroom shown on TV before a real judge. The participants with real grievances have agreed to abide by Judge Wapner's decisions. Eric discovered the show while here last summer. Gives him legal training, he thinks."

"He needs it in this family full of lawyers. Has he ever tried out this knowledge on you?"

"Wouldn't do him any good, Pattee. Coming from a large family, I learned early to argue my case. Eric never had that opportunity. He's an only child."

They found Martha fuming in the kitchen. "Here's my grocery shopping list made out early this morning and no one took it," she said, waving it at Candy. "There's nothing to serve for dinner to all these freeloaders of Miss Nittie's."

Candy attempted to soothe her feelings. "You're quite right, Martha. It slipped my mind. We'll dine out at the Spread Eagle tonight and shop in the morning."

She and Pattee beat a hasty retreat to the main house to inform John and Eric, who were just entering the library. Then, they went upstairs to bathe while there was some hot water available.

The rain had stopped for a while when Claudia, in heavy rainwear, reported in from the meadow. "Daddy, there are silly little men all over the place, lurking behind trees, poking in the old cow shed, dragging the pond, and photographing the ice house. They are disturbing the balance of nature. I'm going to get my bow and arrow and give them a real scare."

Eric reminded her, "Claudia, I don't think that would be wise. We don't want to set off an international incident. Let human nature take its course. They're nothing but a bunch of Keystone Kops. But you had better stay out of the meadows and woods for a few days until they get tired of playing cops and robbers."

"Well, Daddy, what happened at the inquest today to let loose those clowns?"

"We're going to discuss all that after dinner. Uncle John wants to watch 'People's Court' now, and, Claudia, we are going to the Spread Eagle for dinner at six sharp."

# Chapter 5

# A Blessing in Disguise

After their early dinner, the Hassels and Bohners settled themselves comfortably before a roaring fire to ward off the dampness. Thus began the evening's conversation.

Candy: "Has the moose been anchored securely to the wall? I mean its antler."

Eric: "You're out of order, Candace."

John: "Ernest did it. Now let us summarize today's hearing."

Pattee: "Hear, hear!"

John: "Now you're out of order, Pattee. To begin, Peregrine was definitely and unfortunately for us, and of course for him, killed by person or persons unknown."

Pattee: "We know that, dearie. My, just hear that rain beating on the windows."

John: "That's irrelevant and immaterial, except for those out in it."

Eric: "Point number two: The autopsy report stated 'shot in the heart through the back' or was it 'shot in the back through the heart'? That is, when he disappeared last September."

John: "Yes, that figures. Any comments, Candy?"

Candy: "Well, don't look at me. I only took a snapshot, not a shot. I never could have dropped three hundred pounds of Peregrine into the pond."

John: "We are well aware of that. But somebody did."

Eric: "The more intriguing question is how he ended up in the ice house. Was it still in use?"

John: "I don't think so; not since Dottie and Nittie had the kitchen coldroom electrified many years ago."

Candy: "I think, though, they gave someone in the village permission to cut and sell the ice for themselves. You know, for ice cubes. They had that arrangement for the meadow hay."

Pattee: "Do you think the murderer cut off Perry's head? To sort of lighten the load or something?"

Eric: "It would seem more likely that the head was sharply separated from the body while ice cutting was in progress."

Claudia: "Ah, a corpus delicti et caput. . . ."

Eric: "Et caput separatum, Claudia."

Pattee: "Just what does that mean?"

Eric: "Body of the crime and severed or separated head."

John: "To continue; the question arises as to when the remains, or as Claudia here would say, 'reliquiae,' were stored in the ice house, and why they weren't noticed at the time."

Pattee: "How about Ernest and his helper, Harold?"

Eric: "I recall, Horace said they told him they had no reason to be in the ice house."

John: "All right, then. To summarize our little investigation: Person or persons unknown placed the body and head in their separate blocks of ice in the old ice house."

Candy: "We aren't making much progress in solving this mystery. What about the bird-watcher?"

Pattee: "You mean, he might have been waiting and watching for the pond to freeze over?"

Claudia: "Oh, Aunt Pattee, in September? But what about Aunt Nittie's ring down by the pond? Could someone have snitched it to implicate her?"

Candy: "It must have slipped off her finger earlier while taking a walk."

Eric: "I—am—pond—er—ring."

Candy: "You're what?"

Eric: "Nittie's words, remember? Or something similar? Why couldn't she have been talking about her ring? You said she was very fond of it. Perhaps she was trying to tell you that she lost it near the pond. Like, 'I—at—the pond—ther ring'."

Candy: "*Ther* ring? Aunt Nittie doesn't talk like that!"

Eric: "You said she slurred, didn't you?"

Candy: 'True. She was slurring her words, poor old soul. Eric, you are brilliant. We must take it to her tomorrow. Where is it?"

Claudia: "I have it. I'll take it to her."

John: "Now that we have solved that mystery, thanks to Eric, let's move on, or back, to Perry. How is he related to all of us?"

Candy: "Let me see. Perry's mother was a sister of Grandma Amber, thus first cousin to Mother, Dottie, and Nittie; and first cousin once removed to us. Oh, and twice removed to Claudia and her generation. He had a sizable inheritance, I gather, from the way Dottie once sniffed at his never holding a job. He stayed on in Europe after World War I and little was heard from or seen of him except for an occasional passing through Albany on banking business, until he showed up here in September. Nittie wasn't too pleased to see him, but of course let him stay. He seemed very nice to me. But Nittie seemed annoyed."

Eric: "How old is she?"

Pattee: "Who, Nittie? She was ninety-two last October. I remember looking for a suitable birthday card to send her."

Candy: "Did you find one?"

Pattee: "Not really. I had a choice of 'Congratulations on your retirement,' 'Thanks for the memory,' and 'Many happy returns.' I chose the 'Returns,' although knowing there can't be many left."

John: "Have you any more information, Candy?"

Candy: "Perry mentioned being an agent of influence once, whatever that is. A spy, I guess. He said he'd worked for British Intelligence; in fact, had known Philby, Burgess, and MacLean, which I could hardly believe. He knew Dulles in the CIA, too. Oh, and Winston Churchill. I almost forgot that he was called the Falcon; can you imagine that? He thought that funny too, adding that Pelican would have suited him better."

Pattee: "So that's what the bird-watcher was after; big game; so he shot the largest peregrine falcon he'd ever seen."

Claudia: "Oh, Aunt Pattee, you have the biggest flights of fancy!"

John: "Did you ever meet him, Eric?"

Candy (interrupting): "No. Eric returned to Washington before the arrival of Perry. But Perry had expressed interest in Eric's new posting. He mentioned that the father of an old school chum, Harry Snow, had built a house there. And it turned out to be the house that's now our embassy. Everybody we've run into lately seems to have known Harry Snow. He was Grandpa's partner for a time at Amber-Snow, you know."

John: "Ties to Beaulinia, eh. This is getting interesting. Perhaps we should consider . . ."

Suddenly headlights were shining in the windows and a horn was heard with voices and laughter.

Candy exclaimed, "That sounds like Konrad!" She dashed to the front hall, calling back. "They're here," followed by the others to greet Chester and Konrad—and, it turned out, a surprise guest.

Chester and Konrad had reached the valley at nine-thirty. It was cold and raining again, the really splashy kind. Just as they were going to turn off Main to go up Market Street, Konrad spotted a beautiful girl in a trenchcoat and soggy slouch hat, standing at the entrance road of the hospital. He turned to Chester, shouting, "Wait!

Hold it! I've just seen the girl I'm going to marry. Stop the car, Chester!"

"Konrad, are you nuts? What girl? Where?"

"Back up, she's by the hospital road."

Chester stopped the car: "Look, Konrad, it's pouring down rain, we're almost home and . . ."

But Konrad had jumped out and raced back to introduce himself to the lovely stranger and offer her his services (a rather charming, old-fashioned touch), while Chester waited impatiently for him—with the girl in tow—to return.

"This is Lily Blessing. Chester Wackman, my cousin. Lily says she is staying at the Keene Valley Inn, down the road. I've invited her up to the house to meet everybody. Here, Lily, take the seat in front. I'll just drape myself on top of all this stuff in the back."

And so they arrived at the Amber house. On first meeting Lily, Eric and Candy, who were standing in the hall, weren't sure whether Konrad had brought her from England, nor what they should do with her. They were vastly relieved to learn later that she was staying in the village. However, from further polite questioning they also learned that she was a reporter for *The Nonobservance*, which they thought they heard as "The Nonobservant," and could only hope that she would live up to that title. Konrad must be reminded not to divulge family affairs to her, which of course she was after. Anyway, they believed he would be plenty busy in the kitchen helping Martha.

After a late but adequate supper for the newcomers, Konrad drove Lily to her inn in the old Chevie. He returned home too late for Candy and Eric, still worrying about Lily's presence in their midst, to discuss this problem with him. They would do so in the morning.

Chapter 6

# A Black Eye and a Blue Brooch

First thing Friday morning, Candy entered Konrad's room to awaken him: "Now Konrad, you realize it is a bit awkward to have a newspaper reporter as your friend, charming as she is. It will inhibit our conversation and add to our notoriety, especially in that dreadful tabloid, *The Unobservant.*"

Konrad was fully awake. "It's *Nonobservance*. It comes out on Sundays."

"Well, whatever."

"Lily said she'd like to help me in the kitchen, after she heard you tell me I was appointed Martha's helper. That will be perfect. I'll accept the position under those conditions."

"Well, if that's the only way, why I'll increase your allowance so you can take her out, except at dinner time, of course, to keep her away from the house. Take her hiking and down to the club and use all your charm to keep her mind off her job."

"I intend to. I plan to marry her."

"You what? Oh, dear me!"

Eric in the adjoining room called out, "Is that you, Konrad? Your mother and I want to have a chat with you."

"We've already talked, Eric. Konrad has decided to marry Lily."

"So soon? I thought you met her just last night."

"Well, Mummy once said that you and she . . ."

"Quite!" interrupted Eric. "But we don't want any notoriety. I trust you'll find out what her father does."

"He's head of some department in the government. And Lily just graduated from Cornell."

"Splendid. And—she does have a job."

"But not for long, I think."

"Why ever not?" asked Candy.

"She doesn't know how to type."

"Well, how did she get hired as a reporter?"

"They didn't ask and she didn't tell."

Eric replied, "Ah, she sounds like a diplomat."

Candy added on leaving his room, "Don't forget to pick up Martha's shopping list on your way out after breakfast."

The Bohners went down to the dining room to join the Hassels for a do-it-yourself breakfast. It was a lovely day. The sun was shining while the trees around the house glistened and dripped. Claudia had finished eating and told her parents she would first go visit Aunt Nittie this morning and then explore the Ausable River, since the Amber property was out of bounds for her while there continued to be a spy behind every tree.

She was soon at the hospital, where she said hello to old Dr. Cough in the parking lot getting out of his tiny sports car. She thought he must be close to eighty. She had heard that he had arrived in Keene Valley over fifty years ago, to be the only doctor for miles around. He'd always been a colorful character. Claudia remembered when he had treated her for poison ivy many years ago, in spite of Aunt Dottie insisting that there wasn't any in Keene Valley. He'd say to his young patients, "I'm Jack Cough, local M.D. Jack of all trades I gotta be." He used to fly his airplane and still indulged in deer hunting. But now his hands shook at times, and his eyesight wasn't what it had been. She asked his permission to use the lab microscope for specimens she'd collected from the pond, a request enthusiastically granted. But first she looked in on Aunt Nittie to return the opal ring she cherished so. She was dozing, so Claudia just slipped it on her finger, kissed her cheek and tip-toed out.

She thought, *It looks like it will be a gentle ending, like Aunt Dottie's a year ago.* Claudia had always admired those two independent women. *It's so nice to have money of one's own the old-fashioned way, by inheritance,* she sighed, *and to have had their busy lives and many interests and lots of travel.* Their generosity had always been lavish. Nittie, the youngest of the three Amber sisters, had been especially active. *Why, she'd won all those silver tennis cups on the mantelpiece in the dining room, rode her own horse, and had climbed all the high peaks many times. I can just picture her, as Mummy said, always wearing the same hiking outfit: tan shirt, tan knickers, tan high woolen socks, and ankle-high sneakers, like those old Keds; never see those anymore.*

Meanwhile, Mary and Horace had found someone from the village to help with chores and children and decided to take a break for a morning visit to the club. The tennis courts appeared dry enough, so on seeing Konrad and Lily playing, they challenged them to a game of doubles. Fifth game into the match, Horace was at net while Mary was to receive Lily's serve. His mind wandering, Horace suddenly realized that no murder weapon had yet been found and that perhaps the pond should be dragged or drained, when wham! Lily's serve went haywire and the ball hit him in the face, smashing his dark glasses. It gave him quite a shock. Lily was horrified. End of match, and over to the nearby hospital they all went.

After Dr. Cough checked the damage he diagnosed nothing more serious than an incipient black eye. "That's one for the judge," he chuckled. Horace knew he'd never hear the end of it. Poor Lily was so embarrassed. But Konrad reassured her she made a great partner. He had not yet informed her though that he meant in marriage as well. "After all, Lily, Horace is a good tennis player and should have been paying attention. Let's drive over to Lake Placid for lunch and forget about it."

Back at the house, while Candy was trying to pacify Martha, who had presented her with a long list of complaints, including too many people in the kitchen, John and Eric were relaxing on the big porch describing yesterday's inquest to their nephew, Chester, and hoping to gain some hints as to the solution of the case. Chester, a professor of law at Columbia University, advised them to leave it to the proper authorities. John groaned. "You haven't met Lieutenant Whistler yet!"

And with that, in walked the very same lieutenant, so John just repeated himself in a friendlier tone of voice, "You haven't met Lieutenant Whistler yet. This is Professor Chester Wackman. He's an attorney also."

"Lots of legal people around here, Mr. Hassel," remarked the smiling Whistler.

"There's still another one to come. My son, Johnny. He'll be arriving tomorrow. It's like having a Bar Association convention of our own."

"And all in the family," whistled the lieutenant. "I wanted to ask you if you noticed any strangers darting about your property. They aren't attorneys too, are they?"

John laughed: "We thought you'd know who they are. They are a nuisance, and we'd appreciate it, Lieutenant, if you'd tell them to stop messing up the property and the investigation."

"Well, that's sort of why I'm here, sir. We had a phone call from Washington, this morning . . ."

Candy came up the steps from the dining-room porch, interrupting him with a "Why, good morning, Lieutenant. Have you good news?"

"Good morning, ma'am. I was telling the ambassador and Mr. Hassel and Professor Wackman that we received a phone call from Washington this morning informing us that—By the way, you were acquainted with Mr. William Riddle, an aide to Congressman Sam Brasher, I believe."

"Oh, my, yes," replied Candy. "He was in the Congressional party visiting Beaulinia when we heard the news about Cousin Peregrine. We played tennis together. He's a very dashing sort of person."

Whistler continued, "I regret to say, ma'am, that he was shot—in fact killed—early yesterday morning on a tennis court at the Federal Tennis and Squash Club in Washington."

"Why, why, that's a bit unusual, I'd say," said the surprised Eric.

"And he was such a fine tennis player," exclaimed Candy. "You say 'shot'?"

"Yes, ma'am, and killed; in the head, several times."

Then Pattee rushed up the steps from the flower garden, where she had been doing some weeding, asking breathlessly, "Who's been shot?"

Candy explained: "They found Bill Riddle riddled with bullets on a tennis court in Washington."

"Who's Bill Riddle?" asked Pattee.

"I played tennis with him in Beaulinia. He was an aide to Congressman Brasher and a very cool person, really."

Pattee: "Oh, a cool-aide!"

John: "Can it, dearie. Continue please, Lieutenant."

Whistler: "I was hoping that the ambassador or Mrs. Bohner might shed some light on his behavior or activities in Beaulinia. Of course, his case is not in my jurisdiction, but there might be some connection with Colonel Parody."

Eric: "I really didn't have much to do with him."

Candy: "Oh, but I did. I mean, the night of our embassy party, I spotted him in the library snooping around suspiciously. But what has that to do with us?"

Whistler: "Colonel Parody's name was found in Riddle's address book. This address, Keene Valley."

Candy: "Well, he never told me that! But that explains his odd behavior. He certainly seemed to be looking for something. Perhaps the wall safe."

Eric: "Why the wall safe?"

Candy: "That's where we put the packet Cousin Peregrine gave me."

Everybody: "What packet?"

Whistler: "Please explain, Mrs. Bohner. A packet? Do you have it here?"

Candy: "I forgot all about it, but yes, I'll go . . ."

Whistler: "One moment, please. When did you receive this packet from Colonel Parody?"

Candy: "The day I left here last September. He asked me to take it to Beaulinia for safe-keeping, until he could visit us in the spring. I invited him, Eric, I don't know why. He just seemed so alone, and he suggested coming, anyway."

Whistler: "Would you get the packet now please, Mrs. Bohner?"

While Candy disappeared indoors, Eric apologized to Whistler. "I hope you don't believe we'd intentionally withhold evidence. It did seem to slip our minds. Life does get confusing, especially here."

Whistler: "I understand, sir. It's a pretty . . . er . . . perplexing situation."

Candy returned with a small bulky package the size of a candy box. "Look what else I found. It was with that bunch of snapshots I took that day. See, it's of the lane, and there's a strange woman hurrying down it. Eric, lend me your magnifying glass. Thanks. Why, she's wearing a blanket. It must be that hippie boarder of Miss Wall's, the one mentioned at the inquest."

Whistler: "May I see that, Mrs. Bohner? Would you mind if I had a copy made?"

Candy: "Not at all," as she handed it to him, and turned her attention to the packet, reading aloud its label: "To be opened in the event of my death by my attorney,

Casper Swain, of New York City. Well, Perry's dead and, oh, Lieutenant, we learned in New York that Casper Swain died also."

John: "Yes, and that his files were thrown out by his young partners."

Chester (indignant): "They can't do that. Give me their names. They should be disbarred."

Everyone now approved of Candy's opening the package. Eric gallantly assisted cutting the string with his handy pocket knife. Inside were two manila envelopes with writing on them. The first one read: "For my daughter, Jennifer Parody, with love."

Everyone chorused in surprise: "Daughter?"

Candy continued, "Wait a minute, there's more. It says 'These pieces of jewelry belonged to your Grandmother Mary Talcott Parody. Love, Dadders.'"

The chorus surprised again: "Jewelry? Dadders?"

Candy: "Let's take a peek."

Eric: "Don't you dare, Candace!"

Candy set it aside and picked up the smaller envelope. "This one says 'For Candace Bohner, in appreciation of your kindness in Keene Valley. The other package is for my daughter, Jennifer, whom I hope you will get to know someday. She lives with her mother in Pairtrie, England. I was married many years ago to Ann Partridge of Pairtrie, Kent, and Jenny is our only child. Cousin Peregrine.'"

Pattee: "Oh, a Partridge in a Pairtrie!"

John: "Dearie, how do you think of those things?"

Candy: "The name does sound familiar, though. Oh, well, there must be many Partridges in England."

Eric, impatient now: "Well, open your package, Candace!"

She tore it open to discover a diamond-and-sapphire brooch. They were all speechless. Pattee recovered first. "That must be worth several thousand!"

Eric took it to examine under his pocket magnifying glass. "In today's market, I'd estimate ten thousand, at least. Those are good-sized stones." He passed it around for all to admire.

Candy: "How shall we find Jennifer?"

John: "Eric could call someone in the London embassy to locate her."

Whistler decided it was time to leave. "Ambassador, there's no need to worry about withheld evidence, but I'd appreciate it if you would inform me of Miss Parody's whereabouts when you learn of them."

Eric: "Certainly, Lieutenant."

Whistler: "Nor do I believe that Mr. Riddle was looking for jewelry, but something more valuable. That's another riddle, isn't it?" He then made a hasty good-bye to hurry back to headquarters.

Claudia soon appeared. "What did you do to Lieutenant Whistler? He just passed me at the gate going sixty miles an hour, and laughing. Oh, and I picked up the mail at the post office. There's a card from Klara." She handed it to Candy, who eagerly read it. "Listen to this, everybody. Klara writes, 'Dear Mummy and Daddy, David and I had our first glimpse of the mountain, finally. The weather has been appalling. We heard that a New Yorker fell off the Matterhorn into Italy, due to sheer carelessness, of course. Everything is so expensive. David paid six dollars for a small bottle of Listerine. Love, Klara.'"

Eric: "Is that all? Any clue to where she is?"

Candy: "That's it! That's Klara for you. Omits such details. And I can't make out the postmark either. The picture is of a cow in an alpine meadow.

Claudia: "But see, Mummy, there wasn't any more writing space."

"Candy: "She could have omitted the cost of the Listerine."

John: "I think David should drink the stuff at that price rather than gargle with it."

Pattee: "Why would the New Yorker fall into Italy?"

Candy: "The Matterhorn straddles the Swiss-Italian border. Why, she didn't even say if he survived!"

Eric: "Quite. But think, Candace, how much worse it would be if she had written that David fell off, and so on. You really should not permit her to undertake such dangerous—uh—undertakings. I had a college professor who fell off a peak in the Dolomites and . . ."

No one was listening to another one of Eric's gloom-and-doom stories to fit the current occasion. They were telling Claudia about Peregrine's package, Peregrine's daughter, and Peregrine's brooch.

Chapter 7

## The Unhinging of Horace

That afternoon, Henny called her brother Horace from her home in Vermont, wondering if she and Seth and the children ought to come to Keene Valley; a family reunion would be pleasant. Also, since she was a practicing psychologist, perhaps she could be of some help in solving the case. When Horace told her his girls had mumps, the baby was teething, he'd acquired a black eye playing tennis, Martha the cook was threatening to quit—and he wished she would; that Konrad was courting a reporter from the tabloid, *The Nonobservant,* while she helped out in the kitchen, intelligence people were poking around in the woods and meadow, that the moose over the mantel dropped an antler on Detective Whistler, cousins Johnny and Rick were expected tomorrow, or was it today, she replied, "You're all nuts! I'll make it some other time," and hung up.

The younger Hassels did arrive in time for dinner; all seven of them: Johnny and wife, Sally, and Rick and wife, Cindy, plus three little Hassels. Martha had been warned and provided with a large roast to cook, while Konrad and Lily would do the rest. The results were excellent. Afterwards, while Sally and Cindy were getting the children ready for bed and puttering around upstairs to avoid all silly discussions of the bizarre Parody murder by the family, Horace came up the hill to greet the new arrivals and to propose that they gather around the fireplace to sort out the Peregrine puzzle. They welcomed this suggestion and appointed him presiding officer, with Chester to take notes. No, not Chester, no one could read his handwriting. Let Rick do it; as a teacher, he had learned to write legibly. They began:

John: "All right, Horace, as judge of this Court of Latter Day Findings, bring us to order. Do you need a gavel?"

Horace: "Probably, with this gabby family, but never mind. I'll summarize the facts and then each one in turn will have the opportunity to add, amend, or deny. I'll begin by saying that Mary and I were completely surprised that Cousin Peregrine, to be known as the deceased, had been a colonel in British Intelligence and an agent for the American one. Was he really code-named the Falcon?"

Pattee: "Did you know he was married and has a daughter?"

Horace: "Where did you learn that?"

Pattee: "He left a package of family jewels with Candy last fall for safekeeping."

Horace: "Well, Aunt Candy, why didn't you tell the authorities?"

Candy: "I forgot all about it until today, while Lieutenant Whistler was here. It had a note."

Horace: "Well, where is the daughter?"

Eric: "In England. I'm having a reluctant colleague in London locate the Partridges in Pairtrie."

Horace: "Can't you people be serious?" This isn't 'the first day of Christmas, my true love sent to me!'"

Rick: "Hold it. I haven't gotten this all down yet."

Johnny: "By the way, where is Konrad?"

Candy: "We told him to take Lily to the movies in Ausable Forks."

Johnny: "You told him to take out the maid?"

Candy: "Oh, she's not the maid. She's just helping Konrad in the kitchen. She's a newspaper reporter."

Chester: "Konrad found her in the rain in front of the hospital. She had been trying to interview Aunt Nittie."

Johnny: "You mean, you people are harboring a reporter?"

Claudia: "It's love at first sight for Konrad."

Johnny: "And that's why Konrad is banished to the kitchen?"

Candy: "No, Martha needed help, but none of the local girls will work with her. I thought of trying a young man, and then Konrad so conveniently appeared. Such a simple solution, you know. And with Lily in the kitchen, we know what she's doing, and in return, Konrad said he'd help write innocuous reports for her paper. She doesn't type."

Johnny: "Well, that's a pretty rotten thing to do!"

Pattee: "Now, Johnny, he can always marry her if she finds herself in a compromising position; I mean with the paper, of course."

Rick: "Okay, continue."

Horace: "Continue? Let's start again. Since you people seem to know so much, we'll start with, uh . . ."

Candy: "I wish to confess. . . ."

Horace (shocked): "You killed him, Aunt Candy?"

Rick (hurriedly): "Someone read her her rights!"

Claudia: "Shut up, Ricky, and stick to your writing."

Johnny: "Aunt Candy, would you like an attorney?"

Candy: "Please don't interrupt, everybody, or I'll forget what I want to say."

Rick (interrupting helpfully): "It says here that you confess."

Candy: "Oh, yes, or I mean, oh no, not to that. It's just that my explanation of my relationship with Peregrine isn't what I thought."

Eric (sounding suspicious): "What relationship did you have with him?"

Candy: "Why cousinship. I believed he was my first cousin once removed, being Aunt Nittie's first cousin. But I've been mulling it over. His mother is Nittie's first cousin, therefore making him first cousin once removed to her and second cousin to John and me and twice removed . . ."

Eric: "Quite. You've muddled enough for now, Candy."

Rick (reading aloud from his notes): ". . . and twice re-what? How does that go again, Aunt Candy?"

Horace: "Skip it, Rick! Uncle John, have you anything to add?"

John: "I haven't anything even to subtract. I'm lost!"

Eric: "I say, does Horace know about Bill Riddle being murdered?"

John: "No, nor do Johnny and Rick. You'd better explain that one, Eric, since you knew him."

Horace (surprised and growing confused): "Who's this Bull Fiddle? You know, it's a good thing I came up here tonight."

Rick (looking up suddenly): "Hey, what's happened to the moose? Its jaw's open and one antler is cockeyed."

Claudia: "Yeah, the antler fell off and hit Lieutenant Whistler the other night."

Rick: "You mean the moose attacked a law-enforcement officer?"

Horace: "Attention, folks! Let's return to sorting out this muddle."

Eric: "It's Riddle, Bill Riddle, aide to Congressman

Brasher on a junket to Beaulinia to check out Carlos's secret weapon."

Horace (showing utter amazement): "Good lord, who's Carlos? Never mind: I don't want to know."

Eric, continuing: "Candy discovered this Riddle fellow poking around in our library, which is always out of bounds for guests, because it's our private sitting room, our inner sanctum where we can relax and where I work on my research and Candy reads and listens to the radio in the evening. Oh, yes, and where the safe is installed. Candy was suspicious and thought he might be looking for the safe, in which was Peregrine's package, although at the time we had no idea that Riddle knew Peregrine, or that the package contained jewelry he had left to his daughter, Jennifer, who is living with her mother's family, the Partridges of Pairtrie."

Horace, thoroughly exasperated: "If I hear that one more time! Oh, excuse me, Uncle Eric, I know you at least try to be serious."

Eric: "Candy played tennis with Bill Riddle, or Bull Fiddle, as you first called him, and I must say, that's quite good."

Horace: "And?"

Eric: "Well, that's all that happened in Beaulinia, to our knowledge."

Horace: "Didn't someone mention murder?"

Eric: "Oh, yes, but not in Beaulinia."

Horace, impatiently: "Well, where then?"

Eric: "In Washington, on a tennis court. I always said it was a dangerous sport. Never play it myself. By the way, your eye does look black, or is that purple? Konrad told us about your unfortunate accident. You see, Candy, you really should give up the game."

Horace: "How?"

Eric: "How to give up the game? Why it's . . ."

Horace, interrupting: "How was this Riddle killed?"

Eric: "Riddled with bullets."

Rick: "Hold it, everybody. I have a riddle."

Johnny: "That's not funny, Rick."

Rick, continuing recklessly: "And it's no love game!"

Claudia, joining in the fun: "Maybe it served him right!"

Horace: "You know, you two are not witty. You are a pair of nitwits. Go on, Uncle Eric. Any motive?"

Eric: "Why, I imagine so. There usually is."

Horace, raising his voice: "Well, what is it?"

Eric: "Lieutenant Whistler didn't say, unless it was drug-related."

Horace: "So Riddle knew Perry?"

Eric: "But Perry couldn't have killed him, being already dead."

John: "There was some connection, though. In an address book, I believe."

Horace: "Did anyone watch the six o'clock news?"

Chester, who had been reading during most of this conversation, now spoke: "It wasn't mentioned. Both Uncle Eric and I watched for it after 'People's Court.'"

Eric: "Quite. I say, Howard, do you know Judge Wapner?"

Chester: "Perhaps they are hushing it up."

Eric: "Or else Canada isn't interested in that kind of thing."

Chester: "You mean, we had on a Canadian station?"

Eric: "It's the clearest one, I discovered."

Horace: "Never mind. We can turn on the eleven o'clock network news. If I can see it with one eye."

Pattee, who had been silently absorbed in picking up several dropped stitches in her knitting, looked up at Horace who was now standing with his back to the fire: "It must really hurt. Shouldn't we put a raw beefsteak or something on it?"

Candy: "Let's get a cold, wet towel. That's cheaper."

Horace: "Look, Rick, you don't have to write this part down!"

Candy: "Chester, why don't you help Horace down the hill to the Gate House. We can continue tomorrow night. Don't forget to take a flashlight."

Horace: "Thanks, Aunt Candy. We'll try the news tonight for some information."

Candy: "And Eric may learn something from London tomorrow."

Horace: "You know, Henny is right; she said we're all nuts. Oh, I hope you've all had mumps. Our girls seem to have caught them. Good night, everybody."

Eric couldn't recall ever having had them.

Chester and Horace proceeded down the dark road. Chester brought up the same point that had struck Horace on the tennis court before he was struck so ignominiously by a wayward ball. It concerned the murder weapon.

"The inquest report mentioned an ordinary hunting rifle, which is common in these parts, in fact, probably at least one in every household in the village. After all, there are deer, bear, rabbit, raccoon, possum, squirrel, and chipmunk just waiting in these woods and fields to end up on the local dinner tables. Why even Dr. Cough likes to hunt. And Ernest and Harold. I remember, early one summer Aunt Dottie discovered a dead deer behind the barn. She was furious. She suspected Dr. Cough, but hesitated to confront him, since she had no proof, though she did let the villagers know of her displeasure. Could Dr. Cough have seen anything suspicious the day of the murder?"

Horace, exhausted, replied weakly, "Most unlikely on a weekday. He was a busy doctor continually making house calls all over the valley. It was decent of him to come to treat the children today."

"But still," continued Chester, "I'll ask him tomorrow when I visit poor old Aunt Nittie at the hospital."

The village and woods were always so quiet at night that Mary could hear the brothers talking long before they arrived at the Gate House. She called out, "Is that you, Horace and Chester? You're back early." And when she saw under the porch light how battered and weary Horace looked, she added, "Come in by the fire, and I'll fix you a stiff drink."

Chester said good night and departed, while Mary helped Horace inside to the couch by the fireplace.

"Mary," he groaned, "you wouldn't believe what was said up at the house. Those people are something else! There's a guy in Washington named Fiddle, no, Riddle, who got drilled with bullets on a tennis court. There's a daughter of Cousin Peregrine whose mother is a Partridge in a pear tree, whose jewelry Candy has but had forgotten she had. And don't ask me what kind of a 'removed' cousin Perry is. There's someone named Carlos with a secret weapon; we'll skip him. Now, who is Judge Wapner? Uncle Eric asked me if I knew him. And Lily washes dishes in the kitchen while Konrad types up her news reports, which he makes up."

"Well, no one is expected to believe all that nonsense found in a tabloid. It's just for fun."

Horace continued, "Even the moose is coming unhinged again."

"I think you are, too, Horace. Finish your drink and let's get some rest before one of the children wakes up."

# Chapter 8

# Unexpected Departures and Arrivals

Bright and early Saturday morning, the paneled walls of the big house reverberated to the excited shouts of the little Hassels. It was only six o'clock. Martha wouldn't be up and around until eight. Candy, up early as usual, was having her first cup of coffee for the day; her own concoction of hot tap water and instant coffee. It was easier to prepare than going the long distance to the kitchen that early, undressed as yet. Eric too was up, bathed, and shaved, and dressing when he remarked, "I say, Candace, this visit is quite different from what I had anticipated. There has been no bickering. I'm quite enjoying it. Quite."

"That's because the squabblers aren't here." She proceeded to list those who fussed and over what.

"I only commented, Candace. Details aren't necessary."

At breakfast, Candy asked her daily question, "What's the program for the day?" John then invited Eric to drive with him to the Ausable Club at St. Hubert's. "But, John, no golf, please, I don't play. It's a mindless form of activity," warned Eric.

Pattee announced that she would "walk the children to the village to Helen's gift shop for souvenirs, to the library for bedtime reading material, and to the hospital for Nittie to see them, although she probably won't recognize them. She's undoubtedly stopped 'pondering' though. Then on to the club for a dip in the pool."

The children's parents thought they'd take some of the old wooden tennis racquets left lying on the bench in the hall and attempt some leisurely tennis and mild exercise. Chester then challenged Candy and Claudie to a game of doubles. Claudia suggested Horace as a fourth, but Chester didn't believe that Horace, sporting a black eye, would be interested. They could find someone at the club.

Candy reminded Eric to call London about the mysterious Jennifer Parody. "Candace, you know I dislike making long-distance calls."

"Now, Eric, it's an Amber family affair, so you won't have to pay for it."

"You are quite right," he replied and went off cheerfully to the telephone.

John commented on the disappointing, uninformative

television news report of Riddle's murder: "Absolutely nothing." Pattee suggested, "Well, dearie, perhaps when Lieutenant Whistler drops in—he's always dropping in—he'll have more to tell us." They all liked the lieutenant now. He was low keyed, but in control, and most polite. Nice looking, too. They felt comfortable with him, and were looking forward to his next visit.

It turned out the lieutenant was having breakfast with Horace and Mary Wackman at the Gate House. He assured them he had had mumps, both sides. Horace thanked him for clearing the property of inquisitive strangers and then brought up the idea of draining the pond for the murder weapon. "Of course this has nothing to do with the case, but I've heard that Dr. Cough and friends have been suspected of hunting occasionally out of season. And then there's this Bill Riddle in Washington. How does he fit in?"

Whistler told him they were investigating ties to organized crime, but that it wasn't in his jurisdiction.

"But surely Cousin Parody wouldn't be mixed up with that!"

"Hard to say, Judge. Both worked for the same organizations at one time or another, I understand."

"And that bird-watcher and blanket woman connection," persisted Horace. "How's that investigation going?"

Lieutenant Whistler sighed. "Slowly. We're working on it." But he hadn't a clue, and soon departed, as Pattee and her grandchildren walked past the house on their way to the hospital.

After looking in on Nittie, who appeared to be dozing, Pattee observed Dr. Cough making his morning rounds and looking awfully old and shaky, Pattee thought, with tobacco ashes sprinkled down the front of his white jacket. She mentioned this to Miss Jane Wall, the supervisor, who assured her that Dr. Cough could do no harm to Miss Amber and that she and the nurses would give all the care that was needed. Martha came every day to feed "Miss Nittie" her lunch, because she would eat a little something "only for Martha." They discussed the remarkable Martha, a large, beefy Irish woman who had cooked for the Ambers for almost fifty years. Tired now, occasionally ill-tempered and of course distressed over Miss Nittie's condition, her best culinary days were over. Since Aunt Nittie liked her and considered her a part of the family, Martha was treated by the rest with tolerance and circumspection. She was as devoted to Miss Nittie as she had been to Miss Dottie. And she realized that her days of service were almost over.

Pattee took the children outside. She thought, *How fresh and clean the air feels and how clear the mountains look, and the village looks shiny clean too. There's just no place like Keene Valley!* They went next door to the Birch Shop, where Pattee liked to buy maple syrup, but found it closed, with a "for sale" sign in front. So they crossed the road to Carl's garage, where his daughter had recently opened an artisan's shop in the old office. Pattee was expecting the children to select an Indian headdress or a papoose doll, a beaded change purse or a tomahawk. To her surprise, she found herself treating them to dollhouse furniture, a trivia game, and a periscope. She had forgotten that her "toddlers" were growing up. They then headed back towards the club, stopping on the way at the library, her favorite place to visit. After they had all made their selections, they went over to the Keene Valley Grocery for a quart of local blueberries, before they were sold out for the day. "I wonder if there's time to go on to the Mountaineer Shop. I could do with some new boots. No, I'd better get the kids over to the pool now."

While the children dashed to the locker rooms to change. Pattee strolled over to the two center tennis courts monopolized by Bohners, Hassels and Wackman. "What a noisy bunch," she said to herself. "When the family gets together, it's wall-to-wall talk, laughter and . . ."

Chester let out a loud gasp. He and Claudia were partners. The score was six all, with Claudia at net while

Chester served to Candy. Then he dashed forward to take Candy's return just as Claudia swung back her racquet to do the same. The racquet hit Chester's glasses, smashing them and stunning him. Claudia was stunned too. Everybody ran up to view the latest victim of uncourtly behavior. Johnny, who had been playing on the next court, took charge, saying that he and Sally would drive Chester right over to the hospital emergency room and that the rest should remain at the club. Realizing that Chester was not seriously cut up. Rick and Cindy invited Candy, Claudia, and their "fourth," one Fritzie Eschenbach, who had been available and who played extremely well for his age, which was eleven. But Fritzie thought there might be three too many racquets waving about on his side of the court, and said he'd go swimming.

In the emergency room, Miss Wall looked up from her desk as Chester approached and asked, "Are you Wackmans making a habit of this? I'll get Dr. Cough to have a look at your eye. I think he's still around." He was, but not for long.

Chester was led into an examining room where Dr. Cough was seated, writing up a report. Johnny and Sally followed him and stood by the door. Dr. Cough was vastly amused. After shakily examining Chester's eye and laughingly reassuring him that he could look forward to nothing more than a "nice shiner" like his brother Horace's, he suddenly clutched his chest, slid off the stool to the floor, and expired. A moment of deathly silence prevailed. It was such a shocking thing for Dr. Cough to do. Then Johnny bestirred himself to fetch Miss Wall, while Sally leaned over, whispering, "Are you all right, Dr. Cough?" Chester, who could hardly believe his eyes—make that one eye, the other being swollen almost shut—shouted, "Call a doctor! Get an ambulance!" Miss Wall ran in, knelt down over the doctor, and after making a swift examination, muttered, "He's gone."

"Can't you revive him?" pleaded Johnny.

"I'm afraid not. It's his heart, you see. We've been expecting this to happen anytime."

It took only fifteen minutes for everyone in Keene Valley to learn about Dr. Cough's timely demise. And only a few more for John and Eric, sitting on the verandah of the Ausable Club, to hear of it. Eric believed it was typical of the Amber family to be involved and to stir up so much fuss and cause so much trouble in one little village.

On the short drive home, John commented, "Murder, mayhem (if one can call two separate black eyes administered by lethal tennis balls that), and now sudden death. Vacations aren't what they used to be."

"Oh," replied Eric, "I have the impression that this is just a standard one. As you might say, John, 'It's par for the course.'"

John laughed painfully in reply, and changed the subject. "It has occurred to me, Eric, that you might telephone that Congressman Thrasher to find out more about the Riddle case. He might pass on privileged information to you as a member of the diplomatic corps and as his host at the embassy."

On returning to the house Eric gave the matter some thought. He disliked using telephones. He found them an inconvenience. *Ah, but Candace is very good at that sort of thing. She's the one who knows how to persuade a plumber to come immediately, or learns all the gossip in the neighborhood. Candy has talked more with Brasher and his wife—they have played tennis together. His wife! That's whom she should call. Candy has said that one could get more information from the wife, she being the chattier one.*

But when Candy arrived home and heard Eric's suggestion, she did not call Mrs. Brasher. She wanted information "from the horse's mouth, this time," she explained to Eric. However, "the horse's mouth" was difficult to contact, and it took Candy all afternoon. When she finally spoke to the Congressman, he was quite curt; he was "not in a position to discuss the Riddle murder or other related events." *What other events?* Candy wondered, but he had hung up. Maybe this time Eric should have spoken to him. *He probably doesn't like women who interfere in men's affairs.* Eric said he'd think about it. By the time he placed another call, he was informed that the Congressman was out of town for a few days.

After dinner, the family settled around the fireplace for another sleuthing session. "Our Pow-Wow under the Moose," Rick named it. Horace appeared; just couldn't seem to keep away, in fact, and once again would preside, "Now let's begin by listing the suspects. And Rick, would you take notes again?" Horace was just asking for trouble. "Uncle John, you start this time."

John: "Let's see; there's the CIA, British Intelligence—don't they call themselves MI5 and MI6—and the FBI, organized crime, the KGB. They all probably wanted Perry dead."

Pattee: "Dearie, that's a bit far-fetched."

John: "Well then, why not someone who disliked Churchill?"

Pattee: "Why, he died back in the sixties or such."

John: "I mean someone who didn't know that."

Claudia: "I thought of that too, Uncle John."

Pattee: "But, dearie, what would that have to do with Riddle?"

Horace: "Got all that, Rick?"

Rick: "Yup."

Johnny: "There's Aunt Nittie; or is she a no-no?"

Claudia: "Definitely a no. Besides, she went to the hospital before Mummy left that day."

Johnny: "Then it's your mother. How about it, Aunt Candy? Any more confessions to make?"

Candy: "My lips are sealed."

Eric, snorting: "That would be the first time since we've been married. I suspect the mysterious bird-watcher, John, you birdwatch."

Pattee: "But he doesn't fit the description of slim, darkhaired and debonair."
Candy: "Where's Chester?"
Pattee: "He doesn't fit that description either. It's such a clear night that he thought he'd go star-gazing in the meadow, taking Sally and Cindy and the children. A telescope requires the use of only one eye."
Horace: "Any other suggestions?"
Pattee: "I guess we'll have to settle for POPU."
John: "POPU! Tell me, Madame Poupée, what is POPU; one of your dolls?"
Pattee: "No, dearie, it's 'legalese' for Person or Persons Unknown."
Johnny: "Mom, that may be news to the bar association."
Eric: "I say, there's the mysterious Jennifer. Perhaps she's involved."
Just then, the glare of headlights was seen and a motor heard.
Horace: "Now what?"
They all rushed to the front door to find standing there a large, horsey-looking woman of about forty dressed in dowdy tweeds, lisle stockings, and expensive oxfords. She spoke first; "Hi! I'm Cousin Jennifer. Harold Dibble was kind enough to bring me in his truck from the bus stop."
"Come in, come in!" welcomed the astonished Candy and Horace. While Rick and Johnny brought in her bags left by Harold on the steps, the others started talking all at once. "This is a surprise." "Why, we've been trying to locate you," "We're so sorry about your father," "Have you had dinner?" Candy wondered where to put her—"We're running out of bedrooms, but the studio is empty, if you don't mind staying alone up on the hill in the dark woods." Pattee headed for the kitchen to fix a snack for the guest and thought: *Might as well bring something for everybody.* And when the stargazers appeared, she put them to work, too.

Eric was curious to learn how she heard about all this. Jennifer explained. "First, some little man in the Foreign Office called. Then it was splashed all over the London newspapers. The tabloids had a field day with their headlines: 'Ex-Spy Expired'; 'Missing Colonel on Ice'; 'Spy Left Out in the Cold'; and 'Keene Valley, Cuckoo's Nest of Spies.' They called him the Fallen Falcon, or worse, Big Bird. It was very embarrassing. So I flew over and here I am." Jennifer ("Oh, please call me Jenny"), an only child and spinster, was friendly and delighted to find herself a member of a large and rambling family, and happy to answer the spate of questions.

"Why did your father wait so long to return to the family?"

"Oh, some silly feud, I believe, but he never said what. Suddenly, he decided to move back to the States—can you imagine? He was over seventy. But Mummers was against that."

"And how is your mother taking all this?"

"Oh, she's bearing up, but considers the whole affair undignified and a disgrace. Mummers never approved of his profession. I'm a bit hazy about it myself. All that cloak-and-dagger business doesn't fit Dadders at all."

"He appears to have been a colonel."

"That was more a courtesy title, I believe, like your Kentucky one. He did serve in the American army for a time as a code clerk. He acquired his title when he became Winston Churchill's double."

Candy was agog. "Churchill actually had a double?"

"My, yes," replied Jenny in her clipped manner of speech. "After all, Sir Winston couldn't be everywhere at once, so Dadders would stand in for him occasionally on travels and boring receptions and sittings with portrait painters and sculptors. That bronze statue in front of the British Embassy in Washington is Dadders, so he told me."

"How astounding!" was all Candy could think to say. "I must take another look at it someday."

Horace, impatient to get on with things, brought up Perry's funeral. "We thought, Jenny, there could be a funeral service for your father on Tuesday here in the village church, unless you have your own plans."

"Why, that would be just fine, Cousin Horace."

"And as for burial, there is the family plot in Albany."

"I've already arranged for burial at Arlington Cemetery in Washington. I had been informed that he was entitled to that as a war veteran."

"Splendid!" said Horace, much relieved, thinking how his vacation had been an utter nightmare: Perry's body found in the ice house; his daughters with mumps. Why, it was a hangman's holiday. He had to be in court for the inquest, then he got a black eye playing tennis. Next would be the funeral; no, two funerals—Dr. Cough's too. Well, at least he wouldn't be involved with the burial. He departed for the Gate House to tell Mary the latest news, and more coherently this time. He vowed he wouldn't go near the main house tomorrow.

After eating Pattee's filling snack, Jenny was escorted up the hill to the studio, an attractive old cottage perched on a rocky outcrop with a view of the upper meadow and vegetable garden through the trees, and at this moment, of a full moon rising over Giant Mountain. It quite took her breath away. Yes, she assured Candy, she'd be very comfortable here.

## Chapter 9

## Upsets and Questions

Sunday was peaceful. John and Pattee took Jenny for a drive up Whiteface Mountain and a visit to Lake Placid to see the Olympic Arena and ski jump. Chester, Claudia, Konrad, and Lily climbed Baxter Mountain hoping to pick blueberries. The young Hassels took their little Hassels to the Lower Ausable Lake for swimming, rowing, and a short climb up Indian Head.

Candy decided to attend eleven o'clock service at the church in the village. She went to tell Eric, who was struggling over some letter writing in the library. Eric was surprised at her announcement. "Why, you never go to church."

"Let's just say I'm 'casing the joint' before Perry's funeral Tuesday, and picking up the latest village gossip."

"I imagine that we are the subject of the latest gossip, Candace."

"And I think I should say hello to the Reverend Miss Gentle, too, to acknowledge the progressive spirit of this fine community in selecting a woman minister."

"That's a lofty speech! Forget the women's-lib angle. My guess is that her superior qualifications did not get her the appointment, but economics did. Don't women always get paid less for more?"

"Why, Eric, I'm delighted to hear you express such good sentiments."

"Quite. But I do firmly believe women should be paid well. After all, we men marry them. And it's much more sensible to marry a woman with money."

"Well, thanks, Eric."

"Oh, I didn't mean that personally, Candace, I didn't expect any when I married you. I had no idea your family had any. Of course, now, I do not understand why your mother never left you a cent."

"Now, Eric, we've gone all over that. I'd better be off soon. Miss Gentle may want information about Perry, for funeral prayers and such."

"Oh, I'm sure Horace has given her all she'll need."

"But he didn't know much then. She should arrange appropriate hymns and decent music."

"Well, don't ask her what she's going to wear. Are you walking?"

"Of course. It's only half a mile."

"Well, everyone seems to drive around here. It's not like in the city where people are accustomed to getting around on foot."

Candy was to discover how pleasant going to church could be. She had a rewarding chat with Miss Gentle after the service. There was also a bake sale on the lawn with contributions this time by the summer people, who well knew the value of Sunday shopping. Her childhood friend, Mary Hope Diamond, as cashier and bag lady, told her, "Yes, it's unusual to do this on Sunday, but it draws a big crowd. The blueberry pies I baked, early this morning." Candy bought one; then a buttercream and nut cake for Eric and Konrad, their favorite, and on to fudge brownies and sand tarts. She was standing there wondering how to carry all that food home when another old friend, Charmone Clemenceau, approached and offered her transportation. And village news, too, on the way home.

Candy's ears perked up when Charmone mentioned "Bud" Smythe's son, Caine. "Yes, it's actually Lawrence Caine Smythe, but everybody calls him Caine. His father said he used to raise a lot of it when he was young. You know, he bought the old Taylor place, including the chickens, and named it after his mother, Battenkill Ranch. She was Phyllida Battenkill. He plans to raise horses, has his own airplane and invites a few macho friends here on weekends for sky diving."

Charmone tactfully avoided mentioning Cousin Parody, whose forthcoming funeral was announced from the pulpit. But on getting out of the car at the house, Candy did tell her that his daughter had arrived unexpectedly to attend the event and that she seemed very nice.

Candy and Eric spent the afternoon walking up the John's Brook Road to Marcy View and enjoying the peace and quiet. There was no "pow wow under the moose" that evening since everyone was tired from outdoor activity, and then too, Jenny was there. They all turned in early.

The next morning, Eric phoned his chief in Washington to inquire about Bill Riddle. He received a rather unpleasant response. "There's some connection between Riddle and Beaulinia." And, "Aren't you a good friend of Carlos? Well, stay in King Valley."

"It's Keene Valley," corrected Eric. He could hardly believe his ears, when he heard next:

"The State Department has enough problems. We'll call you, don't call us."

Candy found him seated beside the telephone on the window seat of the stair landing looking stunned. On hearing these words from State, she suggested he phone Fred in Beaulinia. He did, but the results from that were far from reassuring. Fred didn't know what was going on. "It's like an armed camp here. State ordered the embassy staff back to Washington on the double. But since Jack and I are Navy, we're staying. You can count on us, Ambassador."

Upset by that news, Eric tried calling Carlos; tried most of the morning, but couldn't get through to him. Then he recalled Carlos giving him a special telephone number. *Now, if I can only find it,* he thought while taking out his bulky wallet stuffed with cards, slips of papers and receipts and notes to himself and—ah—Carlos's very private number. The call went through quickly. Carlos came right to the point: "Those bloody fools in Washington think I've got something to do with pretty-boy Riddle's death. He's connected with a drug ring. Hell, who isn't these days! But those salt-water taffies in the White House think my secret weapon [and he chuckles] is nothing more than the white stuff, Eric, and furthermore believe your embassy is involved after they heard it had been called the Snow House. Hadn't they ever heard of Harry Snow? Now they are threatening to invade my island. MY ISLAND! I'm goin' bananas."

"Do you want me to return, Carlos?"

"Naw, you'd better stay where you are until things calm down. Maybe those loonies will listen to Charlotte. But thanks for calling. I know it's considered highly irregular in your line of work. I'll be in touch with you and send word somehow if necessary."

Now, Eric was thoroughly upset. He was worried about his papers, he told Candy.

"Official papers, you mean?"

"No, no! The article I'm writing on '*Poésies Basques.*' I must rescue them. I must go to Beaulinia."

"Why, Eric, didn't you bring them with you in your briefcase?"

"Ah, quite so; I forgot," he said sheepishly. "Now where did I put them?" and went upstairs to search the bedroom.

"Try the closet," called Candy and then sighing, searched out Jenny to take her for a walk. She was with Claudia in the flower garden, target-shooting with bow and arrow. They started but got only as far as the front steps, when Lieutenant Whistler with a pretty redhaired woman in uniform drove up.

"Ah, Miss Parody, I believe. I'm Lieutenant Whistler from the sheriff's office, investigating your father's death, and this is my assistant, Sgt. Virginia Vitus. So sorry about your father. But thought you might help in giving us the colonel's background and past activities in England. Would you mind answering some questions?"

Candy spoke for her: "Of course, Lieutenant. You can use the library." She led the way back inside and across the hall to a catch-all room of books, television set, boxes of games, a doll house, and collection of old Indian grass baskets, no one knew whose—they must have come with the house. Then she quickly disappeared upstairs to help Eric, still searching for his briefcase.

Jenny asked them to sit down. Lieutenant Whistler, who remained standing, spoke first to the redhaired Sergeant Vitus: "Ginger, are you ready to take notes?" Jenny couldn't help smiling and wondering if with a name like Ginger Vitus, she suffered from inflamed gums. She smiled back, showing a gleaming white set of teeth, and nodding her head.

"Now, Miss Parody, can you tell us if your father came here last September on a business matter?"

Jenny, in her most clipped and British manner, began with, "I do not really know. My father had been retired for some years."

"Retired from what, Miss Parody?"

"I'm not really certain. Employed by the Britsh government seems to cover it best. I believe he had contract work with the Americans too."

"Would you mean contract killer-for-hire, perhaps?"

"Certainly not, Lieutenant. He was not a syndicated criminal. I believe from his schedule of travels over the years, he was involved in courier work. But he had retired; mandatory, you know."

"Could you fill us in on those retirement years?"

"My father traveled considerably. He loved it. My mother never. Sometimes I joined him. He used to joke that he was a 'soldier of fortune,' which I interpreted as not being very important or capable. Sometimes I thought, though, that he did continue to free lance as a sort of odd-jobs man. Why else would he go to such outlandish places as Beaulahland or Zygomar or Beaulinia?"

"Perhaps your father kept a diary," suggested Sergeant Vitus.

"Highly unlikely, although Mother and I did look for one, or at least an appointment book, when we realized his last trip was taking so long."

"Did you know of his visit to Keene Valley?"

"No, nor did I know of all his cousins here. He refused to discuss his American relations. Oh, he did mention he planned to settle some financial matters in the States and elsewhere."

"Elsewhere, like Beaulinia?" asked the alert Sergeant Vitus.

"He did not say. I remember, though, he once had an old friend there, going back many years. It was an odd name I always connected with the drug trade, a thriving industry, as you know, in the Caribbean. Snow: that's it. Whitey Snow, I believe."

"And was this Whitey Snow connected with illegal drugs?"

"Oh, I don't think so. Just his name; that's what's so amusing."

"And a Bill Riddle. Did your father ever mention him?"

Jenny looked startled. "You mean that man wiped out on a tennis court? Yes, that is another curious name. Worked in Washington, didn't he? I read about him in the newspapers. But I cannot say whether my father ever met him or not. Are you suggesting that my father . . ." Jenny began to bristle, "my father's courier services involved drugs? Why, that's just out of the question, Lieutenant." Jenny stood up in anger.

"I beg your pardon, Miss Parody; it's a mere formality to ask. There have been some pretty odd connections turning up lately. And, I might add, the FBI and intelligence people won't even give me the time of day."

Jenny sat down again. "Sorry, Lieutenant. Of course my father was a respectable man."

"I'm sure he was, Miss Parody. But if you recall further information, would you get in touch with me or Sergeant Vitus at this number in Elizabethtown? The second number is my home." Lieutenant Whistler handed her a card.

Jenny, calm and collected once again, glanced at the card and said good-bye to the good-looking lieutenant and his colleague as she saw them to the front door.

Candy came downstairs when she heard the motor start, "Jenny, you look as if you've been through the wringer. Let's go walking now. Anything in particular you'd like to see?"

"The ice house and the pond, Candy. Perhaps you can tell me about Dadder's last day here as we walk around."

Candy thought Jenny looked a trifle grim. "Good heavens, Jenny, you surely don't suspect me, do you, because I was the last known person to see him?"

"Oh, Candy, no." Jenny relaxed as they proceeded down the short driveway to the ice house and the barn nearby and then down and around to the meadow and the pond. "It's such a lovely place, like an English meadow, but with all those mountains around!" exclaimed Jenny with pleasure.

They turned off the lane below the pond and trudged up a muddy road past the overgrown pasture to the upper meadow and vegetable garden. Ernest was busy weeding, so Candy just waved to him, telling Jenny, "That's Ernest Middleton, who tends the garden, takes the trash to the dump, and brings in the firewood. By the way, I hope there's firewood in the studio for you to use if it's chilly."

"Oh, yes, I'm very snug there, but haven't needed a fire."

"Now those rickety wooden steps over there along the rock lead up to the studio. Let's try them. I'll lead, just in case." They reached the top of the steps and rock safely, and with a few more steps reached the studio porch. It was a large, hexagonal one holding a huge table in the center specially made for picnic parties of many years ago. They sat awhile to chat and admire the view of Giant by sunlight and shadow.

"It's all so conveniently laid out," said Jenny, as they wandered back down the road blanketed with soft tawny pine needles, past the log playhouse, converted to a cabin, where Chester liked staying, and finally reached the house. They cut past the kitchen and dining-room wing and into the garden, calling first to make certain that Claudia would not shoot them.

Jenny asked, "By the way, Candy, what happened to my father's things? I'd like to take them back with me."

"Of course, Jenny. They must still be in the Gate House. I'll ask Horace to find them. Though I hope you plan to stay on longer after the funeral."

## Chapter 10

## Two Funerals

The funeral of Peregrine Parody was scheduled for two o'clock at the Keene Valley Church on Main Street. The Rev. Doris Gentle was to officiate at a short, simple service, which the family would augment into a near-disaster. Although it was not the family custom to have open coffins and viewings, Jenny had requested that the coffin not be sealed until she had viewed its contents. As Candy explained to Eric when they arrived at the church, "Of course Jenny wants to be certain she's at the right funeral, and that her father is attending, too, so to speak." Candy and Jenny were shown into a small anteroom containing the coffin before the service began. Candy was particularly curious to see if the head had been replaced properly. It had. However, she was surprised to find Perry's beard and mustache had been shaved off. He did look like Winston Churchill.

John and sons, Johnny and Rick, found their way to the Parish Hall to don choir robes. Jenny had expressed a wish that the family participate in the service, since her father's sudden demise had happened at the time he was returning home "to the bosom of his family." John offered to join the members of the small choir, while Rick and Johnny agreed to perform Handel's "The Trumpet Shall Sound," accompanied by the organist, Jessie Brown; Rick to sing tenor and Johnny to play Mrs. Brown's son's trumpet.

The small church filled rapidly. No one in the village wanted to miss "the goings-on." "You never know what might happen with that Amber bunch!" said one old-timer. Also attending were Lieutenant Whistler, other and anonymous law enforcers, a hearty sprinkling of summer residents, and even a station wagon load of tourists passing through, it was learned later.

After the coffin was brought in. Miss Gentle took her place, adjusted her glasses and solemnly began: "I am the Resurrection and the Life," followed by "The Lord is my Shepherd," which "of course she knew backwards," Candy said later; but appearing a bit rattled, recited one line as "Yea, though I walk through Keene Valley of the shadow of death, I will fear no evil." The mourners understood.

Then bravely carrying on, she read "For what is life?" concluding with "for it is soon cut off and we fly away." Candy thought that was a nice touch, since she had told her that the headless Perry was called the Falcon.

Miss Gentle continued, "O come let us sing unto the Lord, Hymn number Two hundred and Sixty-three." It did show a sensitive awareness of the spy in their midst. They all sang out: "Once to every man and nation/ Comes the moment to decide/ In the strife of truth with falsehood/ For the good or evil side." There followed another prayer about "the stranger in our midst, and a sojourner" and "O spare me a little that I may recover my strength before I go hence"; another hymn, page one hundred and ten. "Where shall my wandering soul begin/ How shall I all to heaven aspire/ Should know, should feel my sins forgiven/ Blest with this ante past of heaven."

Candy whispered to Eric, "Miss Gentle is really covering the subject well, to include Perry's favorite antipasto. But now what is she saying?"

". . . To quote from a poem about Lincoln by Edwin Markham. 'And when he fell . . . he went down/ As when a lordly cedar, green with boughs,/ Goes down with a great shout upon the hills/ And leaves a lonesome place against the sky'."

"Well, that ought to take care of all three hundred pounds of Perry," Eric whispered.

"And now for our Concluding Affirmation, a recitative, 'Behold, I tell you a mystery' and air, 'The Trumpet Shall Sound,' performed in the name of the Lord by our sons, Richard and John Hassel, Junior." This was greeted by a clap of thunder that shook the rafters, followed by a cloudburst. But undismayed, off went the two soloists; Rick reciting a mystery, joined by Johnny sounding the trumpet.

Now unfortunately, Rick had awakened that morning with a swollen tongue, his old reaction to blueberries, which produced a "slurring" of speech. By the time he reached "and at the latter day/he shall be saved," he could only sing it as "he shall be shaved." Every time that refrain appeared it came out "he shall be shaved." Candy, who the day before had helped them practice, knew the words well, and whispered in annoyance to Eric, "Why is he doing that?"

Poor Eric was struggling to maintain a solemn demeanor while recalling Candy's telling of Peregrine's face having been shaved. Lieutenant Whistler, also in the know, couldn't contain himself and hastily slipped out to wipe off tears of laughter. It did not help the performance for the trumpeter to find Rick's enunciation funny also. Johnny struggled valiantly to purse his lips properly for his brief trumpet solo interludes.

Mercifully for all, they reached the end. Miss Gentle rose and came forward to bestow the final blessing, "Depart in peace." *More like in pieces,* Candy thought, watching Eric shake with silent laughter. To spare further embarrassment, she quickly led him out a side door. Even Jenny, who joined them, was trying hard not to smile. Candy turned to her and said, "I suppose we should have arranged some refreshments for this crowd." But Jenny replied, "Oh, they've gotten their money's worth. I'm sure." She went to thank Miss Gentle.

The downpour was over and the sky was clearing. They were gathered out front now. John noted, "The Falcon must have made it into heaven all right; in fact, I'd say blasted into it. We should have spent more money on Johnny's trumpet lessons in school."

Pattee, standing beside him, added, "Never mind. Ricky 'shaved' the day!"

Miss Gentle and Lieutenant Whistler were invited to the house to join the family for tea and cake, while Chester took the flowers from the church to Nittie in the hospital across the road.

Dr. Cough's funeral took place the following day. Lieutenant Whistler, who lived outside of Elizabethtown, said he'd bring his mother, who had once been a neighbor of the doctor's sister. The Amber family was just dying to meet Whistler's mother.

It had been decided to hold the funeral in the auditorium of the Keene Valley Central School to adequately accommodate the expected crowd. Once again the Reverend Miss Gentle would officiate, and there would be a "swell bash" in the cafeteria afterwards.

Whistler and mother arrived as the casket was brought in and placed at the foot of the stage. After finding a seat for his mother along the back wall, he quietly moved around greeting familiar faces with a nod here and a smile there. He became intrigued watching Miss Wall bring forward Dr. Cough's battered stethoscope to lay it on the casket, followed by her brother, Elmer, the Doc's old drinking buddy at the Spread Eagle Bar, laying the Doc's rifle at his feet. The Hassels, Bohners, and Wackmans were sitting quietly, not lending their talents to this service, which consequently went forward without incident.

Afterward, Whistler thought he might just have a look at that rifle. It was a Plattsburg 1963 Anniversary Special, "a dime a dozen around here, I guess. But the only one I've seen so far." He managed to borrow it discreetly and get it to the lab in Plattsburg. Later, he would learn to his surprise that tested bullets matched the one found in Parody's body.

That night, Nittie Amber died peacefully in her sleep. Someone was heard to mutter, "Oh, no, not another funeral! Call Miss Gentle to see when she can fit it into her busy schedule." This dampened everyone's spirits. They all had been fond of Nittie. And she was the last of the Ambers. It was the end of an era. She would be buried in the family plot at the Albany Rural Cemetery.

John called his absent sisters to inform them of her death and of the funeral planned for Saturday. First he talked with Peaches and Honey in Florida, who felt it was too far and too expensive to come and they didn't like to fly. Then he called Fran in Greenwich, who complained that it was inconvenient, but of course she'd be there, arriving on the Friday afternoon train at Westport, and that someone would have to meet her. This produced no enthusiastic reaction.

Meanwhile, shortly after the Spread Eagle opened that Thursday, Lieutenant Whistler entered to question Elmer Wall in his customary place at the bar. Of course Elmer could hardly be expected to remember a single day of last September, or whether the Doc was doing a bit of pre-season deer hunting. "But he did like to get ahead of the game," chuckled Elmer. Whistler gave up and next tried to locate Ernest and Harold, whom he found eventually sitting on Judge Wackman's porch and willing to be more informative now that the Doc was dead.

As Horace was to explain later to the family, "Ernest and Harold found Peregrine's body slumped over near the pond. Believing that Doc Cough had been hunting the previous evening, they assumed he had bagged Peregrine accidentally. They explained 'Doc was gettin' awful near-sighted, ya know.' Not wishing to see Doc in any trouble, they weighted the body with rocks, and with the little row-boat, dragged him out to the center of the pond and dumped him. That winter while resuming their annual ice-cutting chores, Peregrine's body appeared to their utter horror in the ice. But keeping their heads, although forced to cut off Peregrine's in the course of sawing blocks, they carted him off in ice to be buried, so to speak, under the sawdust in the ice house. Sorry about that, Jenny."

The family, for once, was speechless. Then Chester inquired, "What will happen to those two, Harold and Ernest? There will have to be a hearing."

Horace could only reply, "Who knows? This is a small community. Ernest is an old man and Harold has a vacant mind. As Whistler said, 'Case closed probably,' Do you or Johnny want to offer your legal services, if necessary?" They did not.

Then Jenny spoke: "Are those two to be believed? Why couldn't one of them have accidently shot my father?"

No one could answer. It was a disturbing idea. But a far less sinister solution.

## Chapter 11

## Fran Amber Arrives

Eric departed for Washington early Friday morning. It was a tiresome trip by bus, with a change in New York. But he just couldn't take another funeral. Furthermore, he was worried about Beaulinia. Candy would remain for Nittie's funeral and burial, although she was as anxious as Eric to find out what was going on in the State Department, Beaulinia, and Eric's foreign-service career.

During lunch on the dining-room porch, she asked for a volunteer to drive her to Westport to meet Fran's train, the four-twenty from New York. There was silence. Finally, Rick offered. On the drive over, later, Rick brought up the subject of the Amber family. "You know, Aunt Candy, Dad was never a great one for discussing the family. He always acted as if he'd like to forget the whole set-up. Oh, he was fond of Dottie and Nittie, but not close to them the way you and Aunt Fran and Aunt Liz were. Now, who is, or was, this Cousin Peregrine? How did he fit in?"

"Oh, dear me. Let me see if for once I can get it straight. Cousin Peregrine's grandmother was a sister of Grandma Amber, your great-grandmother and Nittie's mother. His mother, daughter of his grandmother, was first cousin to Aunt Nittie, and of course, Aunt Dottie, and my mother or your grandmother, Kitty. That made Peregrine a first cousin once removed to Nittie and her sisters, and second cousin to your father, me, and Aunts Liz and Fran, oh, and Peaches and Honey. Now Nittie's cousin would be twice removed to me, and thrice removed to you. Can that be right?"

"Uh, thanks, Aunt Candy. That's clear enough."

"Oh, well, after the war, Perry remained in England where he had been stationed, rarely returning to Albany, his hometown. His father left him a comfortable income according to Aunt Dottie, who thought it a disgrace that he didn't hold down a regular job, but just traveled around the world. Of course she didn't know and wouldn't have believed that his traveling was subsidized by an intelligence department. I can't picture him as a spy, though. Weighing over three hundred pounds would tend to make him conspicuous, I should think. Do you always drive this fast?"

"The speedometer reads only thirty-five."

"On these winding roads, it feels like sixty."

"I thought you'd like the scenic route. We have lots of time."

"Oh, I do. Now let me see. Jenny must be your father's and my second cousin, which makes her a second cousin once removed to you and twice removed to your children and I don't know what!"

"Let's get out of the removal business. Tell me about Great-grandfather Amber and the Keene Valley place."

"Grandpa, that is, my grandfather, made his money in the drug business in Albany. Oh, dear, that sounds bad these days; pharmaceuticals is the word I want, I guess, for epsom salts, witch hazel, rubbing alcohol, and, oh, and soda fountains! Yes, I remember being told that the soda fountain in the old drug store at the foot of the hill in Elizabethtown was an Amber-Snow one."

"Who was Snow?"

"By the time I came along, he was a defunct partner, long gone. But it's quite a coincidence that our embassy in Beaulina is a house he built and lived in." Candy was enjoying the presence of a good listener. Eric always wanted her to get to the point in one sentence.

"Did Grandpa build the K.V. house?"

"No, he bought it around 1906 from the Brazilian ambassador, named Mendonza, who had been recalled after a change in government. The house hadn't as many rooms then. The kitchen was in the cellar, and the family ate in the living room. Grandpa added on the two back bedrooms and bathrooms over the porch, and added the entire dining room and kitchen wing with maids' rooms upstairs."

"What about the studio and playhouse?"

"We believe the studio was on the property before the Mendonzas bought the place. The playhouse was built for us to play in when we were young. We loved it. The Gate House used to be the old caretaker's house. There was a wash house for doing laundry beyond the barn. And of course the small ice house where poor Perry was found."

"What happened to the Amber-Snow Company?"

"It was bought by a large Chicago firm when Grandpa died. But the building is still there in Albany, I think, a couple of blocks up Broadway from Union Station."

"What's going to happen to the K.V. property now?"

"I don't know the terms of Nittie's will. I'd hate to see Fran get it, now that Aunt Liz was killed in that air disaster some years ago."

"What's wrong with Aunt Fanny?"

"You'll find out soon enough. But don't call her Fanny to her face."

"That's what Dad said. You have to admit she's still a good-looking person, and managed to hook three husbands!"

"Oh, she's got the looks, the brains, the style . . ."

They pulled up beside the quaint old Westport Railroad Station as the train appeared around the bend and scrambled out of Rick's Toyota to locate the Pullman car section. Fran always went first class. The train slid to a halt. A conductor called out, "Westport" it seemed to them, and alighted. Rick remarked that they already knew it was. Then Fran appeared. "Looking stunning as always," sighed Candy. Fran was wearing a beige silk turban and a beige cashmere coat with beige fox fur collar draped over a beige silk dress. Her beige leather shoes and handbag matched too.

"Cand!"

"Fran!"

They kissed the air in the vicinity of their cheeks.

Candy spoke first: "This is Rick, in case you didn't recognize him. He'll get your bags." The conductor was lifting them off the train. Rick grabbed them and put the large pieces in the trunk and the overflow in the front seat. Fran struggled to get into the back. Candy remarked, "Fanny first."

Fran turned sharply around to stare at her. "You know I do not like being called Fanny."

Candy replied calmly, "I meant that's the way to get into one of these small cars: fanny first."

Rick felt perhaps he should apologize for owning such a small, uncomfortable, plebeian vehicle.

Fran sat back and lit a cigarette in an ivory holder so long that Rick, now seated at the wheel, worried that he would be stabbed in the back of the head. She turned to Candy, sitting beside her and began in her husky voice:

"Well, Candy, it does seem we get to see each other only at family funerals. I didn't expect Aunt Nittie to die this quickly. I was planning to visit her as soon as the divorce was final. You can't imagine how fatiguing and difficult divorces are; and this was a friendly one, you might say. Of course the lawyers make it so complicated, but worthwhile. I did get the large house in Greenwich. Rick, you're not going the right way."

"It's a detour, Aunt Franny. There's some road construction ahead."

"Would you mind rolling up your window, Candy? It is blowing the cigarette ashes on my coat. I thought I'd wear it to Nittie's funeral. I hope you have something suitable to wear. Put on weight? But then you always did tend to look dumpy. Short legs do that. How's Eric? Absentminded as ever? I plan to visit you this autumn in Beaulinia.

I met someone from Washington who had just returned from there and he said it was just divine. Everybody wonders how Eric was so lucky to get an ambassadorship there after all those years of struggling along in such minor positions. But tell me, Rick, what are you doing these days? Still teaching? I heard you write poetry for the *Banter Digest*. That always was a peculiar magazine."

And on and on "chattered" Fran. And faster and faster drove Rick. He now understood why no one else wanted to meet Fran's train.

Fran continued, "You know, this whole Parody affair is bizarre! Imagine Cousin Perry in the ice house! And then a mysterious daughter, what's her name, appears...."

"Jenny," contributed Candy.

"Ginny? For Virginia, I suppose. What is she like? Very English? Odd, her appearing out of the blue. Is she staying at the house? Who all is there? Will there be a reading of the will after the funeral, the way they do it in motion pictures? Of course Liz would have inherited the K.V. property if she hadn't gotten herself killed in that air crash, along with Lance too, and leaving their children orphans."

"Oh, Fran, those 'orphans' were all grown up and married and successful in their fields when that happened."

"Yes, but she was Dottie's and Nittie's favorite. They always felt protective of her 'children' after that. How are yours? Is Klara still out digging in the deserts of New Mexico? I can't imagine anyone choosing to live with the Aztecs."

"Navahos," corrected Candy.

"Oh? Well, Claudia doesn't have any such ideas, I trust. Has she blossomed out into someone pretty, or does she still look like you? At least you managed to send Konrad to London for some veneer. And, Rick, how is your father? Still living in that démodé house in East Syracuse? Well your mother is a pleasant woman; she has a lot to put up with. Always looks so tired."

Candy noticed the side of Rick's face and the back of his neck growing red. "Rick, have you a radio? Let's listen to the news."

With relief, Rick switched on the radio, deciding any station noisy enough would do. Disc Jockey Jay from Ausable Forks in his hayseed drawl did just fine. There was silence in the rear—for a few blessed minutes. Candy, curious about Fran's daughter, Sandra, who had eloped with a Las Vegas gambler ten years ago and going from bad to worse she had heard, opened her mouth to ask but then realized she'd start the torrent of words again, and so remained silent. But Fran didn't.

"The Wackmans are there in full force, I dare say. Where is everyone staying? The house must be overflowing. And small children everywhere. How's the cooking this year? Martha still there?"

Rick turned up the sound of Disc Jockey Jay's music. Candy didn't feel answers were necessary since Fran didn't wait for them.

"Rick, dear," Fran continued, "isn't the radio a bit loud? You know, Candy, these murders, and one in our own backyard, I must say, is so déclassé for the family. It's humiliating to be dragged into it. Do you realize that Bill Riddle, a gangster no less, was a great-grandson of Harry Snow? So I heard, anyway."

"What!" exclaimed Candy, remembering Riddle poking around in the embassy library. "Why, he . . ."

"They called him the Snow King."

"Who?"

"Bill Riddle, of course. He was a dope peddlar, into cocaine or heroin. I can't tell them apart, except that one is supposedly more expensive than the other. And selling it in the halls of Congress no less. Really, people these days have no standards. Of course, Grandpa's Amber-Snow Drug Company gets its share of publicity and disparaging remarks. Perhaps that is why Snow retired early to Beaulinia. And there you and Eric are, established in Harry Snow's old house. People will say that Eric's appointment was a 'snow job'."

"Oh, really, Fran!"

"Well, they say there is a connection between Cousin Perry and Bill Riddle. Why couldn't that daughter of his, Ginny . . ."

"It's Jenny for Jennifer."

". . . be involved too. And you have permitted her to stay with us? Well, she'll have to leave."

"Jenny seems like a nice wholesome girl—er, woman. She's like one of the family, really, Fran. Well, here we are!"

They were whizzing past the stone gates, tearing up the short, steep hill, coming to a jolting halt at the front steps. Rick jumped out of the car, grabbed Fran's bags from the trunk, dashed up the steps, dumped them in the front hall, and disappeared.

John and Pattee then came out, followed by their grandchildren, who ran down the steps to the fountain behind the car to sail some toy boats they had found. Torpedo galloped out of the woods to join them.

In amazement, Fran greeted John. "Really, John," she sniffed, "all those children running and shouting. No sense of decorum. And that reminds me, Candy, this Lily you told me about helping Konrad in the kitchen? We can't have your son and his girl friend carrying on there. Really, you should know better. And in Nittie's house too! It's shocking. Whose wild dog is that? Horace's? Tell him to tie it up down by the barn."

They were silent as they escorted Fran into the hall to meet Jenny. Then she was hastily taken upstairs by John and Candy, who informed her she would be in Dottie's old room, the one with the telephone. Claudia had moved out to share Candy's room, now that Eric had departed.

Fran sniffed. "I can't take Dottie's dark and cramped room. I've had the tower room for years. John, you and Pattee must move out. I know if Nittie were here, that's where she'd put me. I need the adjoining bathroom. You can't expect me to creep down the dark hall in the middle of the night to one of those bathrooms in the back. Returning, I might go past my door in the dark and fall down the stairs the way Eric did once."

John was outraged at being ordered out of his room, but did not wish to raise a fuss. Candy saw it differently; she'd "raise the fuss," and did so, diplomatically. "Now, Franny, you know that bed has a dreadful mattress, the original, probably a hundred years old. And with John's grandchildren next door, up early and always popping in, you'd never get a wink of sleep. Let's put you in the back bedroom, that's next to a bathroom. You used that one as a girl. The mattress is innerspring, too. It will be quiet there. After all, you're not planning to stay long, are you?"

"Well, yes, I am. Nittie's affairs will need straightening out. And I'll need a room with a fireplace."

"And so you shall have it, after we leave in a few days. But the weather is warm, just now."

"I really had not expected such a houseful. And all lapping up Nittie's hospitality. It's disgraceful!"

"Well, Franny, we were requested to come for Peregrine's inquest, and then everything else happened."

"That's just it. And you are all laughing and chatting as if it were nothing serious. It's really so disrespectful."

Candy's patience was wearing thin. She took Fran to the back bedroom. "I'll get the boys to bring up your luggage. Then you'd probably like to say hello to Martha." She hastily departed, chuckling to herself at the thought of arrogant Fran and irritable Martha having a most unpleasant chat. She assured John that Fran was under control and ordered him not to move out or she'd kill him.

On her way to see Martha, Fran had to pass by the four young Hassels, chortling away on the porch as Rick gave a word-by-word description of the drive from Westport.

Johnny said, "Well, I don't think that's so bad. She

doesn't seem to have any complaints about me." He was lounging in the hammock, when Fran appeared and greeted him.

She then added, "Aren't you a bit heavy for that, Johnny? It's sagging dreadfully. Really, it's just for the children's use, you should know. And you could make yourself useful by carrying my bags upstairs. Don't be as clumsy as Rick was." Then turning to Sally and Candy, "Now let me see, which is Cindy and which Sal? I never can tell you two apart. Did you know that your children were splashing about in the fountain unsupervised?"

She then continued on her way to "beard" Martha in her den. There was silence, until Fran was out of earshot.

Sally, mimicking Fran, began: "Really, Johnny, you mustn't put your feet up on the hammock. Can't you lounge sitting up? You're a big boy now," and giggled.

Cindy, who had been practicing aerobics before Fran appeared and had remained silent until "Hurricane Fran" passed on, found her voice now. "Are you sure she's an Amber? She seems so different; sophisticated-looking and disagreeable-acting. Let's all go home tomorrow."

Johnny, standing up to fetch Fran's bags, answered her, "But, Cindy, we can't miss the funeral. Besides, I want to see the expression on Miss Gentle's face when she encounters her."

It was a welcome relief to have Col. Abel Smythe drive up right then. He had happened to be in Keene Valley on an errand at the Baxter Gun Shop when he learned of Fran's arrival. He was told, "Ya know, she writes an advice column in one of them ladies' magazines under the name of Fran Amber." The colonel's heart beat with joy. He'd been very fond of Fran before the war parted them. He drove right up to the house to invite her out to dinner. This pleased everyone. He was still tall, slim, and handsome. This pleased Fran.

## Chapter 12

## Two in a Row, One to Go

Of course, the Parody case was not closed, as Horace thought. Lieutenant Whistler had decided he must check the whereabouts of Dr. Cough on last September 29 and 30. Miss Wall, an efficient being and a stickler for keeping accurate records at the hospital, produced the day book for that period. Dr. Cough was "taking the waters at Saratoga Spa" those two days. She remembered that when he returned, he discovered his rifle was missing but he did get it back.

"How was it returned, Miss Wall?"

"As I recall, my brother Elmer told me that Harold Dibble found it on the Amber property."

Whistler groaned inwardly. "Miss Wall, can you tell me where Harold lives?"

"Oh, with his mother, Daisy Dibble, across the road from the Amber's gate. But of course, he may be attending Miss Amber's funeral."

Whistler thought to himself as he left the hospital, *Now surely Harold couldn't see straight enough down a gun barrel to shoot anyone. But why didn't he mention finding the gun? Probably because I didn't ask. Well, I'd better ask him plenty this time, and find out if he'd noticed any unusual strangers; no; just strangers, since everyone is* unusual to him. *Then I'll check the guest records at the Keene Valley Inn and Sarah Alice Wall's Guest House.*

To any detective comes the ultimate challenge. Whistler believed that was to be the backward Harold. How does one match wits with the witless? One cannot bring him to his senses, like sobering up a drunk.

He found Harold's mother in the front yard feeding the chickens. He introduced himself and requested to see Harold, if he might. "Harr—oold!" shouted Daisy, and added, "He's out back, feedin' them pigs. Mighty slow about it, tho'."

"I'll just slip around back, Mrs. Dibble, if you don't mind. I know you're busy."

No sign of Harold, though, until the lieutenant peered over the railing of the pig pen. There he was, face up in the mire, with an arrow through his eye. Two portly pigs were noisily feeding at a trough in the far corner and looked up menacingly when Whistler started to climb over the railing. The lieutenant changed his mind, telling himself, *Not in a pig's eye could he be alive.*

He rushed into the house to call headquarters. "Look, Chief, this whole case is getting out of hand. Got another victim, in a pig pen this time. Shot in the eye with two pigs looking on." (pause) "With an arrow!" (pause) "No, I'm not joking! I need the medical examiner and some troopers, preferably pig-handlers. And if that deputy assistant, Carl, could tear himself away from his garage, I'd like his help, too. He knows something about pigs, I think. I'm at Daisy Dibble's place on John's Brook Road."

Then he had to break the news to Harold's mother. As soon as some troopers arrived, he gave them the usual instructions not to muck about and destroy evidence. It would be the medical examiner's job to get mired in details.

He thought he'd better find Ernest, who would either be at the funeral or up in the Amber vegetable garden at this time. He'd try the garden first since it was close by. As he drove up to the top of the pasture road, he could see Ernest's truck parked by the tool shed. And so was a dead Ernest, slumped over the steering wheel. There was no sign of violence. It appeared to be a heart attack.

All in all this was an unforgettable day for Whistler. "I'm being surfeited with red herrings and smothered with corpses," he moaned. He called his chief again, on the car phone this time, for more assistance.

The Amber family members, having been at the church attending their aunt's funeral, were unaware of these tragic developments. However, they would all have to be requestioned, "just routine, of course." Whistler would let Carl handle that, while he inquired around the village.

The family was horrified on hearing the news from Carl. Why, that meant two more funerals coming up in addition to Nittie's burial yet to be. As John said, "It was a grave situation."

Carl was most apologetic about coming at such a time. Miss Nittie and Miss Dottie had been most kind to him and his family. And Keene Valley would never be the same without them. He'd be as brief as possible. The family had collected on the main porch for Carl's official questioning. "Incidentally, Mrs. Bohner, is your son around?"

"Gracious," exclaimed Candy, "I forgot all about him. He's probably in the kitchen struggling with the mousse."

Carl thought that a bit strange for a moose to be in the kitchen, unless Konrad was a taxidermist. He would check that out later—if he remembered. *These people were always confusing*, he thought. *Their minds and their tongues went clickety-clack, and you could hardly keep track of all the silly things they said.* Before he could continue, Konrad and Lily appeared with coffee and cookies and offered some to Carl too. They then returned to the mousse. He went on thinking. *At least they're polite and not stuck-up.*

Carl cleared his throat and began: "Judge Wackman, would you mind telling me who all is staying here, and where, in which of the various houses on the property, I mean."

Horace replied, "There's myself and family staying in the Gate House. In the main house here are my uncle and aunt, John and Pattee Hassel, whom you know, with their children and grandchildren."

"Are they around?" interrupted Carl.

John replied, "My son, Johnny, is seated next to you, Carl. The others are in the library watching TV or playing trivia. We told them to stick around. Do you want Johnny to get them?"

"That's all right, Mr. Hassel. I'll talk to them, when I finish here."

Horace continued: "My Aunt Candace you know. Her husband, Eric Bohner, is the ambassador to Beaulinia."

*What do these people say?* wondered Carl to himself. *Bulimia! Isn't that a dieting disease? Forget it.* He then said aloud, "I don't believe I see the ambassador."

"He left for Washington yesterday, so he's not a suspect," said Horace cheerfully.

"I've met Claudia in the village many times," went on Carl as he smiled at her. "Now, that young woman in the kitchen?"

Candy answered, "She's Lily Blessing from New York, a reporter for the *Not Observing*, staying at the inn, and, as a friend of Konrad's, helping in the kitchen."

Carl thought that a rather odd combination of activities, but decided he did not want to hear a fuller explanation. It wouldn't clarify anything, the way they talked. *However, what has happened to that old cook?* Aloud, he asked, "Is Miss Amber's cook still here?"

"Martha? Oh, yes. Would you like to question her?"

Carl remembered Martha and would wait until later— much later, "Ah, here's Chester Wackman. I got your flat tire fixed. You can come pick it up any time."

"Thanks, Carl." Chester added, "I'm staying in the play house. And this is our newly discovered cousin, Jennifer Parody, from Pairtrie, England."

"Miss Pairtrie. Oh, excuse me; Miss Parody. Sorry about your father."

"She is staying in the studio. You probably remember that from the days you used to help your grandfather in the garden."

"Yes. Is that steep wooden flight of stairs along the rock still there? I used to like running up and down it as a kid."

John spoke next. "And, Carl, do you remember my sister, Fanny Amber Hassel—uh, what do you call yourself now, Fran?"

"It's nice to see you again, Carl. I'm using my professional name, just plain Fran Amber. My, you are very active in village affairs."

"My wife enjoys your articles, Ms. Amber. Now, just for the record, Mr. Hassel, I need to know where you all were this morning before the funeral."

"Oh, just around here. Seemed more appropriate. After breakfast, we stayed in the house or on the porch until early lunch. Claudia and Chester helped Martha and Konrad and Lily in the kitchen. My grandchildren were playing in the library. And Cousin Jenny, I believe you went out walking for a while?"

Carl was jotting all this down. He had felt uncomfortable at first, not knowing how to address each of them. First name or last? Although he'd known the older members all his life, they were somehow strangers. He concluded that last names would be more professional. They were older folks due some respect. He then made his way to the kitchen.

After questioning a truculent Martha, he departed. She then appeared at the top of the steps from the dining room to announce: "We're out of milk, Mrs. Bohner. That Konrad just can't remember to pick up everything on my market list!" and went back down the steps, muttering. "Send a boy to do a *woman's* job!"

Johnny responded: "Come on, Chester, let's us men go to Valley Grocery and get the stuff. How much, Martha? And anything else?" They went down the steps, trailing Martha, to confer with her. "Two attorneys to grill Martha," laughed Pattee. "Will she fry them?"

Now Claudia noticed that her archery target had fallen over and was lying in the tall grass at the edge of the garden. On investigating, she spotted someone lurking in the encroaching woods. It scared the wits out of her, at first. Then she grabbed her bow which she found lying at her feet, and brandishing it, shouted: "Get out, get out! Who do you think you are?"

It turned out to be a local news reporter, Claudia called to Uncle John who had just reappeared on the porch from seeing Carl to his car. She was furious. "The nerve of that guy!" John, who was watching the snooper tear through the underbrush down the hill to the meadow, called belatedly, "Need any help, Claudia?"

Dinner was soon ready after the two lawyers returned from the store. The family agreed with relief that Aunt Nittie's funeral was nicely done by the Reverend Gentle. "Practice makes perfect!" Having her nephew and five great-nephews as pallbearers was a nice touch. In spite of their struggling to lift the casket into the hearse. For once, nothing embarrassing happened. They were quite pleased with themselves. Even Fran refrained from criticizing. The will was not mentioned.

But Candy was curious about Fran's "professional life," and after dinner, while strolling around the circle in front of the house with Pattee, she questioned her about it.

"Oh, didn't you know, Candy? A couple of years ago she got a job with one of those women's magazines, the kind sold at supermarket checkout counters, *Family Square* or *Just a Housewife;* no, it's *Homemakers' Own*. She runs an advice column."

"She what? An advice column? Pattee, you're joking! With her snippy manner? What kind of advice?"

"Oh, on manners, etiquette. It's quite good and quite arrogant. But the readers seem to like that tone."

"I can just picture it. Pattee. 'Dear Miss Amber, I found a shoelace in my soup at a fancy dinner party, the other night. Should I have returned the soup to the kitchen, complained to my hostess, or . . .'"

"Swallowed it?" added Pattee, laughing. "And signed, 'Joe Banana' of . . . of . . ."

"Tyelace Corner, Virginia," contributed Candy. "Now, how would she reply? 'Dear Mr. Banana, Are you sure you hadn't tied one on? What kind of shoelace?' Your, turn, now, Pattee."

"All right. 'Was it dirty? No matter. Under such circumstances, for health reasons of course, with your elbow, knock the soup plate, as if by accident, so that it drops to the floor.'"

"And," added Candy, "'Please try to avoid splattering the guest sitting next to you.' I must get a copy of the magazine."

Pattee wondered: "Now how would Fran answer a letter such as 'Dear Miss Amber, Last night I found a body in the ice house . . .'"

Fran suddenly appeared. "What are you two laughing about?"

"Why, Franny, I just learned that you write a successful etiquette column. Pattee and I were wondering how you'd handle a letter starting with 'Last night I found a frozen body in my ice house. What should I do?'"

"You two are never serious! All right that's a challenge!" Then smiling, Fran went on, "For you two sillies, first I would run through a list of alternatives such as: 'one , try thawing; two, better than in an outhouse; three, was it a relative? And four, better not reuse that block of ice.'" Then turning serious, "It is strange, Ernest and Harold finally admitting to placing Perry's body in the ice house and now getting killed."

"Ernest had a heart attack."

"I wonder. We'll have to wait for the autopsy results. After all, Harold was definitely killed by an arrow. Even he could not have done that to himself. Now, Candy, do you suppose that daughter of yours, Claudia, was over there shooting game with her bow and arrow? She does have some odd hobbies. And she is always wandering around in the woods."

"Why, Fran, what a dreadful thought! Why would she kill Harold, or anyone, for that matter? She's hardly the type."

"Well, you seemed to have brought up your children in rather gypsy fashion with all that traveling from pillar to embassy post." Then noticing Candy's grim facial expression, she added, "Of course it would have been an accident."

Candy was flabbergasted; in fact, ready to commit a bit of murder on her own.

Pattee cleared the atmosphere by suggesting they go see what all the "fellers" were doing this evening. They marched back to the house in silence.

Chapter 13

# A Chase and Photo Finish

After Sunday breakfast, Konrad found his mother sitting beside the telephone on the stair landing. She was pondering whether to call Eric in Washington about the latest deaths, or not. She decided on "not." "Why upset him yet? I'll tell him when I see him tomorrow evening."

Suddenly she was aware of Konrad standing there. He sat down.

"Mummy, I have a favor to ask."

"Oh, dear!" sighed Candy.

"Lily wants to get a picture of everybody before they all leave."

"Oh, Konrad, that won't do. We don't want that kind of publicity."

"We've got it already. And think of the awful pictures other newspapers may dig up." Konrad always produced solid arguments with his requests.

"Thank goodness your father isn't here. But will the others be willing?"

"I thought you might persuade them. That's the favor. Lily's afraid of losing her job if she doesn't have something to show for it."

Candy did dislike refusing her children their requests. They were always reasonable ones, she felt. "What news has she—or should I say have you—been sending this weekly tabloid?"

"Oh, we've been going to the Pipe and Book shop in Lake Placid to buy some English newspapers and just rewrite the stuff. Of course they don't know what they're talking about but that doesn't seem to matter in England. I should have bought a Paris one for you to read. It sounded so funny; *Le Faucon en Glace,* and Keene Valley was called *La Vallée de la Mort,* Death Valley."

"But Konrad, isn't Lily's tabloid suspicious?"

"It's not called *Nonobservance* for nothing! But she does feel the need for a touch of accuracy. She has taken pictures of the house, the garden, pond, ice house, and now Harold's and Ernest's houses. We'll have to think up some lurid stories to go with those last two."

"Why, you are the most irresponsible journalist I've ever met, Konrad!"

"Now, Mummy, you told me to keep Lily out of the way."

"And so you have, Konrad. The meals have improved, too. We appreciate all that. I know! When we are all gathered around the fireplace tonight, I'll tell them you want to snap a few photos—informal shots—none of that media-type photo session stuff—for Lily."

"Thanks, Mummy."

"Oh, by the way, as you know I am returning to Washington tomorrow and taking Jenny. I don't want any hanky-panky in the kitchen."

"Are you referring to my passion for Martha? But seriously, Mummy, I wouldn't dare. I don't want to scare away Lily. She takes a pretty dim view of the family as it is. 'Wacky' and 'eccentric' are words of hers that slip out. Oh, I've got to tell you; Martha put up a sign at the foot of the kitchen stairs up to the maids' rooms that says: 'There is to be no hank and pank up there.'"

"Oh, Konrad!" Candy was laughing. "I must go over to have a look."

"No, please don't. Lily is so embarrassed."

"I have been meaning to talk to you, now that you have had a vacation. . . ."

"A vacation! Why I've been slaving in Martha's galley as chief cook and bottlewasher!"

Candy continued, "You will need to look for a job soon. When are you planning to return home?"

"Lily plans to stick around a few more days for the latest funerals and any more murders that crop up."

"Konrad! Don't say that!"

"Anyway, Chester has offered to drive us to New York next weekend. First, he wants us to climb a few mountains with him."

"Isn't that where Lily lives?"

"Huh? Oh, New York. She's thinking though of moving to Washington where she says the action is."

"If she wants action, she had better remain in Keene Valley."

"Well, let's get to the club now. Remember, Lily and

I challenged you and Jenny to the tennis match of the century. I should say of the last century, since the only racquets we have are those old wooden ones."

Meanwhile in the village, Whistler, confused at this point, went looking for Elmer Wall. He wasn't at his usual place at the Spread Eagle when it opened for the day. Nor did Jane Wall at the hospital know of his whereabouts, she said. So he crossed the road to catch Carl at his garage. He'd need his help and he could read over his notes and use Carl's telephone to find out the results of the autopsy on Ernest Middleton. "Just had to be sure," he told himself. Therefore, on hearing the report, he was stunned. So had been Ernest, electrocuted by a stun gun. "A stun gun?" he asked the medical examiner.

"Yeh. It's a small, hand-held box run by a nine-volt battery with two prongs which when pressed against the skin give a nice fifty-thousand-volt jolt. It left two minute marks on the back of the victim's neck like mosquito bites."

"So Ernest was murdered. Now the question is," Whistler was telling Carl, "is Elmer the next victim or a suspect? We'll just keep this under our hats for the time being."

Claudia, after leaving off the tennis players at the club, pulled up just then to a gas tank in her Volkswagen convertible. The top was down. She waved hello to the lieutenant. He thought, *Now there's the only normal one in that Amber family. Not shallow; looks like her mother—and her father, too—but beautiful. Her eyes are so expressive; how they light up when she describes crystals and "shapes in nature" and what all lies beneath the surface.*

"Good morning, Miss Bohner," he called. "Nice day for a drive."

"Yes, I thought I'd take some pictures, it's such a clear day. Say, that's too bad about Ernest dropping dead in the middle of the vegetable garden. I'd been up there before breakfast that day to photograph the dew on carrot tops and glistening spider webs on the grass."

"Did you notice anything unusual?"

"Not particularly. The tool shed door was wide open. I assumed the catch was loose. I closed it. My cousin Jenny came down the steps from the studio and watched me. We didn't stay long."

"Perhaps your cousin noticed something. I'd like to talk to her."

"Oh, she's leaving tomorrow for Washington. Her father is going to be buried in Arlington Cemetery."

Lieutenant Whistler sighed as he turned away. The investigation was going nowhere and everywhere. He still had to find Elmer. Suddenly he heard Claudia exclaim, "Oh no!" He wheeled around to discover her slumped down across the front seat. In horror, he called, "Miss Bohner, are you all right?"

Claudia looked up with a smile and a wink. "Shh, there's Bunny Munchkin in front of the Birch Shop. I don't want her to see me." But of course, Bunny had, thanks to the lieutenant.

"Yoo hoo, Claudia," Bunny called. "Don't go away. I'll be right over." She was. "Claudie, you're just the person I want to see. Tell me all about what's been happening in K.V.!"

As Claudia was introducing Bunny to the lieutenant, a screeching of rubber tires was heard, and Dr. Cough's Porsche was seen tearing out of the hospital driveway and heading north. Elmer Wall was at the wheel. Lieutenant Whistler dashed to his car, turned on the flashing red light and siren and took chase. Actually it turned out to be not very thrilling. Elmer did not know how to drive a foreign car, while Lieutenant Whistler's old Dodge had problems. It became a chase in slow motion.

"Come on, Claudie, let's follow!" exclaimed Bunny as she started to climb into Claudia's car.

"Wait, Bunny, it's still attached to the gas pump."

"Never mind. I'll drive mine." Bunny ran across the road to her car and took off after the lieutenant.

While Claudia was paying for her gasoline, Chester

drove up in his battered blue Plymouth and asked, "What's all the excitement?"

After Claudia explained that Elmer Wall had stolen Dr. Cough's Porsche and was being chased by Lieutenant Whistler, and was followed by Bunny, he set out after them. When Claudia then saw Carl drive out of the garage in his tow truck and head in the same direction, she decided she might as well join the fun too.

The procession proceeded through the village, past the airport, where a half-dozen sky divers were lining up to board "Captain" Caine Smythe's training plane, across the bridge over the Ausable River, and headed for Spruce Hill. Elmer suddenly swerved off on to a side road leading to the Keene Valley dump. By the time Lieutenant Whistler bounced his way into the garbage area, he could see that the Porsche was empty. The dump was littered with mounds of smoking trash, abandoned autos, rusty bed springs, piles of bulging plastic garbage bags, and three huge furniture packing containers. Ah hah! The lieutenant heard a rustling sound coming from behind one of the boxes. By this time, Bunny, Chester, Carl, Claudia and a few villagers scenting excitement on a quiet Sunday ("It sure beats going to church, especially since we've been goin' to church all week for funerals.") had arrived. They stayed back when Whistler drew his gun and shouted at the container, "Come out and with your hands up!" There was a suspenseful pause. Then out lumbered a bear on her hind legs, waving her forepaws. She was followed by two cubs trying to imitate her. The lieutenant actually swore as he retreated to his car in haste, as did the others. After the bears moved off to sweeter and less eventful pastures, the lieutenant stood up and surveyed the area. "Now, where is Elmer? Probably in the woods beyond and headed up East Hill."

Carl picked up a cap near the Porsche and told Whistler it looked like Elmer's. Whistler decided to radio for troopers and dogs. They were a long time in coming. *All this fuss,* thought Whistler. *All I want to do is question him. What is going on in that soggy mind of his?*

While the lieutenant and his deputy, Carl, sat down for a smoke and a wait, their followers, one by one, departed. The chase resumed when dogs and troopers finally arrived. The cap was sniffed and off they went. The sound of yapping dogs and cursing men could be heard on that quiet Sunday, as they crashed through the underbrush up East Hill. After covering a breathless distance, they reached a clearing with a brown shack standing neatly in the center. The dogs charged ahead. A man sitting on the tiny porch looked up to see the arm (and legs) of the law swiftly approaching, and deciding the situation looked unhealthy for him, retreated behind a screen door. Lieutenant Whistler once again drew his pistol and shouted, "Come out, Elmer, with your hands up!"

The voice from inside called back, "I ain't Elmer. And call off them dogs first."

Lieutenant Whistler, at first puzzled, discovered that it really was not Elmer, but none other than Old Man Phipps, berry picker and supplier of same to the summer folk. As he stepped out, he said, "I see you found my cap. Thanks."

Lieutenant Whistler, disappointed but undaunted, decided on a new plan. "We'll disband, men, for now, and we'll leave the Porsche at the dump where Elmer can find it. He hasn't any place to go. He's not guilty of anything, yet. He'll probably return to his sister at the hospital if given a chance."

Carl added, "There's going to be a replacement for Dr. Cough starting tomorrow. I'll warn him." Then they all dispersed.

During dinner, Claudia announced that there was a suspect, Elmer Wall.

"Elmer?" exclaimed John.

"Who's Elmer?" inquired Jenny.

"Miss Wall's brother. She's the supervisor at the hospital. But how could he be a killer? He's never sober enough to lift anything but a bottle. With a gun or bow and arrow, he'd miss the side of a barn."

Claudia described the chase. When she reached the part where Mama bear appeared with her paws up, Rick interrupted with "Maybe she's the murderer." His brother Johnny suggested. "This bears looking into."

Claudia continued, "Cut it out, you guys. I haven't finished." But when she told them what she had later learned from Carl about Old Berryman Phipps's cap, even John was moved to state, "Well, that caps all!"

Martha, who was in the dining room to listen to the dinner conversation, began to laugh. This startled them. They had never heard Martha do such a thing before. Konrad was busy writing all this down for Lily's newspaper.

As the family collected around the fireplace after dinner, Horace and Mary joined them, bearing astonishing news. Lieutenant Whistler had phoned them that Ernest Middleton had been killed with a "stung" gun. All were curious to know what a "stung" gun was. Horace, explained: "It's a small electronic device which fits into the hand. You press a button, and, presto, two antennae pop out and sting the victim. But when Ernest got stung, it was too much for him, fatal in fact."

Rick, the trivia expert, added, "It's called a *stun* gun. Horace. A weapon used by police enforcement to overcome unruly suspects. Of course, anyone can buy one. Just the thing to fit in a lady's purse for street protection. But it might be considered a concealed weapon then."

Pattee joked, "I think I'll stick with my poisoned umbrella."

After the chatter and banter subsided, Candy mentioned Konrad's request of a photo session for Lily's tabloid. Sally and Cindy jumped up, taking their children into the library, muttering, "We only married into this family. Count us out!" and several other disparaging remarks.

But John, who liked Lily, suggested, "We could sit reading or doing crossword puzzles, Pattee, while Chester and Rick and Johnny huddle in one corner deep in conversation, and Franny, Candy, and Claudie could lounge around or knit in a natural-looking way. Horace, you might stand under the moose with Mary."

Lily was waiting out on the porch until Konrad could set up tripod and camera while performing a comic routine of "lights, camera, rolling," that had them all in stitches.

Horace added, "Be sure to get in the moose. And, Jenny, don't hide behind Claudia. Fran, show your profile."

Fran's next remark echoed the thoughts of the others. "Candy, this is one of your worst ideas. We'll have to approve the proofs, Konrad. The smudgier, the better."

Konrad then called Lily in to join them. She blushingly thanked them. Somehow, they did not expect her to last long as a reporter. Later, they would be astonished to learn that she had been given a raise and praise for the fine job she was doing. *The Unobservant,* as they called her paper, had never had such quality coverage before.

## Chapter 14

## Grave Situations

Aunt Nittie's burial was scheduled for noon on Monday. The family planned to leave early for a leisurely drive to the Albany Rural Cemetery, where all Ambers finally came to rest in peace. Transportation arrangements were made with voluble deliberation and sudden abandon. John and Pattee would take Jenny and Candy. Chester offered to drive Horace and Mary and Fran. But certain members felt that Chester's old car looked pretty derelict and not dignified enough for a funeral. Therefore, Horace suggested they go in his Audi. Fran agreed, but Chester questioned Horace's driving ability. Then Col. Abel Smythe arrived in his long green convertible, inviting Fran to ride with him, since he was going to Albany anyway on an errand. Chester decided to drive himself, leaving Horace and Mary a twosome in the Audi. John asked Candy if she'd like to make some changes before they started, but she replied that his driving and his Cadillac would do.

The young Hassels with their little ones also departed, but for Syracuse. Konrad and Lily were going to take photographs of the village. Claudia sighed with relief when all had finally gotten off. Sitting on the Gate House porch talking to the Wackman's babysitter, she remarked on how peaceful and lazy the summer day seemed. Then Bunny, that bundle of fun and energy, appeared. "Come on, Claudie," she called. "You promised to show me the scenes of the crimes. Which house across the way is the Dibbles'?"

"The one with the chickens in the front."

"Let's snoop around."

"Forbidden territory. Mrs. Dibble would probably take a pot shot at us trespassers. We'll go on down the lane to the pond."

As they trotted along, Claudia explained how Cousin Peregrine had been shot in the back by Dr. Cough. She corrected himself. "No, it turned out it couldn't have been the Doc. Maybe it was Elmer; but he disappeared at the dump. Then Ernest and his helper, Harold, discovered the body, suspected Dr. Cough of shooting him by mistake for a deer, and dumped it in the pond. After all, the victim wasn't a regular summer person. Then in the winter, while cutting ice, they found the frozen remains, and accidentally cut off the head in a block of ice. They cut a huge oblong for the body and put them in the ice house, which collapsed this month, waking up Horace. I'll show you that later. Now we'll go up the hill to the vegetable garden. That's the old cow pasture on the left."

"I'm confused, but this is a beautiful place."

At the upper meadow, Claudia showed Bunny the tool shed, next to which Ernest had parked his truck and in which he had been found dead from a heart attack. "No, it wasn't a natural one. He had been stunned to death. That's why he wasn't at Aunt Nittie's funeral, although no one had noticed, except Lieutenant Whistler, I suppose."

"It seems awful complicated. Is that lettuce and beets and carrots and cabbage growing? Oh, Claudie, I ought to get my rabbit costume and let you take a picture of me in the cabbage patch."

Claudia suggested, "And munching on a carrot. We could call it 'Bunny Munchkin Was Here.'"

"Or, 'One Giant Hop for Bunny.'"

"Even better, 'One Giant Bunny Hopping Mad.'"

Convulsed with laughter, the two girls turned away. Bunny, always curious, pointed as she asked, "Where do those steps go, the ones up the rock?"

"Up to the studio. I'll show you. They're sort of rotten, so don't hop up, Bunny."

On reaching the studio porch, Claudia said, "Let's take a peek inside. Uh oh, there's Martha. Now what's she doing here? Hi, Martha."

Martha came out the door carrying rumpled linen, grumbling to herself. On noticing Claudia and Bunny, she complained, "I don't know why I am called upon to straighten up here. What with Miss Nittie gone and all, what's going to become of all this? But if you two are going inside, don't make a mess. Here's the key, so, mind you, lock up afterwards and return the key to its proper hook in the kitchen." And off she lumbered with her laundry basket.

Bunny was enchanted with the cozy living room and dining-room wicker furniture, brass bed in bedroom, tiny kitchen and bath. "Sort of primitive luxury. Who stays here, Claudie?"

"Usually the overflow of guests. Cousin Jenny is the latest."

"Who's she?"

"She's the daughter of the victim, whom we never knew existed, from England. She's a second cousin once or twice removed, so Mummy says."

"Oh, what's this?" Bunny stooped to pick up a crumpled piece of paper under a chair near the fireplace. "Hey, Claudie, look at this!"

Claudia took the paper and read the almost illegible scrawl. "It says, 'and don't forget to settle the riddle, diddle and middle.' That doesn't make much sense." She did not tell Bunny about more writing on the back.

Bunny, excited, said, "Another mystery. A mysterious message. Let's see what else we can find."

But their search turned up nothing more than a mouse trap under the stove, fortunately empty, and an old leather glove behind a cushion on the dining room windowseat. Claudia decided to keep the note. After Bunny's departure, she took it out of her pocket to read the reverse side: "If Diddle and Middle are just Pollution, then Riddle must be the Final Solution." She mulled over that for a bit, wondering if she'd be silly to show it to Lieutenant Whistler.

Meanwhile, John and Pattee and Candy and Jenny were enjoying their drive to Albany. Pattee had mentioned some schoolgirl incident that had happened to her years ago at St. Agnes School. Jenny replied laughing, "That reminds me of when I taught at a posh girls' school in Somerset, also named St. Agnes."

"Oh, what did you teach?"

"Gym; hockey, archery, pseudo judo. But those girls were such a limp, disinterested gaggle. One day, I lined them up to scold them and an idea suddenly hit me. Drill, that's what they needed. I showed them how to march in formation. Thought a taste of army discipline would serve them right. Well, they just loved it. Voted to buy uniforms, and eventually requested a rifle range. Then I got fired, to be replaced by a drill sergeant from a nearby army base."

John asked, "What'd you do then? Join the army to improve your teaching skills?"

Jenny chuckled, "No, I became a travel agent, but not for long. I made out a ticket to Auckland instead of Oakland. They sound alike, you know. It took the traveler— he was from Brighton, but none too bright—two days to realize he wasn't in California but in New Zealand. When he did, and called the agency, reversing the charges, I got the sack."

"What are your plans now?" John wanted to know.

"I thought I'd spend some time in Washington after Dad is buried, and perhaps New York and Miami, very popular with British tourists. I'd love to take a Caribbean cruise and drop in on you, Candy, in Beaulinia. I love cruising. Once on a Mediterranean one I discovered that my cabin was to be shared with a man. It was an Italian ship, where English was only half understood and my Italian not at all. I sought out the purser to explain this embarrassing mistake of theirs and to request a single. The purser, shrugging his shoulders, got me to understand that they were overbooked even, and then smiling and winking told me how 'lucky lady' I was."

"What did you do then?" they all wanted to know.

"Nothing. My 'roomie' turned out to be a perfect gentleman. And so good-looking, Latin type, so suave and a marvelous dancer. We divided up the area, his and hers, and agreed not to invite in friends. We still correspond, that is, until recently."

By this time, they had reached the cemetery and were pulling up to the large family plot near the North Gate. The hearse and the Reverend Smoak, pastor of Nittie's church in Albany, had just arrived. The freshly dug grave was in the front row nearest the road. In the center stood the large headstone of great-grandfather Wain Amber, once a prominent Methodist missionary, flanked by the smaller stones of wives one and two. Pattee said later that she felt like singing "O beautiful for spacious skies" when she saw those Amber graves of Wain.

Candy was surprised and delighted to find Honey there. She was carrying her beloved little dog, Snowball, a miniature Boston bull terrier with a round white head and two bulging eyes, nearly blind, though. And at the last minute, Henny and Seth arrived and stood beside the other Wackmans. But Fran never appeared and probably wasn't missed.

Then, all approached the unfamiliar but holy Dr. Smoak and introduced themselves to him and a few faintly familiar faces of Nittie's vintage standing behind him. Grouping themselves around the casket, hovering over the open grave, they listened to a short service admonishing them to take due warning and consider the shortness of human life, the awful realities of eternal life and other lugubrious matters "for the Lord giveth and taketh away" all the way to "ashes to ashes and dust to dust." And then it was over. They really felt that Dr. Smoak could have sounded hopeful with more fire and less brimstone. They duly thanked him, and returned to living.

Candy could hardly wait to talk to Honey. As Honey explained, "Family feeling got the better of me, I guess. The last of the Ambers. I'm terribly curious too about the mad killer of Keene Valley. Aren't you afraid, Candy? And with Konrad and Claudia still up there?"

Candy hadn't been until now, and began to feel some alarm. But Honey always was such a worry wart, she told herself. Still . . .

Snowball, who had been resting in Honey's arms, was set on the grass to roam about a bit.

"How did you get Snowball on the plane?" Candy now asked.

"Put her in a carry-on bag. She was doped up and sleeping. I was afraid she might snore, though."

"But how did you get her through airport security?"

"Just sent her through in the bag on the treadmill. No metal parts. I'd removed her collar."

While they were talking, the still groggy Snowball had sniffed her way over to the open grave and promptly fell in on top of the casket. John, who had been watching her, quickly scooped her out, hoping that no one had noticed. But all eyes were on him and the redeemed dog just risen from the dead. "Paying her last respects," he muttered to Honey as he handed Snowball to her.

Before separating, they'd have lunch together. They were soon piling into a nearby Howard Johnson's. A table for ten was arranged and the fun began. John remarked, "Of course with all those witnesses, Snowball's descent into the grave will be reported all over Albany by nightfall. Think what a newspaper headline could do with that: 'Dog Overcome at Great Aunt's Burial.'"

Pattee picked up the spirit with "Unleashed Terr(i)or Attack at Cemetery."

Honey, who'd recovered from the shame of it all, joined in with "Where There's Smoak There's . . . uh, uh . . ."

And Charlie suggested, "Snatched from the Jaws of Death."

Henny, still recovering from a strep throat which had prevented her from attending Nittie's funeral in Keene Valley, took a more serious view. "You're all nuts," she announced. Seth, her husband, never having attended a family affair before, sat and stroked his beard. He was fascinated with this Amber Bunch. And looking at each one, he discovered how much they all resembled one another. Even newcomer Jenny. All had blond or light-brown

111

hair, all had wide-spaced blue eyes and high foreheads; with or without glasses and mustaches. And even into the next generation with his own children. "Amber genes run deep. The results of a matriarchal family," he decided.

On parting, they all thanked Honey and her acrobatic Snowball for making this a memorable day. Honey was going to see a man about a dog; she wanted a vet to examine Snowball before returning to Florida. They then went their separate ways. John and Pattee deposited Candy and Jenny at the Albany Airport before driving home to Syracuse.

Chapter 15

# The Root of All Pain

Candy was anxious to get home, to tell Eric the latest news and happenings. She had invited Jenny to stay with them, but Jenny declined. After arriving at National Airport, they caught one of those filthy cabs with a driver who barely understood English. Candy left Jenny off at the Chancery Hotel on Massachusetts Avenue and continued on a few blocks to her house.

She knew Eric would be alone, because he had given Bertha a few days off. Wanted privacy, he'd said. He had inherited Bertha (as he had worded it), his mother's housekeeper for many years. Not knowing quite what to do with her, although Candy did, since she disliked housework, he had fixed up a tiny apartment in the basement, installing her mainly as a housesitter for the frequently empty house.

He had felt that installing bars on doors and windows was not enough security against Washington's burgeoning crop of burglars.

As Candy entered the house, she was greeted by Eric, coming down the stairs with, "I think I'm going to be fired."

"Now, Eric, how can they do that?"

"They're treating me like a leper. Those arrogant fools won't answer my calls and refuse to see me. I don't know what to make of it! Did I greet you?" and pecked her on the cheek, adding, "I have a terrible toothache!"

"Why didn't you say so? When did it start?"

"On the bus from Keene Valley; dreadful trip. Changing buses in New York was a nightmare. The passengers boarding there looked like street people."

"I'd better call Dr. Dorian."

"He wouldn't be in his office this late."

"I'll call him at home."

"Do you think we should disturb him?"

"Do you think you should continue to suffer? I'll dial but you'd better talk to him to describe it."

Dr. Dorian was home and prescribed a codeine painkiller and an early morning visit. Candy rushed over to a drug store on Connecticut Avenue to procure the relief for Eric. She didn't want Eric to visit Dr. Dorian in such a wretched condition. A patient in pain upset the dentist. She was almost glad she would be escorting Jenny to her father's burial instead of taking Eric to the dentist the following morning.

He was sent off early in a taxi, still in great pain. Dr. Dorian whisked him into the chair and began to probe his teeth with a shiny instrument while chatting away. "So, Ambassador, you have been in Keene Valley. Lots of news about that place. A three-hundred-pound spy in a block of ice because he was a dope courier for some Congressman's aide is not your run-of-the-mill stuff. That Riddle guy lost his match and his life on a tennis court. His sister is a patient of mine."

Eric replied, "Aagh ee ah hee-a-ed oo a fahhy."

Mrs. Dorian, who assisted her husband, was standing there to translate. "He said he was related to the family."

"Who, Riddle was?" Dr. Dorian removed his hands and implement in surprise from Eric's yawning jaws.

"No, the spy, Peregrine Parody."

Back into the mouth went saliva tube, hand and pick. "You know, Ambassador, you need to have a root canal done. This old tooth has given you trouble before."

"Buh Ah muhs ahen a fooha."

"He says he must attend a funeral, Vic."

"When?"

"Oohay."

"Today."

"Well, Ambassador, I'll fix you up for now and make an appointment for you with Dr. Raffle. I don't do root canals. It's better that you see a dental surgeon."

Eric, his mouth free of encumbrances, spoke clearly and decisively, "Not Dr. Raffle, though. His hands shake. A neighbor of ours went to him for an extraction. She was sitting in the waiting room when he appeared and called her name. She said he seemed so old and shaky that she just didn't identify herself, but got up and casually walked out."

"Now that you mention it," went on Dr. Dorian, resuming work, "he has been practicing for almost fifty years. That's much too long, especially if he is shaky. But you know, old—I mean old, old, patients don't notice that because they're shaky too. And they prefer an oldtimer and keep him in practice longer than he should be because he'll take time to listen to them."

Eric wondered to himself what he could listen to except "oogh" and "aagh."

"These young dentists just want to get the job done and move on to the next patient. Well, there's Dr. Deeth; he's in his forties. Dr. Morris Deeth. It's spelled D-E-A-T-H, but pronounced Deeth, like in teeth. He doesn't want to frighten away patients."

While Dr. Vic (as in pick) Dorian left the room to telephone, Mrs. Dorian removed the bib and asked Eric what he thought of the two latest deaths in Keene Valley.

"What latest deaths?" Candy had forgotten to tell him about Ernest and Harold because of fussing with his toothache. And Eric rarely read a Washington newspaper. He assumed Mrs. Dorian was referring to Aunt Nittie and Dr. Cough. His reply seemed a bit odd to Mrs. Dorian: "Oh, they were expected and natural in the course of events. But I try not to get involved. I'm just anxious to return to Beaulinia."

"Oh, yes, that's where you are. I read in the papers that all this dope here is coming from there; big warehouses full of the stuff. And that President Carlos, I think his name is, has a secret weapon to defend his drug market."

"That's just rubbish, Mrs. Dorian. The papers, as usual, have gotten it all wrong. I've seen no dope. And Carlos exports bananas."

But Eric was upset and later on leaving, bought a newspaper to read in the taxi taking him to Arlington Cemetery. There was time to attend Perry's burial before his appointment with Dr. Death (as in teeth). And the pain was temporarily gone.

He arrived at Peregrine's grave site as the flag was being folded to be given to Jenny. He slipped in beside Candy standing next to Jenny, wondering who those beefy-looking strangers were behind them. "Our old law-enforcement friends, I suppose."

There was another ceremony commencing close by. While Candy and Eric and Jenny, the only mourners, walked over to the waiting limousine, their on-lookers turned to the next plot to join that burial contingent. Candy caught a glimpse of Congressman Brasher and his wife.

"Good grief, are they burying Bill Riddle next door to Perry?" Jenny heard her remark and looked shocked. "Cousin Eric, would you mind asking someone whose burial that is?"

Eric returned quickly with the words, "Yes, it's Riddle. Let's get out of here."

Candy wondered why they'd waited a week to bury him. "Poor Jenny, you look all in. Do you want to come home with us?"

"Thanks, Cousin Candy, but I think I'll just return to the hotel. I'll call you later."

By that time, the Novocaine had worn off and Eric was painfully silent. Candy decided they'd better go right on to Dr. Death's office, even if they would have to wait for an hour and a half.

That evening, the Bohner's front doorbell rang. Candy was dining with Jenny at her hotel. Eric, still in some pain, had declined her invitation, to suffer alone in peace with no appetite. He opened the door expecting to find Candy having forgotten her key.

"Why, Lieutenant Whistler, this is rather unexpected."

"Good evening, Ambassador. Forgive my intrusion. I should have telephoned first, but I am looking for Miss Jennifer Parody."

"Please come in. She's staying at the Chancery Hotel, not far from here and dining there with my wife." Eric did not feel like talking more than was painfully necessary. "I expect both of them soon."

"Would you mind if I waited, Ambassador?" Then noticing his robe and slippers. "Unless you were planning to retire."

"No, it's due to a root canal. I'll take another painkiller. Perhaps you would like a cup of coffee."

They both went to the kitchen for codeine and coffee. Eric asked, "Anything new turn up, Lieutenant?"

"I believe so. Your daughter Claudia found a curious note in the studio where Miss Parody had stayed." He showed it to Eric. "She said you were clever at solving riddles."

That pleased Eric. "Let's go into the living room and work on it." After reading the Middle, Diddle, Riddle rhyme, he said, "Surely Riddle is easy."

"Bill Riddle, you mean? That's what I thought. Incidentally, while I am in Washington, I hope to find a picture of him. I've had no cooperation from the FBI over the telephone. I believe he is probably Mrs. Melville's bird-watcher."

"I wish I could help you with Washington authorities, but I am having problems of my own with them. Ah, but my dentist knows Riddle's sister. Let me give you his telephone number."

"Thank you, sir. Now what about Middle and Diddle?"

"Oh, I say. That caretaker's named Middleton."

"And his helper, Harold Dibble, but not Diddle."

"Oh, that matters not in such matters. 'Ds' and 'Bs' are interchangeable. How does that go? 'Don't forget to settle . . .' I say, that looks rather bad for Cousin Jenny. And this 'final solution' for Riddle. Isn't that an expression for killing? Oh, Lieutenant, my wife is dining with her. We must do something." Eric jumped up.

"Easy now, sir. It may not be what it seems."

The doorbell rang. Eric dashed to the front door, struggled with the bolt, and opened it after viewing Candy and Jenny through the peephole. He reached out and grabbed his wife, pulling her in, and then hastily slammed the door. Jenny was left standing outside in utter amazement.

Whistler, by this time also at the door, reopened it. "It's all right, sir." And to Jennifer, "Please come in, Miss Parody. It's the Ambassador's toothache that's bothering him." He led her into the living room and explained to her why he was there, while Eric hustled a surprised Candy up the stairs and into their bedroom, shushing her exclamations until he had closed the door. He was shaking.

117

Candy just stood there with her eyes and mouth wide open in silence while Eric stammered, "She's the killer. She did it. Riddle, Middle, and Diddle."

"Now, Eric, what on earth are you jabbering about?" Eric in his customary convoluted fashion slowly informed Candy what he had learned from Whistler.

"Well, at least she didn't kill her father. Remember the bird-watcher?"

"I think three murders are quite enough," snapped Eric.

"Nonsense. Jenny's not the type. In any case, what do we do now? We can't stay up here. We have guests."

"We'll wait a bit. Sit down and turn on the television or something. Whistler wants to question Jenny."

So they waited awhile, but in silence, hoping to hear what was said in the room directly below. Candy's thoughts were rattling around in her head and she thought to herself, *On the drive to Albany, Jenny mentioned teaching archery and rifle practice at a girls' school. Better not tell Eric that. He'd have a fit. But then Claudia too could be a suspect with her bow and arrow. Poor Harold Dibble met his Hastings like King Harold in um, 1066, or thereabout, with an arrow in the eye. But look at Eric; he has his own rifle range at the embassy. Of course, one should have a motive, it seems to me.* Then she turned to Eric, sitting in the other chair facing the blank television set, and whispered, "Can you hear anything?"

"He asked her if she knew William Riddle."

"What is her reply?"

"I can't make out. But it's not short. Why must people mumble so! Ssh! Someone's calling."

"Candy! Eric! I'm going now." That was Jenny. Candy and Eric rushed down the stairs to find Jenny and Lieutenant Whistler standing at the front door. "Oh, must you leave so soon?" Eric inquired politely out of constant habit, and not meaning a word of it.

"Lieutenant Whistler is taking me to police headquarters to get my statement written down."

"Oh, Jenny," gurgled Candy, "don't say anything until we get a lawyer for you. Isn't that so, Lieutenant?"

"This is just routine, Mrs. Bohner."

"Did he read you your rights, Jenny? You don't seem terribly upset!"

"It's all right, Candy."

"We'll get a lawyer for you. Where shall you be?"

Lieutenant Whistler gave Eric the address and departed with Jenny, down the steps and into a waiting car. *At least she's not in shackles,* thought Candy.

Eric and Candy were speechless, but not for long. "Candace, I really don't know how your family continually gets into these scrapes. Think of it! Hauled off to the police station. Arrested for murder! And that brazen hussy as calm and collected as if she were taking a moonlight stroll."

"But she's hardly a relative, only a removed sort of one we never knew existed until now. She's English!"

"Well, that's exactly what I mean. Those mad English are always into murder. Look at their newspaper headlines: 'Bog Killer Bags Another Body' or 'Yorkshire Pudding Poisons Party,' and what about that 'Acid Bath Found in Nursing Home'!"

"Now, Eric, I'm sure all that doesn't help your toothache."

"Oh, I say, I've forgotten all about it."

"Good; now, how do we go about finding a lawyer for Jenny at nine o'clock at night?"

"Don't they have some free ones hanging around courthouse doors? Of course you do have a whole family of them."

"True, but they don't practice in D.C. What's the name of the lawyer who did our wills?"

"Pendleton, I think. Nicholas Pendleton. And don't say 'Where there's a will, there's a way.'"

"I could phone him."

"If he handles wills he certainly won't handle a murder. He deals with the more respectable form of dying."

"I know, Eric, but surely he could suggest a defense lawyer."

"Do you have any idea what one of those would cost? But then, Jenny would be paying for him. All right, you'd better try him. You are better at that than I am."

"You know, Eric, it is not difficult to get people to do your bidding. Instead of saying, 'If you think perhaps you might be able to come, although I know it is an imposition, but we are having a bit of a problem, you see. My wife sort of shot our next-door neighbor—dead, I'm afraid, and well, she might find herself in some difficulty since she is being charged . . .'"

"That's enough, Candace. You've made your point. I do tend to understate. But you overstate so—so—efficiently."

"Why, thank you, Eric. That's a nice compliment."

"Now don't you think you ought to call Mr. Pendleton, before Jenny is tried and convicted?"

"All we have for Pendleton is an office number," Candy called to Eric. "You'll have to look up his home number; the print's too tiny in the directory for me to read."

"Which one? Does he live in the District, Maryland or Virginia?"

"I don't know." Just then, the telephone in front of Candy startled her by ringing. "Hello?"

"Mummy? This is Claudie. Konrad and Lily and I are leaving K.V. for home tomorrow. Konrad wants to know if you can put up Lily for the night."

"Is she still working for that tabloid? Oh, I guess so for one night. Tell Konrad just one night, though, as we are having complications at this end. I can't say what, now."

"So are we, Mummy. Horace and Mary have moved up here to the big house with their children, while Henny and Seth have brought theirs. Chester and Aunt Fran are still here."

"Well, that's the way it goes, Claudie."

"But that's not why we're leaving. There's been another murder, or reasonable facsimile."

"Oh, mercy. It does sound like Death Valley. Who's the latest?"

"Elmer Wall. Horace found him."

"Horace seems to have a knack for that. Where? In the washhouse this time?"

"No, in the dump. He had to take over bags and bags of trash and garbage, which had been piling up on the kitchen porch, because the racoons had gotten in through a hole in the screen and made a terrible mess. He said that when he got over to the dump, the latest bulldozed hole the size of a tennis court was almost filled up and ready to be covered over with dirt. Near the edge he saw a bag with a shoe hanging out. Smelled pretty awful, he said. But what was worse, the shoe had a foot in it. He couldn't recognize the foot, but on gingerly opening the bag did recognize the face. He came back here to call Lieutenant Whistler, who doesn't seem to be anywhere around."

"That's because he is here in Washington. He's a part of our complications."

"Is Daddy in trouble? I mean, arrested or something?"

"No, he just has a toothache."

"Well, why would Lieutenant Whistler be interested in Daddy's toothache?"

Candy paused and then spoke more softly, "I didn't want to tell you this over the phone. He's interested in Jenny."

"Daddy's interested in Jenny?"

"No, Whistler is."

"You mean Whistler is in love with Jenny?"

"No, he took her to the police headquarters downtown. . . ."

"Oh! My piece of evidence, the Riddle."

"It would seem so. But goodness, Claudie, I must hang up. I am trying to locate a lawyer for Jenny. See you tomorrow and drive carefully. Oh, and Claudia, don't tell

Konrad and Lily or anybody else. Good-bye."

Candy was rattled. She did not want to upset Eric. "I'd better not tell him until tomorrow after the kids have left K.V. He'd fuss all night that they were in danger and recall from his past some similar family he knew years ago who was murdered in their beds by a mad killer on the loose and stuffed in trash bags to be collected by . . . and he'd keep me awake all night, too."

Fortunately, Eric had retreated to his bed, exhausted and doped. She located a magnifying glass and pulled out a telephone book, when the bright idea came to her to call Pendleton's office number, no matter how late, because it probably had a recorded message of where to locate him. This had really been a trying day for both Candy and Eric. For once, Candy agreed with him that they should return to Beaulinia as quickly as possible. They deserved a rest. "But first, get Jenny out of jail and Eric out of pain."

She dialed the number of the office, learned the home number and was soon speaking to him. "Hello, Mr. Pendleton? This is Candace Bohner. Sorry to bother you so late, but we have a sort of problem," which she wearily explained to him. He said he would send his son, Miles, or was it nephew, Candy couldn't remember later, to see about bail and that Candy in her confused condition needn't be there, too. He would call back if necessary.

Candy thought, *If Jenny is freed on bail, where will she stay? With us? Eric would never permit that. Oh, dear! Well, what would he suggest? He'd say, "Let her rot in jail."*

## Chapter 16

## The Muddler's Theory

Meanwhile earlier that same day, Chester was sorting out papers in Aunt Nittie's desk in the library of the Keene Valley house. He discovered a list of personal items she wished to have distributed to her nieces and nephews. At the top of the list was her opal ring; it was to go to Fran. Chester sat up with a jerk. "Cripes, what happened to the ring? It must be the same one found by the pond. Claudia said she had returned it to her. Did she?"

Claudia was soon found and questioned. Yes, she had, and furthermore had seen it on Nittie's finger the day before she died. Perhaps it was in the hospital bag in which the nurse had packed Nittie's personal effects. The bag was located upstairs in Nittie's old room, but not the ring. Claudia, wanting to clear herself of any latent family suspicion, told Chester to ask Martha if she had seen Nittie wearing it. They trooped down to the kitchen to ask her. "Yes," said Martha, "Miss Nittie was wearing it her last day when I went to feed her her lunch. She would brighten up when I'd admire it." No one knew whether it was a particularly valuable stone (probably) or just a sentimental one (definitely). She had brought it home from India many years ago.

Horace was consulted next. He drove right down to

the hospital to ask Miss Wall. He soon learned that no one remembered if she was wearing it when the undertaker came. A telephone call to the firm in Elizabethtown elicited the information that it is against the law in New York State to bury a person with jewelry other than a wedding ring, unless specifically requested, and hence any jewelry would be removed and returned to the family. The undertaker in Albany who had arranged the burial was next called and gave the same answer, but added that of course slip-ups could occur.

Now Fran, the interested party, had been following this search from the beginning and therefore saw no alternative but to have Aunt Nittie exhumed, to leave no stone unturned in their search. Claudia was shocked. Mary was shocked. Horace and Chester found it distasteful, but called Uncle John for his opinion. That was unprintable. However, Fran was adamant. She wanted that ring. The argument raged all day. She was offered as a substitute the silver bracelet, also from India, Nittie always wore and her grandmother's gold watch pin. Still it left everyone feeling uneasy if not guilty. As Fran pointed out, "What if it's a clue to Cousin Perry's murder? And if it isn't in the coffin, then who took it?" But the judge decreed, "Case postponed temporarily," to which they all agreed. They did consider it a private matter, though, and never informed Lieutenant Whistler. "Let Nittie rest in peace for now."

Claudia did not get a chance to tell all this to her mother over the phone, since Candy was anxious to locate a lawyer for Jenny just then. Claudia was eager to make a very early start the following morning for the long, hot drive to Washington. But when Konrad told her he had to pick up some luggage left at the Wackman house in Bronxville, she had to wake up Chester to get his door key, and then change their plans to spend a night there. At least they could let off Lily in New York to report to her office.

At the same time, Eric awoke from what he called "a black hole of drugged sleep." "How can people become addicted to such dreadful stuff?" he remarked to a sleepy Candy, who had spent half the night downstairs by the telephone. She hoped that Eric wouldn't mention Jenny.

"How's the toothache?" she asked.

"Much better. Now if this Dr. Horace Death . . ."

"It's Morris," interrupted Candy.

Eric continued, ". . . can finish up the root canal job quickly—and he did mention one other visit—we can take off for Beaulinia. The only question is how."

"How what?"

"How we find transportation to Beaulinia, and secretly. President Fellow has banned all flights to and from."

"No problem. Call Carlos."

"He's probably being tapped, and so are we, now that I think of it. But he was trying to tell me something the other day. He talked about nearby islands and then asked if I remembered the game we used to play on the sidewalk in front of his house. Didn't make much sense."

"Well, what did you play?"

"Marbles, jacks, skin the cat."

"Skin the cat? What's that? We girls used to jump rope and play hopscotch and . . ."

"Hopscotch. That's it! Island-hop. Where's the atlas?"

By this time Candy was wide awake and pattered downstairs for some coffee, while Eric went in search of an atlas. She knew she's have to start calling around for flight information. But, no. Eric said the phone might be tapped. She must go in person to a travel agency. She'd do that while Eric was at Dr. Death's. She'd have to visit Jenny, too, without his knowledge.

Eric decided at breakfast to call his chief, "that pompous Appleby," at State, to find out his "situation, position, or status," if any. At least his call went through this time. "Ah, Bohner, sorry about your toothache and family problems. Just take it easy for a few days. And then I'll be in a position to fill you in."

Those pleasant words upset Eric more than the previous rebuffs had done. He was now convinced the government was up to some skulduggery, at Beaulinia's expense. "Candy," he called to her in the kitchen, "work out our itinerary and get our tickets today."

Candy joined him in the dining room where he was pacing up and down. "But, Eric, Claudia and Konrad are returning home today and I'm not certain just when we could plan to leave."

"I am going as soon as possible, Candy, with or without you." Then noticing her expression of distress, he added, "Preferably with you, of course. By the way, what is happening to Jenny?"

Candy's heart sank. "Nothing much." And thought to herself, *Here it comes!*

"How can you say that? She was arrested, wasn't she? Did you find a lawyer? Has she confessed? Who'd she murder?"

"No one. At least, I don't think so."

"I'm afraid it's too much to hope not. You can't trust these English women. If they aren't writing about crime, they're committing it. And here she is, a relative to boot. I simply do not understand why your family causes so much trouble in so many ways. Now, there's your mother . . ."

Candy fairly bristled. "Let's not discuss my mother. She's taboo with you."

"Taboo is right!" was Eric's parting shot as he left the room.

*Well, I'm certainly not going to tell him about Jenny until curiosity gets the better of him. Then he'll have to beg for information,* Candy consoled herself. *And I'll just postpone getting those air tickets too!* She marched upstairs to make up the beds for the children.

The doorbell rang. Candy ran down the stairs, peered through the peephole to discover Lieutenant Whistler on the steps, and hastily removed the chain. She pulled back the stiff bolt with difficulty, turned the knob, and opened the door and iron grill. "Good morning, Lieutenant."

"Morning, Mrs. Bohner. You sure go in for security here. Steel bars on all the windows, too."

"It's the new wave of house decorating in a crime-ridden city," joked Candy. "Please come in."

"Is the Ambassador in?"

"Just a minute and I'll get him." She ran up the stairs and returned shortly with Eric, who greeted the lieutenant with pleasure. He had told Candy, "Splendid fellow. Enjoy his company."

They invited Whistler into the dining room to sit down and have some coffee. He declined at first. "I've come to say good-bye. There are new developments in Keene Valley now that Elmer Wall's body was found in the dump by your nephew, Judge Wackman."

Eric, who hadn't heard of this before, almost fell out of his chair. "That's just too much, Lieutenant. Is there anyone left alive in Keene Valley? But I have been giving these murders some thought. It's a tit-for-tat theory, I call it."

"Now what would that be?" asked Whistler with a twinkle in his eye.

"It's like dominoes. Riddle kills Parody. His daughter, Jennifer, then kills Riddle in revenge. Or perhaps over drugs."

"Oh, no!" exclaimed Candy.

"Don't interrupt, Candace. Now Ernest Middleton and Harold Dibble think Dr. Cough killed Parody. Well, Dr. Cough's gun did. Then Jenny believes Ernest and Harold, the Middle and the Diddle, killed her father, so she killed them."

"But, Eric," Candy interrupted again, "you just said Jenny thought Riddle killed her father."

"Oh, yes. Well, then, of course, Jenny could have first believed Riddle was the culprit and then changed her mind, alas, after killing him, by learning about Harold's and Ernest's involvement, so she had to kill them too, to get it right. Then she had to bag Elmer because he was suspicious or perhaps witnessed her crimes of revenge."

"Now, Eric, not Elmer the bagged man. He was alive on Sunday."

"That fits. Jenny didn't leave K.V. until Monday."

"Nonsense, she was with us all day."

"Ah, but what about Sunday night after everyone was asleep? She was staying quite alone up at the studio, out of sight and sound."

Whistler just sat there, astonished at this dialogue.

"That's true," Candy conceded, "but why would she kill her father?"

"I didn't say she did. You're getting confused, Candace. I repeat, Ribble did. And she killed Ribble, which is why she was arrested."

"It's Riddle," Candy snapped. "Not Ribble."

"Let me finish, Candace. I do stand corrected. Elmer Wall must have killed Ernest and Harold. He probably thought they were implicating his old drinking companion, Dr. Cough."

"All right, then, correct yourself on who killed Elmer Wall in the dump."

"Candace, you ask the worst questions. Perhaps in a drunken stupor he fell into a bag in the dump and smothered. End of chain reaction."

Lieutenant Whistler did his best to maintain a straight face, and now managed to get in a word. "That's very interesting, Ambassador. I do have one other matter to ask Mrs. Bohner about. Would you know what might have happened to Colonel Parody's luggage?"

"Oh, his daughter, Jennifer, asked me about that in Keene Valley. He arrived with two large leather satchels, very smart-looking and new. And tan colored, I recall. I asked my nephew, the judge, to get them from the Gate House, but he couldn't find them, even in the cellar."

"What about the barn?" suggested Eric.

"Why, that was locked. Nittie and Dottie stored a lot

of furniture in it, along with their Buick. That's a good place to look, but I don't know where the key is kept."

"We can see to that, Mrs. Bohner. You are of real assistance."

Eric suddenly wondered, "What is going to happen to this Cousin Jennifer Parody?"

"That was very thoughtful of you to send her an attorney, Ambassador, but she has not been charged and was returned to her hotel after giving us a statement. Her alibi for the time of Riddle's death seems adequate."

"Beware of the ones with alibis, Lieutenant."

"I agree, Ambassador. I hope your toothache has subsided. Now I must be going."

So he departed, leaving Eric stunned that Jenny should be let loose in this city. "What if we are next on her list?" he asked Candy.

"Now, Eric, it's probably all drug-related; nothing to do with us."

"But there is Snow House in Beaulinia and your family's old drug firm, Amber-Snow and . . ."

"Eric, I think you made more sense when your tooth hurt. Lieutenant Whistler seems to know what he's doing."

"Perhaps he came to warn us."

"You should be getting ready to leave for Dr. Death's, who rhymes with seethes. Want me to come along?"

"No thanks, Candy. You'd better be around in case the children call."

While Eric Bohner kept his appointment with the dental surgeon, which rhymes with gentle sturgeon, Lieutenant Whistler was on his way back to Keene Valley. Every so often, he would let out a chuckle. "Those Bohners! They don't make people like them any more. Well, of course *she* comes from the Amber family, which explains a good deal. But I wonder how she managed to make such a perfect matrimonial match. He's a real muddler!"

He began mulling over Jenny's statement: "Met Riddle on a cruise four years ago, but didn't know he knew her father. Their meeting must have been intentional, even to planning the cabin-sharing. Or *was* it that way? But Riddle knew her father and Riddle was a drug dealer on Capitol Hill. Could Parody have been a courier for Riddle? Or for anyone? Was he smart enough to do that? And he was hardly inconspicuous, weighing over three hundred pounds—without ice." Whistler chuckled again. "What a case! Bohner may have a point about several killers in spite of his muddled reasoning. That's all I need, unless they're killing each other off. 'A gingham dog and calico cat theory,' as the ambassador might have said." He chuckled again. "Well, let's see what's in the colonel's satchels. First, we must find them. Then I'll have to question those Wall sisters about their brother Elmer. Strange for such respectable women to have taken in hippies as boarders. There is always the drug angle. And I am still not satisfied with Miss Jenny's statement. She denied knowing anything about that riddle-middle-diddle paper, and made a point about not being that stupid to leave incriminating evidence around, if she were guilty. Now, who else was in the studio? Ah, Martha, the cook; not a butler, but a cook." He chuckled once again. "I need a cold beer, but guess I should settle for coffee. That Washington climate of heat and dripping humidity! Surely it must cook the brains of our national leaders. Give me the cool, peaceful mountains. Only not so peaceful now with bodies all over the valley."

He pulled up to a roadside restaurant, and then the idea hit him. He went directly to a telephone to call Washington, with the request (he didn't have the authority to order) to have Jennifer Parody brought in again for further questioning. He would explain when he got back there. His second call was to the M.E. at Elizabethtown, to get the autopsy report on Elmer Wall. He let out a whistle, "That ambassador pretty much hit the nail on the head: Elmer suffocated while 'under the influence.' But was it accidental? Did it happen at the hospital or the dump?" A third call put through the order to find those two Parody satchels—search the Amber barn—and bring them to Washington, pronto. He would return now to Washington, but first, one iced coffee to go.

## Chapter 17

## Overdose

Eric was walking slowly home from the dental office, up Connecticut Avenue to Dupont Circle, then on to Massachusetts Avenue, approaching the Chancery Hotel, when he noticed a crowd of people, television cameras and police cars. There he spotted Jenny being escorted out the door and into an unmarked car, "with one of those red whirlygigs on top," as he explained to Candy the minute he entered his house.

Candy asked, "Did she see you?"

"I don't think so. I slouched behind some bushes. Well, Candace, your cousin Jenny is going to be a television celebrity on the six o'clock news."

The telephone rang. Candy went to answer and quickly returned to the hall where Eric was leafing through the usual junk mail. "It's for you. Asked for Ambassador Bohner."

Eric reluctantly went to the phone. "Hello."

"Ambassador Bohner, I'm Mike Fine from Network News, and want to ask you about your cousin, Jennifer Parody."

"She is no relative of mine. You have the wrong number." He slammed down the receiver.

The telephone rang again. "Don't answer, Candace. It will be that news fellow again. Let it ring."

"Of course, Eric, he'll probably appear at the door soon."

"If he does, I'll call the police. Or better still, where is my cane? I'll give him a good thrashing for good measure. Oh, there's a postcard from Klara and David on the hall table."

Candy snatched it eagerly and read it aloud: "Dear Mummy and Daddy, David should be well enough to leave the hospital tomorrow. We lost almost everything in the mudslide on Verblüffenberg."

Eric interrupted, "Let me see that. She can't have the name correct. It means, ungrammatically, Mt. Baffle. Well, go on."

Candy continued, "Everybody kept telling us it was *erklimmbar*. We didn't know that meant 'unclimbable.' We do now. No need to worry. Love, K and D." She handed the card to Eric.

Looking at the picture side, Eric remarked, "It reads *Parkplatz im Grindelwald*. That's the parking lot in Grindelwald."

"What does she mean, Eric, 'not to worry'? Why can't she ever give us a few details! Well, now I am worried. What happened to David? Was she hurt? Does she need money?"

"Stop fussing. I'm sure everything is all right. She and David are very competent. She should be worrying about us."

Candy laughed at that and cheered up, only to worry again about their own problems, when Eric asked, "Did you arrange the itinerary, Candace?"

"Oh, Eric, I haven't had a chance. Besides, we must sit down together and work out a tentative route, so that when I talk to the travel agent, I'll sound as if we were just planning a simple, romantic escapade to avert any suspicion."

"Escapade? It's an escape!"

"You know Eric, I must get more food in the house, what with the children coming and all. But now I'm almost afraid to go out for fear of that newsman waylaying me. I wish Jack and Fred were here to help."

"This isn't primitive Beaulinia. Call up a market and have the stuff delivered."

"Of course, I'll make out a list right away. I wonder if they'll take a check. And while I am doing that, take a look at the atlas."

Eric opened the book on the dining-room table. "Candy, what was the name of Beaulinia before Carlos bought it? This is an old atlas."

"Oh, I don't know. Wasn't it the same? It's one of those Windward Leeward islands, I think."

"Really, Candy, it can't be both." Eric studied the map of the Caribbean area. The phone rang. "Don't answer it, Candace."

"Now, Eric, I must. It might be the children," and went to the phone. She was right. Claudia was calling from Bronxville to explain her overnight stop there, and that Lily wouldn't be coming to Washington. She continued: "Say, Mummy, did you hear how Elmer Wall died? He fell into a laundry cart for discarded hospital stuff, got bagged and taken to the dump, so Bunny told me. Almost got burned there and then. We think it should be named the Elmer Wall Memorial Dump. And I found my first killer bee, I believe. It's bottled and I'm . . ."

"Is it alive or dead, Claudia?"

"Oh, it suffocated before I could punch holes in the top. But it's pickled now in bee-eer, at Konrad's suggestion." She laughed at her little joke. "See you tomorrow. Oh, how's Daddy's toothache?"

"We've forgotten all about it. He's being treated."

"Konrad wants to speak."

"Hello, Mummy? I popped the question."

"What question, Konrad?"

"I asked Lily to marry me and she accepted."

"But you have no job, Konrad."

"Perhaps Daddy could use an economic consultant in the embassy."

"We'll discuss it tomorrow. But congratulations. She's very nice. What would you like for supper tomorrow night?"

After hanging up, Konrad sighed, "Mothers never change."

Candy next ordered the groceries and then returned to Eric, still poring over the atlas.

"You know, Candy, I can't understand why we haven't heard from 'Near' and 'Far.' They could at least write, if unable to phone."

"You mean like Klara? 'Dear Mrs. Bohner, Fred should be well enough in another day. We lost the embassy in a hurricane. Not to worry. Jack.'" Candy thought she was being amusing, but Eric did not.


While the Bohners were coping in Washington, matters were no better in Keene Valley. Two state troopers arrived at the big house with a search warrant for the barn. Judge Wackman was indignant, saw no necessity for such a document, was always willing to cooperate with the authorities. Of course he'd unlock the barn door as soon as he could find the key. After a lengthy search, unsuccessful, in the Gate House, Horace trudged up the hill to the main house and started going through Aunt Nittie's desk drawers. Fran came downstairs and hearing noises in the library, went to see who was "snooping."

"Horace, what are you doing?" she demanded in a peremptory manner.

"Looking for the key to the barn, Aunt Fran," and he continued searching.

"Well, you won't find it there."

"We've searched the Gate House." He was becoming exasperated.

"Well, Nittie always kept it hidden under the lower corner of the barn ramp on the left-hand side," sniffed Fran, as if he should have known.

Without even a word of thanks, Horace dashed out of the house and back down the hill to the barn, thinking. *Of course, Aunt Nittie, growing forgetful, would place it in an obvious place.*

The barn door was readily opened.

Just then, Col. "Bud" Abel Smythe drove onto the property, heading for the house, while waving and calling, "Halloo!" Sporting a green beret (to match his green convertible, no doubt) and obviously courting the still-beautiful Fran, he raced up the hill to find her waiting on the steps. They were off for a game of golf, the bags of clubs casually tossed into the rumble seat. To the group at the barn, as they passed, they looked like a picture of the vintage 1930's. The sight was refreshing.

But not the sight in the barn. On the right stood Nittie's and Dottie's big blue Buick, with its trunk slightly open and a white powdery substance spilling out. It seemed to Horace just a forgotten bag of sugar or flour. On the left was a jumble of odd pieces of battered and torn furniture, and littered about the floor a dozen or so dead rats.

Chester happened along just then from a stroll in the woods and turned pale at the sight of those rodents. "Ugh! They must have been poisoned."

The troopers continued searching back in the horse-and-cow stalls, where the satchels were easily found. They were not keen about climbing up to the loft, but decided they'd better be thorough, what with the judge and the professor both there. With relief they found the hayloft empty. They had what they came for, the satchels. But they decided the Buick bore investigating.

The interior looked fairly clean, and empty. The key

135

was in the ignition. Now to the trunk. Officer Wilkins gingerly lifted up the trunk door, while the other three peered in to view the expected bag of sugar and perhaps other forgotten groceries. Instead, they found a torn brown paper bag containing small, torn plastic bags, the source of the white "stuff."

"Holy smoke!" muttered Officer Strang. "Looks like heroin. Nobody touch a thing. Wait, you'd better call in headquarters. This'll have to be photographed, tested, and fingerprinted."

Chester, now fascinated by the lifeless rats, asked, "You don't suppose they died of an overdose, do you?"

"Highly likely," replied Horace, "It's hard to believe, though." He was grateful that Lily Blessing had departed. He could just imagine the headlines she'd write for her paper: "Judge Caught with Dope behind Barn Door" or "The Amber Cache of Heroin."

Carl soon appeared in his tow truck. "Where's Whistler?" he asked.

"He'll be along," answered Officer Wilkins.

"I think he's in Washington," replied Officer Strang.

The Wackmans retreated to the porch of the nearby Gate House to sit and wait for the arrival of the criminal division.

Eventually, word was sent to have Lieutenant Whistler call Elizabethtown as soon as he arrived back in Washington. Jennifer was put behind bars, after calling her attorney. No one thought to inform the Bohners until evening, when Chester phoned, interrupting their map-reading session.

"Look, Eric, if we took off from Miami to Jamaica to Puerto Rico . . ."

"Not Puerto Rico, that's American-owned."

"Haiti, then."

"Avoid that place."

"All right, Dominican Republic. Their embassy is close by here."

"You mean the one that gets fire-bombed occasionally?"

"It's been quiet lately. And from down there we could call Carlos. Oh, my, just look at all these islands—and their names: Turks, Inagua, Mayaguana, Exuma—that one's for zombies. Oh, there's the phone."

"Don't answer it, Candace."

"Hello?"

"Aunt Candy? This is Chester, I thought you ought to know what's happened here."

Candy's heart sank. What more could possibly happen!

Chester described the barn search, the dead rats, the bags of heroin, Nittie's car dusted for fingerprints and then towed away, Cousin Perry's satchels carted off to Washington and . . ."

"For goodness sake, Chester, try to hush it up. If you people in Keene Valley do one more thing, Eric will divorce me!"

"But, Aunt Candy, we haven't done anything. It's all due to the vicissitudes of life, or perhaps death in this case. Horace just keeps discovering objects of criminal activity. Believe me, we aren't happy over it. What's happening to Jenny?"

"My goodness! I don't know. Eric saw her being arrested at her hotel this morning. We haven't heard another word."

"Does she have an attorney?"

"We got one for her last night when Lieutenant Whistler took her downtown for questioning, but he later released her."

"So now she is back in custody! You have to admit, Aunt Candy, that news isn't too good at your end, either. We'll keep in touch. 'Bye."

Candy returned to Eric who had turned to the gazetteer to study the place names, and as casually as possible passed on the latest Keene Valley news. He jumped up, dropping his book, and cursing the Amber family in general and Perry and Jenny Parody in particular.

"Now, Candace, first thing tomorrow while I'm at Dr.

What's-his-name, you betake yourself to a travel agency and get our tickets. And plenty of traveler's checks too. By the way, how's our bank account?" And off he stalked, upstairs, probably to pack. Candy shrugged her shoulders, knowing he would cool down shortly. She turned on the television for the early news, hoping that Eric would not hear it. He had had enough upsets for the day.

The Hassels in Syracuse, blissfully unaware of developments, also turned on the news, and were very much surprised to see a picture of Jenny being escorted out of her hotel and into a police car. John went to the telephone and dialed the Bohners' number. It rang eight times before Eric upstairs decided he had better answer it, since Candy hadn't heard it with the television on in the living room. He crossed the bedroom to the phone by the bed and reluctantly lifted the receiver.

"Ambassador?" John asked when Eric answered.

Not recognizing John's voice over the phone, Eric thought it was another newsman and said, "Sorry, wrong number," and slammed down the receiver.

John was baffled over Eric's odd behavior, being usually so polite. He tried calling again. Eric again answered, prepared to give this persistent nuisance a piece of his mind.

John began: "Ambassador?"

Eric, raising his voice: "Look here, young man, I told you before that you had the wrong nu—"

"Eric, Eric! This is John, your brother-in-law."

"Oh, I say, John. I didn't recognize your voice. Good of you to call—er—twice. How's Pattee?"

"Fine, fine. We want to know what's going on in Washington?"

"John, it's been a nightmare. I've had a toothache for days, until finally a root canal was performed to relieve it."

"I'm sorry to hear that, Eric, but I meant, we just saw Jenny on television being hauled off by police for Bill Riddle's murder; drug connections, too."

"Hold on while I go downstairs and get Candy. She can give you all the details."

"And I'll put Pattee on the extension to catch all of them."

Pattee and Candy and John, who could hardly get in a word edgewise, talked for half an hour, while Eric paced the floor worrying about the cost of this long-distance call, until he remembered that John had placed it. Then he recalled his suspicions of the phone being tapped, and worried that Candy would mention their secret plan to return to Beaulinia. He snatched the phone to tell John and Pattee of his suspicions and added that Candy could call from a pay phone, collect, if they wouldn't mind. Pattee suggested they come to Washington for a visit. In fact, since her curiosity knew no bounds, she decided then and there that they would fly down first thing in the morning.

They arrived after lunch the following day, which cheered up Candy and Eric, who were feeling rather helpless, now that they had acquired their air tickets.

"But, Eric, why do you want to get back to Beaulinia just now? I thought it was in quarantine or something," remarked Pattee. She and John were seated with Candy and Eric around the Bohner's dining room table having coffee and some banana cake Pattee had baked and brought along. She called it her Pattee Cake.

"Pattee, only trade relations are broken off," corrected John.

"He left his antique clock collection there," Candy contributed.

"Now, Candace, Pattee doesn't want a silly answer, although true in a way. But my most important research books are there. Also, being in Keene Valley again after so many years of not being there has made me appreciate the charms of Beaulinia. You've never visited us there. You must come. I hope it's not too late."

"Well, so you are going back now," added John, "and you are worried."

"It's that idiot, President Fellow. I think he wants to invade the island."

"Whatever for? I thought it was just a banana republic!" said Pattee, who thought her banana bread highly appropriate under the circumstances.

"That fool Fellow doesn't like Carlos."

"But that's no reason to invade," John commented mildly.

"Our gung-ho president will find one." Eric was becoming indignant over the arrogance of the entire federal government, and explained, "Carlos has a secret weapon, which the government would very much like to get its hands on without having to buy it."

"Secret weapon," piped Pattee. "Why, what is it?"

"Ah, that's a secret." Eric replied, smiling. "But Carlos thumbs his nose at big brass and pushy politicians, and that can be dangerous."

"He's an old school friend of yours, isn't he, Eric?"

"Yes, and that doesn't help my situation in the sabre-rattling State Department, either. I was appointed ambassador only because Carlos insisted. Now I am regarded with suspicion by the powers-that-be in the Foreign Service Office."

"Oh, a spy," chirped Pattee.

"Wrong department, dearie."

"Well, Pattee may be half-right. They may doubt whose interests I'm taking care of."

"Eric, that's ridiculous. You are an honorable and honest person."

"I must admit that my sympathies lie with Carlos, although he's a bit of a buccaneer. I do admire his panache. He wanted an island, bought one, and now rules it."

"Is he an American?"

"He was born one. I don't know what the State Department considers his status now. Probably a traitor."

John dryly commented, "Your president may claim him as an American citizen and therefore claim his island as part of the U.S."

"There's that. But I think they'd use the drug angle, so popular these days. It would be typical of those bumbling bureaucrats to decide the secret weapon was cocaine or heroin. With the embassy still called Snow House by the older natives, it would be enough to set off the Washington 'trivia set' into believing the worst."

"And heroin in the K.V. barn isn't helping you any. Now what do we do about Jenny?" concluded John.

"I'm not going near that woman," growled Eric. "And, Candace, I forbid you to, too."

"Now, Eric, I somehow do not believe she can be guilty of anything."

Pattee suggested, "Dearie, why don't we go down to the jail and find out what's what."

"Dearie" (they called each other that, but John's face expressed some pain), "one doesn't just walk into a jail like a hotel."

"Well, that lawyer could help. Let's call him."

"Oh, do, John" pleaded Candy, "please do. We won't learn a thing sitting around here."

"Now, Candace, you are not to go with them."

"I know, Eric. Besides, I must be around for Claudia and Konrad. They should be arriving soon."

After John got hold of Pendleton, he and Pattee took a cab downtown.

## Chapter 18

## Departmental Doings

Now unbeknowst to the Bohners, plotting and planning their furtive getaway, a meeting was being held that same afternoon at the State Department. Four men were present: Secretary of State (SOS) Willard Mayday, James Appleby, Eric's Chief in the Foreign Service Office, Stan Taylor, Chief Drug Enforcement Officer, and General Ted Troupe, Liason Chief from the Pentagon.

"All right, let's hear the latest on Bohner, Appleby."

"It's hard to believe, Secretary, but Mrs. Bohner has bought two air tickets to Miami, Kingston, and Santo Domingo."

"That's quite a jaunt. No Beaulinia?"

"No, sir, but obviously they're headed that way, in a roundabout fashion."

"A bit of deviousness to avoid your orders?"

"Well, sir, Mrs. Bohner explained to the travel agent that she and her husband were looking for a romantic escapade. And then inquired about several other islands and local flights."

"Well done, Appleby. Shall we let them have their 'romantic escapade'?"

"Why not! Chief Drug Enforcer Taylor here can— er—tail them, of course."

"Actually, Secretary Mayday, DEA feels this might

throw more insight on the Parody-Riddle-Middleton-Dibble-Wall Case."

"Not Wall, Taylor. Looks like he drank himself to death."

"Well, Congressman Brasher believes Carlos has a secret processing plant on his island and Bohner has a secret room in Snow House—I mean, in the embassy," continued Taylor.

"What do you think, General?"

"It could fit neatly into our plans. If the Bohners were there, they would be our excuse to protect our embassy and rescue them."

"What about those two naval aides?"

"Oh, they don't seem to know what's going on. But you want me to call Admiral Bullock and have them removed?"

"Naw. Let's keep it normal-looking for the Bohners."

Appleby then asked, "Should I call Bohner to give him permission to return to Beaulinia?"

"Let's keep him in suspense and let him continue in his subterfuge. What's she call it? 'Romantic Interlude?' It could be Bohner's final boner." They all laughed.

The Secretary continued, "Any more reports, General, from that retired friend of yours in Keene Valley?"

"Oh, Colonel Smythe. Expect one anytime."

"That last one was a dilly! Do you think he's—um—reliable?"

"Bud was always a bit potty, but I think he's accurate about the Amber family, don't you, Taylor?"

"He's also potty over that Fran Amber."

Mayday exclaimed, "But that's good. He gets the inside dope—er—information, then."

Taylor remarked, "I can't figure out how nothing seems to bother that family. Bodies in ice house, pig pen, truck, trash bag, and heroin in the old lady's car! And no one ever noticing enough to report that Colonel Parody was missing! They carry on like this happened every day."

"Maybe it does," chuckled Mayday. "Now that detective?"

"Whistler, I believe."

"I hear he's becoming a nuisance."

"We'll try to steer him to Beaulinia, too, if you'd like," said Taylor.

"Is he on to Brasher yet?" asked Troupe.

"Not that I know of. I can check."

"Yeah, you'd better," replied SOS Mayday, "and let me know. President Fellow is taking a keen interest in this affair. He's even code-worded it 'Caper.' I'm having a supper meeting with him soon. Well, if that's all, gentlemen, we can adjourn."

As the Secretary's visitors filed out, they could hear him chortling to himself, "That Bohner is a born loser!"

Taylor began to feel some sympathy for poor Bohner, but reminded himself that he had his own job to do in Drug Enforcement. He sighed, "In England, they call this the silly season."

At 6:00 P.M., President Fellow (as in "jolly good") greeted his committee in the Round Room for a round-table discussion. Besides SOS Willard Mayday, around the table were seated Felix Wino, Secretary of Aggressive Defense (called SAG); Fellow's good friend and financial advisor, C. L. Raymond of Radar and Lasar Industries, the largest defense contractor in the Pentagon stables; Dan Russki, head of NIDS or National Inter-Departmental Security; and Counsel General Art Chessman, top law-enforcement advisor. The topic of discussion was "Caper." The purpose: "To acquire Carlos's secret weapon by friendly persuasion." "And," added Chessman, "to bring him to justice for harboring warehouses full of heroin."

"For what!" exclaimed Russki, "And how?"

"Oh, Willard and Felix will think of something," replied Fellow. "First, I'd like to hear a progress report from 'Clunk' Raymond."

Raymond cleared his throat and began, "Now, gentlemen, R & L Industries has made Carlos a very generous offer."

"I hope it's an offer he can't refuse," interrupted Fellow. "By the way, what is this secret weapon?"

"He calls it BULL, but I don't know what the letters represent. He says it's the ultimate defense weapon."

"What's that got to do with the warehause full of heroin that Art mentioned?" asked the president.

Chessman spoke up. "Yeah, that's what I'd like to know!"

"Well, Brasher reported it to you," reminded Mayday.

"But I don't think that has anything to do with his secret weapon," Chessman replied.

"No, but you're to get the DEA to confiscate it when we invade," reminded Wino.

Chessman asked, "Is this Carlos still an American citizen?"

Mayday said, "That's debatable. His passport expires next year."

"Gentlemen, we'll go into that later. Please continue, Raymond."

"Well, Mr. President, Carlos is being cagey. And R & L Industries will brook no competition. We've offered to merge with him. It's a sound business practice we call a 'take-over.' Carlos just laughed at us."

Wino added, "Since the military functions on the same forward principle, Clay Raymond and I with best intentions decided to merge business and military forces and do a 'take-over' of the island."

"Now just a minute, Wino," spoke up Mayday. "We at State prefer the negotiating route. Are you trying to butt in?"

"Just how far have you gotten, Mayday?" snapped Wino. "You sent that Bohner as ambassador, and what does he do? Writes an article about Basque influence on

Creole and receives an honorary degree from the university there."

"Hold it, Wino! Carlos wouldn't accept anyone else but his old school chum. It's the old-boy network at its most outrageous, but we had to go along with it."

"Haven't you ordered Bohner to negotiate?" asked Fellow.

"I don't trust him," muttered Mayday.

The group fell silent at this unusual remark.

"Where's Bohner now?" resumed Fellow.

"Here in Washington, but he's planning a surreptitious and roundabout return to Beaulinia on Monday."

"What's he doing in Washington?" demanded Fellow.

Mayday sighed, "It's a long story, Mr. President. One to put anyone to sleep."

"Try me."

"Two weeks ago, a relative of Mrs. Bohner was found frozen in the ice house on her family's property in Keene Valley, so . . ."

"Where's that?"

"Keene Valley? Adirondack Mountains, in northern New York. Uh, near Lake Placid, where the winter Olympics were held."

"Ah, yes. We won some gold medals."

"The Bohners went up there for the inquest since she was the last person to see this Colonel Parody alive."

"Who's this Parody?"

"Mrs. Bohner's cousin, a retired spy and perhaps dope runner."

"So she killed her cousin? Good grief, what next!"

"No, she was cleared. But Brasher's aide, Riddle, may have been involved. But then maybe not. He's dead now, anyway. Two more people got killed and Mrs. Bohner's aunt died, and so did her doctor. The Bohners have been pretty busy attending funerals and burials. Oh, and now the daughter of the first victim has been arrested here in Washington."

"So that's why Bohner is in Washington?" interrupted Fellow.

"I didn't want to bore you with details," replied Mayday.

"Just tell me, Mr. Secretary, where does Bohner fit in?"

"Justice and DEA are keeping an eye on him, Mr. President," spoke up Counsel General Chessman. "We figure he must know something!"

"I wouldn't count on that," answered back Mayday. "He's not too aware of what goes on anywhere."

"Then why don't you get rid of him?"

"Because of his close connection to Carlos, as I've mentioned."

"But you believe that is an impediment?"

"Yes and no. You see, he's the only one in foreign service who looks the way an ambassador should; tall, distinguished, soft-spoken, knows a dozen languages; and his wife is well connected. She comes from a staunch Republican family."

"Oh, I do see. Well, put some pressure on him."

Wino remarked, "It's a little late for that. We're collecting battleships, marines, anti-personnel tanks, missiles, and non-motorized airmen, discreetly of course, in Puerto Rico."

"Does Bohner know?"

"Of course not!"

"But he's returning?"

"*C'est la guerre.* That means, 'too bad, fellow, but that's war.'"

Dan Russki, head of security, who had been dozing through all this, suddenly piped up in his high, nervous voice, "War! I haven't seen any mention of that in the newspapers."

"Is that where you get your information?" snapped the president.

Wino turned patiently to Dan and said gently, "It's

all very hush-hush. We aren't allowing any of the media on this 'rescue mission'."

"Oh, it's a rescue mission. Who or what?" asked Dan.

"Number one, our ambassador when he gets back there. Number two, Carlos's secret weapon, which is a threat to our defense industry. And number three, dope addicts from heroin. There may also be some American medical students there."

President Fellow added, "And, Dan, it's time we showed the world once again that we Americans stand proud and tall in our fight against communists."

Russki, fully alert now, squeaked, "What communists? Are there any in Beaulinia?"

Wino answered with determination, "We'll find some, Dan. Count on that. This will also give us the opportunity to test Clay Raymond's new equipment. We must find out just how good Carlos's defenses are."

"That makes sense," Russki meekly agreed.

"Anyone want any more sandwiches or pastry? No? Well, Felix, give me a collision date for 'Caper' as soon as possible."

The meeting was over. It was definitely the silly season.

# Chapter 19

## Back to Square One

Jenny would have agreed. It was a very silly season in Washington. She decided that Americans were mad, absolutely mad. "Here I am in jail, all because I came over from England to bury my father and meet his relatives. Murders then occur 'left, right and center,' as Dadders would say, or pig pen, vegetable garden, and tennis court. This solicitor is a dolt. And that nice lieutenant such a disappointment. Why haven't Candy and Eric come? Or surely my embassy should help. Sir Malcolm Stairs could at least have the courtesy to call or send a representative."

Aid soon came. The young Pendleton, with Hassels in tow, arrived and learned she was free to go, and then wondered what to do with her. They were embarrassed to admit to her that Eric forbade her presence in his house. She couldn't return to the notoriety of the Chancery Hotel. But Pendleton found her a room nearby in a small, quiet hotel on New Hampshire Avenue where John and Pattee helped her get settled. She was to remain in Washington, of course. Pattee showed her how to change her hair style, add makeup, and wear her reading glasses when she left the hotel with them for an early dinner at a restaurant. The "disguise" seemed to work. That gave Pattee the perfect explanation as to why the Bohners couldn't be with her. Since they were recognized everywhere, she would be too if seen with them.

Jenny would have liked an apology, or at least an explanation, from Lieutenant Whistler. However, he was stretched out on a couch in a back room at police headquarters, catching up on some sleep. Traveling, interrogation, heat, and fruitless examination of the satchels had taken their toll. Those satchels had been a terrible disappointment to him. Nothing incriminating or informative was found, just a jumble of clothes, books, toilet articles, an old, ragged blanket, and a pair of overshoes. Undoubtedly it had been searched long ago and some contents filched. The lab had no better luck; no fingerprints of use, no grains of heroin or anything else; no wallet and no gun. Yet he felt deep down that Jenny was withholding information or lying outright. Well, Riddle's death wasn't in his jurisdiction. But he was certain that it was linked to the rhyming "middle and diddle." If only he could find the missing link. Well, he'd return to Keene Valley and start again, after a short nap, to dream about cavorting rats having an orgy in the Ambers' barn.

In due time, feeling rested, he set out once more for Keene Valley. Early the next day, he was seated on the sun porch of the hospital, waiting for Jane Wall to see him. He picked up a copy of the *Valley News* and began reading idly about summer residents arriving, the Birch Shop up for sale, "regrettably a loss to the community," *etc.*, and then a long article about "The Unusual Demise of Keene Valley's Most Colorful Character, Elmer Wall," whose "presence would be sorely missed at the Spread Eagle." Next to it was a small headline, "Brasher Wins Again." It went on to state, "For the third straight summer, our own Congressman Sam Brasher took the winner's cup at the Ausable Club Golf Tournament." He hadn't realized that Brasher had ties to this area. *But it says here that he has rented a cottage at the club every summer for many years.* Whistler swore to himself at his own oversight. Where was Brasher now? *I must check that out when I'm finished with Miss Wall.*

But it was more like Miss Wall finishing him. No, she had no idea how Elmer ended up in a bag of disposable linens to be taken to the dump. No, she had no knowledge of Elmer's taking Dr. Cough's automobile. No, she didn't know of her sister's boarders being hippies. "They were well behaved and clean," she remarked crisply. No, she had never heard of Bill Riddle. Now, perhaps, Mr. Brasher, but she'd have to consult the hospital log for that. And so on. Of course she'd like to help, but she knew nothing. Whistler admitted to himself that he was up against a stone wall.

Brasher was no better. In fact, he wasn't even there, at the Ausable Club. Mrs. Brasher, very pleasant, said she expected him to fly up tomorrow evening. He flew his own plane, she added. Kept it at Marcy Airfield, at the other end of the valley, you know. Yes, he knew the field. So that's whose plane he'd frequently seen there! Must be fun flying over the high peaks. Who else flies around here? He'd have to check it out.

Back in his car, he groaned at remembering those bags of cocaine in Miss Amber's Buick. *It was cocaine and not heroin as had been believed. How had they gotten there? And why? It was a good hiding place. But someone's plans had gone awry, all right! Better find out how long those barn rats had been dead. Clues are so scarce.* He wished those prima donnas at the FBI would be more forthcoming with their information, too.

He pulled into Carl's garage to get some gasoline, thinking, *I'm going to have a look around Miss Wall's house. Wonder what boarders she has now. After all, they might know something. And that sister of hers, too. Their house is close to the Ambers' stone wall, and only a stone's throw from the pond. Would the old ladies or their boarders have gotten into the barn? More likely, Ernest and Harold, who obviously knew more than they ever told. That was a pretty far-fetched story of theirs about finding the gun and covering up for Dr. Cough's near-sighted accident! But the Doc had been out of town that day, Miss Wall had said, "taking the waters at Saratoga." Kind of a quaint way to say he'd been attending the races there. Then there's the account of Riddle watching the hippie in the lane. Can I connect Riddle to the barn? No. Those bags haven't been in there that long. Probably placed there shortly before the Wackmans arrived.* He continued to think about the bags of cocaine while waiting at the gas pump.

"Have a Coke!" he heard a voice say.

Startled, he turned to see Carl standing at the car window, offering him a can of Coca-Cola.

"I was just thinking about that. Thanks. You know, I was wondering, Carl, if you could do a job for me this evening."

"Sure, Lieutenant. Need an overhaul?"

"No, it's an undercover. You know everybody around here pretty well. I'll stop by later to fill you in."

"Got some hot leads?"

"Nope, but I'm hoping you'll find 'em. I'm going to check out some things at the airfield now, and then go over to the dump to look at those packing cases the bears seemed to like. See you later."

## Chapter 20

## Bohner Comings and Goings

To return to the previous day, before Whistler left Washington, Claudia and Konrad returned home safely, much to their parents' relief. At dinner they were told the Tale of the Twelve Bad Rats and finding it frightfully funny, rephrased the story as: "And then, the grocery bag of dope is discovered by the ring leader, Bonzo Rat of the Keene Valley Highs. He throws a barn party that night. Let's see. Who comes? Well, his girl friend, Titty Tat and his brother Democ."

"Democ?"

"Sure, for Democ-rat,"

"Don't forget Autoc-rat."

"How about Temperate. He's mean."

"Then there's the gambler, Baccarat."

Eric stopped the fun. "That's enough. It's pronounced 'baccarah.' Now, let me remind you that Uncle John and

Aunt Pattee are here for a day or two, so your mother will let you know who uses which bathrooms. And, Claudia, is your car parked in a legal space? We want no more parking tickets. I know it's not your fault that you can hardly ever find a space in front, but we must take extra care to avoid attention at this time. And both of you be careful about answering the phone. Find out who is calling; if strangers, hang up. And don't talk about the murders or our plans. I believe the phone is tapped."

"Oh, Daddy, that's ridiculous! You'd hear something sort of strange. I'm going to try it." Claudia did and came back to the dining room in a few minutes saying, "I guess you're right."

"Whom did you call?" Eric was suspicious.

"Just the weather. But it did sound 'off.' Maybe that's due to this awful humidity. Aren't you supposed to hear a clicking sound, though?"

"Dad," asked Konrad, "would it be all right to call Lily in New York?"

"Oh, I guess so, but make it short. By the way, congratulations. Any plans for supporting a wife?"

"It would help if you knew of an opening in the State Department."

"I don't believe that State wants another Bohner, Konrad. But your mother will probably think of something, I'm sure."

Then, the doorbell rang. "Don't answer that, Konrad!" ordered Eric. But Konrad had already gone to the front door and was peeking through the tiny viewer. "Dad, it's only Dr. and Mrs. Harper." He opened the door for them as Eric stepped into the hall.

"Eric, old friend," greeted Johann, "we are bringing you an unusual epistle from your secretary in Beaulinia, that intelligent young man . . ."

Margy interrupted to simplify his statement. "It's a letter for Candy, from her secretary, Jack."

Candy appeared from the kitchen. "Did I hear my

name spoken in vain? Oh, Marge and Hanno, how nice to see you. Out taking a walk? Come in."

They settled themselves in the living room, which Margy had always admired; piano in the bay window large, baroque cabinet filled with Eric's curios along one wall, and grouped around the fireplace four blue-and-gold-upholstered but hard-cushioned chairs. Eric disapproved of slouching.

Margy, looking through the door of the dining room, said, "Where is all your silver?"

"It's in storage. We're afraid of burglars again, since that master thief escaped from prison. Why, the first night Eric got back, he was in the upstairs library and thought he heard him on the back stairs. But it was only the cat."

"Well, I'm glad to see you've left the family portraits hanging. That one over the mantel does resemble Claudia."

"She is a great-great-great-grandmother Amber. The one behind you is her son. He looks like Konrad, don't you think?"

Margy went on, "We should have called you first, but when we got home a short while ago, we found . . ."

Hanno took over the explanation. "We have just now returned from Grafton, New Jersey, where we spent the night attending a wedding of the daughter of Margy's Congressman and good friend, Greg Grey. It was a simple ceremony in their home, actually in the garden, since it was so soon following the death of the groom's grandfather. The uncle of the groom, Eduardo Cooke, is the mayor of Grafton and performed the marriage. There were just a few close friends and family. . . ."

When he paused, Margy explained. "We arrived home half an hour ago to find this letter from Beaulinia. A short note from Fred Nearim asked us to deliver Jack's letter to you in person, Candy. We thought that odd and were wondering if you and Eric were in trouble." She handed the letter to Candy.

"Well, Candy, what does it say?" Eric was impatient.

Candy read: "Dear Mrs. Bohner. Fred and I are holding down the fort. Carlos will help you now to return to B., if you so desire. Catch Saturday's only flight from Kennedy to Martinque Airport, where someone will meet you to take you the rest of the way. . . ."

"But we've bought tickets to Kingston and Santo Domingo!" cried Eric.

"We'll just have to change them. Eric. My, what a relief to hear from those two."

"Continue, continue, Candace."

"'Fred says he's finished the ambassador's typing and cleaned his guns, but could use some more oatmeal soup. Respectfully, Jack.' But what on earth is oatmeal soup? Oh, it must be soap. He cleans guns with oatmeal soup? I mean soap?"

Eric was now excited. "Guns! That reminds me. I'm going to take along those old pistols of Uncle Frank's. If only you hadn't thrown out the ammunition, Candace. Well, Konrad can make himself useful and dash over to Virginia to buy some."

"Now, Eric, you'll do no such thing! Those guns aren't going on an airplane. They'd never get through security. And then we wouldn't, either. Think of the attention we'd get. And State . . ."

"Confound it, I thought this was a free country! Well, there's the diplomatic pouch."

"Not this time, Eric. We're going incognito, so to speak. And no luggage, either. Only carry-on bags."

"Candy, I don't believe I am hearing you correctly. You mean you will travel without the usual two or three overweight bags you always take for your 'bare necessities'?"

"They were only heavy because of the books—and the food. And the answer is yes. We don't want to draw attention to ourselves. Anyway, most of our clothes are in Beaulinia."

"Well, my briefcase goes."

"Of course, and shaving kit and clean odds and ends.

You can take the small carry-on and I'll take the large one. Isn't this exciting!"

Johann finally had a chance to speak. "You have tomorrow to get ready. But we'd better be going back home."

Margy added, "Candy, let me know if there's any way I can help. That reminds me. Greg Grey asked me a curious question: how well did you know Sam Brasher in Keene Valley? I don't think he thinks much of him."

"I didn't. Ah, but you don't know all that's happened since you were in London, do you? Come to lunch at one tomorrow and we'll tell you the whole story. And Hanno, we want to see snapshots of your trip. I'm sorry that Bertha, or Big Bertha, as Hanno calls her, isn't here to make the chocolate soufflé he likes."

They departed and Eric and Candy returned to the living room where Konrad had just turned on the television.

Eric asked, "What about the children?"

"You told Bertha to return Sunday night. Claudia returns to work Monday. And Konrad?" She looked directly at him.

"Oh, I'll be busy, with resumés and helping Lily move down here."

"Not to this house, Konrad," Eric stated firmly. "What is she doing about her job at the *Non-Observation Post?*"

"She plans to give notice. Conflict of interest, she feels."

"That's a relief. Where does she plan to stay?"

"With relatives in Arlington, I think. Say, Dad, any chance of my getting a car?"

"None at all, until you have a job and need one."

"That's what I thought."

"Now remember, you and Claudia are not to mention our trip to anyone. It's rather delicate."

"How are you getting to New York, Dad?"

"I expect your mother will work that out. That's where her talents seem to lie."

The Hassels soon returned and were promptly given the details of the Bohners' change in travel plans, pushed back from Monday to Saturday. John and Pattee kindly offered to stay on a few more days until Bertha was back and fully in charge of kitchen. Konrad and Claudia, of course, were plenty old enough to manage on their own. But Bertha could be counted on to lock every window and bolt every door at night.

The phone rang. Once again Eric shouted. "Don't answer that, Candace."

So John, seeing Candy's annoyed frown, did. He came back from the pantry, saying, "It's for you, Candy. A Cissy Blake. Know her?"

"Oh, my, yes." She dashed to the telephone to greet her old friend: "Cissy, coming to Washington?"

"Candy, how did you guess? Didn't know whether you'd be there or on that island paradise of Bahlonia. Shoestring Tennis here in Houston is sending me off again to another conference. I think it's because Houstonians can't understand my Boston accent, but Washingtonians can."

"For Shoestring Tennis? When are you coming?"

"Would Monday be too short a notice? Just for two nights."

Candy paused. She could not tell Cissy over the phone that she and Eric wouldn't be here. "Let me check with Eric."

"But of course she can't," replied Eric on being asked.

"Then I'll have to give her a reason."

"Well, make up one."

"Candy," spoke up Pattee, "John and I will be here and we can explain to her when she arrives that you were suddenly called away on diplomatic business."

"Thanks, Pattee." Then, "Cissy? Sure, come ahead. Will Herman be with you?"

"Are you kidding? Herman says he's no longer an improper Bostonian, from down east. His roots are now in Texas and his head's in a ten-gallon hat. But what's this string of murders in Keene Valley all about? Isn't that the place you're always talking about?"

"It's a long story, Cissy. I'll tell you when I see you." And Candy wondered when that would be.

"Herman sends his best to you and Eric. See you soon. 'Bye."

Pattee wanted to know what Shoestring Tennis was. "A new kind of racquet using laces?"

Candy explained that it was a low-budget organization to help handicapped children acquire the feeling of achievement by learning to play tennis. "Cissy devised an unusual method of teaching them. She starts them hitting beach balls, I believe."

Pattee wanted to know how large were the racquets.

"Really, Pattee. It's a regular-size racquet. Just the ball is large, so they can't miss."

John suggested that method might help Pattee's game too.

They talked well into the night about what to expect on Beaulinia. They could hardly be expected to actually know.

## Chapter 21

## Beaulinian Idyll

In Beaulinia, it was a busy day for Fred and Jack at the embassy. Expecting the Bohners' arrival the following day, but finding themselves understaffed, actually unstaffed, since every Beaulinarian was preparing for invasion, they set to with dust cloth, mop, or sweeper in one hand and a bottle of beer in the other, to tidy up the place without overexerting themselves.

Relaxing after finishing their household chores. Fred jumped up on hearing a roaring sound. "Jack, the invasion's begun!"

"Steady, Fred, that sounds like Carlos in his jeep with full escort."

It was. "Greetings, Far and Near," called a jovial Carlos to the two aides sitting in the shade of the side verandah, "I've brought 'vittles' to please the discriminating palates of the returning ambassador and his charming lady."

Jack felt that didn't quite fit the facts. The ambassador was a picky eater and the madame, as he liked to call her, didn't care what she ate, as long as she didn't have to prepare it. But he and Fred would enjoy Carlos's bounty to the full. In fact, they'd have a taste of it that evening.

Fred, the worrier, asked, "Any news about the invasion? If the Marines land before the Bohners do, Jack and I are going to look like deserters from the U.S. Navy."

"Not to worry," smiled Carlos. "My friends in Puerto Rico tell me it will be a week before they'll be ready to move this way. We're ready for them now."

Fred, hardly reassured, suggested, "One lone plane flying over can do a hell of a lot of damage. And that volcano, Mont Dieu Merci! I thought it was extinct, but I've heard it rumbling. This is getting to be a pretty hot spot."

Carlos grinned. "My young friend Fred, trust the Secret Weapon. Beaulinia won't blow up. But your president might in frustration," he added. "Well, *bon appétit!*" he called as he drove off.

Jack and Fred rushed to the truck to help Carlos's men bring the "vittles" into the large, old-fashioned kitchen, and then offered them some beer, which they accepted. But the men soon departed. Duty called.

"Well, Fred, what shall we dine on tonight? Callaloo? Cassava pie? Jug-jug, tum-tum, chip-chip . . ."

"Jack, are you making those up?"

"Not at all. My *Creole Cookbook of the West Indies* tells it all. Callaloo is crab stew, jug-jug is ground meat with peas, and tum-tum is mashed green plantains. We'll skip that one. Chip-chip tastes like clams. Oh, here are some mangoes. And let's have pepperpot soup. It's in a can, so you can prepare that, Fred. Later, we'll have a real rum punch. Oh, we'll live it up today."

"That's right, Jack, and be merry, for tomorrow we die," added Fred gloomily.

"No, just diet," quipped Jack, as he shook open a folded apron, which he donned, and then added a chef's hat. Ever the professional was Jack.

"Hey, Jack, I've a great idea. Let's wear those nutty operatic guards' uniforms tomorrow for the Bohners' arrival. Cheer 'em up and all. And let's have a taste of this sherry now. Surely this beautiful bottle is not for cooking. Oh, and maybe we oughta get in some target practice after dinner." Fred was cheering up.

"We'll be too looped to tell a bull's eye from a cow's. And that reminds me. I'm busy, so you'd better milk the ambassador's cow." Jack was getting out bowls from the cupboard and measuring and beating ingredients.

"When?"

"When she moos."

"Aw, Jack, you know she doesn't like me."

"Bessay will have to put up with you, Fred. And when you finish, take the milk down the hill to that family with all the kids. I think it's their turn to get the milk today."

"Honestly, all this milk and cream. Bessay'd make a nice steak and roast."

"She belongs to the ambassador, so just do what you're told. As a reward, I'll make avocado ice cream. It's your favorite."

"Bejeesus! There it goes again, that rumbling. Maybe Carlos has a secret rocket down in the volcano crater."

"No, I think it's electronic."

"The rumble?"

"The secret weapon, Fred. I was down by the windmill talking to Carlos's son, Don, yesterday and he mentioned he'd studied electronics at MIT with Commander Groper's son, who incidentally, flunked out."

"Ah, those windmills! And with their signs reading 'High Voltage,' which doesn't make any sense. Should be 'High Windage' to blow away invaders. That's a joke, Jack."

"I'm glad you are in a good humor. The Bohners should be too, after a peaceful time in the Adirondacks. I hope they take us with them next time."

"Those whirring windmills may blow us up there."

"There you go again, Fred. Anyway, Mrs. Bohner was looking forward to a family reunion. She says it's lovely there, and quiet. The kind of place where nothing happens."

"That's where we should get ourselves stationed, Jack. And we thought Commander Groper was doing us a big favor shipping us here. What do we do when the shooting starts?"

"Don't fire 'til you see the whites of their eyes," shouted Jack, imitating the commander's voice.

"Gee, we can't shoot at our own navy!"

"You've got a point there. I know! We'll dash down to the cove when the time comes and dig a foxhole and stay out of it. I mean stay in the foxhole and out of the fighting."

"We can't desert the Bohners," remarked Fred.

"I should think they'd want to join us."

"Listen, Jack, you know that dinghy on the beach? If things get rough, we could row them out in it toward the ships, sort of look like rescuing them."

"Freddy, you're a genius! We'd be home free and get a medal to boot. I hear Bessay mooing. Get the bucket. Don't kick it. And when you finish and take the milk down, see if Doc Duval would care to join us for an early dinner."

Just then, they heard Don shouting, "Hey, you guys, anybody home?"

Jack shouted back, "In the galley, you landlubber, and

wipe your boots before entering. I've just swabbed the deck."

Don appeared at the kitchen door. "Hi! I've come to hitch back up your electricity."

"*Merci Dieu*, will wonders never cease! You mean we must give up dinner by candlelight?" laughed Jack.

"Listen, fellas, I'm sorry Pop did this to you, no lights, no radio, no telephone. But it's called security," he said, "You can always explain at your court-martial that you were captives of war," Don joked. "But now the ambassador is returning and our defenses are all in place, so I've brought you a gift from Pop. Come on out to the jeep and tell me where you want it."

They all trooped out to the front drive. Wondrous to behold, stood a television set.

"You mean we get to watch TV for bein' on good behavior?" asked Fred.

"Not exactly. We've installed a satellite dish. Pops has decided he should watch the 'news events of the world' before he starts makin' news himself."

"Where do you think, Fred?"

"In the library. Can you install that, Don?"

"*Mais, oui, monsieur.* I am ze chef ingeneer of Beaulini-eer," mocked Don, remembering the story of Jack's tour-guide imitation. "Now this set will give you some trouble. It's an R & L. We had to take what we could find. Those R & L people are also the biggest defense contractors. They couldn't even make a Mickey Mouse watch that would run for a million bucks. Then they'd have to charge two million for maintenance. But lemme get the juice flowing and the telephone going. Oh, Pops says, lay off the phone, though. This is goin' to take me awhile."

"Well, stay for dinner. Your 'pops' provided," Jack said.

"I thought you'd never ask. Thanks."

Jack continued working on his "*nouveau cuisine.*" "Fred, I hear Bessay calling."

Don asked, "Wha'd you call her?"

"Bessay. It's for 'Bésame Mucho.' You know, that old latin song, meaning 'Kiss Me Much' in Spanish."

Fred added, "I translate that as Bessay can moo a lot."

"It's Fred's favorite song."

"Yeah, but not my favorite cow!"

"Why does the ambassador keep a cow, anyway?" Don wondered. "Got an ulcer?"

"He just likes cream in his coffee, whipped cream on his pastries, and ice cream every afternoon."

"Gee, doesn't that bother his wife?" persisted Don.

"She doesn't have to milk Bessay," complained Fred.

"But she would if no one else did," added Jack. "Whatever the ambassador wants, she sees he gets it."

"That sounds sort of old-fashioned."

"Oh, they are, believe me," said Jack. Then he remembered that he wanted to ask Don about the windmills all around the island. Fred had gone a-milking meanwhile. In a mock accent, he continued, "Hey, Don Quixote, why you tilt at windmills all zee time? You in for shock. They high voltage."

Don laughed and explained, "I'm in charge of them. Pops is smart. They're his first line of defense. He calls 'em the Beaulinia Air Force."

"You mean, those 'huts' lift off the ground?" Jack asked in amazement.

"Not quite. I'd better get your power turned on now." Don went out.

Fred soon returned to the kitchen with half a bucketful of milk, which he slammed down on the table. "That old biddy wouldn't cooperate. Kicked me twice—that song must mean kick me much and not kiss—and then whacked me with her tail. You'll have to put the squeeze on her, Jack. She likes your style better."

"Fred, it takes a light touch. Go back. Oh, never mind, I'll do it myself. Show Don where the phones are." Jack swung out the door with the bucket, calling, "Coo coo,

Bessay, my moochoo. Jacques will *sauvez vous.*" He began singing, "Kick me once, and kick me twice, and kick me once again. It's been a long, long time."

Fred went to find Don and take him to the library. Don remarked, "What a swell room! Look at all those bookshelves, made of solid mahogany. There used to be lots of those trees here." Don ran his fingers down the side of one and suddenly touched a hidden button, causing a five-foot-wide unit to swing slowly open. "What the . . . ! What's this, Fred?"

Fred just gaped. "Beats me. Looks like the ambassador has a secret room. He never told me. And I'm his private secretary. Maybe he doesn't know about it, either."

Don turned on a switch inside which lit up a closet lined with shelves along one wall. It was empty except for a small, dusty carton on the floor, Fred stepped in, bent down, and opened it. "Just some white powder," he told Don.

"Let me see that. Hell, Fred, do you think it's heroin?"

"Taste it."

"Not me. Besides I wouldn't know the taste of the stuff."

"I'll ask the ambassador when he gets here."

"What would you say to him? People kill for that," remarked Don.

"Holy mackeral! Do you think he's a dope addict? Let's get rid of it."

"Ya better not, Fred. He'd kill yuh for doin' that too."

"Gee, and we've left fingerprints. I'd better wipe them off." Fred went back to the kitchen to find a rag.

Jack returned just then with a full bucket of milk and lovely cream for the evening's dessert as Fred dashed in, looking agitated.

"Hey, Jack, come take a look at what we found. I need a rag."

Jack followed Fred with a rag, saying, "You forgot to clean . . ."

"A hidden closet!" exclaimed Jack at the library door. "Any skeleton?"

"No, but a bag of white powder."

"Ah, a skeleton ground up in a blender, no doubt. Dust to dust, you know," Jack decided.

"I've got to dust off our fingerprints, Jack. Don and I suspect dope rather than a bag of old Bohner bones."

"You're kidding! Why would the Bohners . . . It's probably been in the house for eons."

"Okay, I'm finished with the dusting," said Fred. "Let's close up." But the shelves wouldn't budge when they tried pushing them. "Now what do we do?"

"Get Don Quixote to tilt at it," suggested Jack.

Don soon found the closing mechanism, adding, "Nothing but an open-and-shut bookcase. I'll ask Pops if he knows anything about it."

"Anyway, I say the ambassador is not guilty until proven." Fred's argument for the defense seemed to settle the matter. Jack returned to the kitchen, Don to telephonics, and Fred to delivering the bucket of milk and inviting Doc Duval for dinner.

Chapter 22

## The Flight of the Humble Bs

The Bohners departed very early Saturday morning. Claudia would take them to National Airport to catch a flight to Kennedy. She had parked her car around the corner in front of Ruth Baker's house. This gave Candy an idea.

To avoid being seen or followed she arranged to sneak out their back gate and cut through Ruth's adjoining yard and house. It worked beautifully. They were soon on their way, crossing the Potomac and pulling up to the main terminal of National, with only an hour to wait. On arriving at Kennedy, they had a two-hour wait, so Candy suggested eating a late breakfast or early lunch, in case this was a cheap flight which served only a stale sandwich and a tough apple.

Eventually they boarded to take their seats in the rear section. Candy had concluded many years ago that in case of accident the tail had a higher rate of survivorship. While waiting for take-off and before buckling up, she walked back to get a drink of water. Sipping it, she noticed on the aisle seat of the last row a sinister-looking passenger whose coat pocket bulged with what looked to her like a revolver with its handle sticking out. She hurried back to Eric to whisper to him what she had seen, adding that she was certain the man was a hijacker.

Eric, ever alert to danger, unbuckled his seat belt, grabbed his folded umbrella and hissed at Candy, "Follow me and grab his gun the instant I tell you." They marched single file back to the restroom area. Eric then wheeled around and rained umbrella blows on the suspect's head, shouting, "Grab it, grab it, Candy!" By that time the victim was slumped unconscious and bleeding across the vacant seats in that row. An attendant, hearing the commotion, rushed up the aisle. Eric handed her the gun and pointing to the prone figure, calmly informed her, "I believe he is a terrorist. Here is his gun, better search him for grenades."

He proceeded to brush past her, Candy following, and returned to their seats. By this time, the plane, loaded with vacationers, was in an uproar. The purser wiggled his way up the crowded aisle to request Eric to explain his bizarre actions. On hearing Eric's somewhat rattled account, he wisely decided to move the Bohners forward to empty seats in the first-class section.

They never learned the outcome of their assault. Was he, or wasn't he a hijacker? However, they had an unexpected and enjoyable first-class flight to Martinique. Although Eric did fume, "Now you see, Candace, I could have brought along Uncle Frank's pistols! Look how that terrorist got through security. You shouldn't have talked me out of it."

"You know," Candy mused, "he might have been an air marshal."

Eric spluttered, "But you said he was . . ."

"That's what I suspected," interrupted Candy.

"You mean, we might be arrested for attacking an armed man?"

"It doesn't look so. We are getting first-class treatment. Want some free champagne?"

They didn't get congratulated, either, but were left with what Candy called "one of life's little mysteries." She had lots of them.

They were permitted to disembark unhindered at Martinique. After going through passport control, they glanced around for the "someone to meet them." Eric did make an observation in passing that "I imagine they'll ban umbrellas now on board aircraft." They turned around on hearing a voice say, "I'm the Candy-man." Eric, surprised but quite quick-witted, replied. "And are you the Eric-man too?"

"Ah, Monsieur Bohner and Madame, I am your escort." He handed Eric a short note from Carlos explaining that Captain Candiman would be assisting them for the remainder of their journey to Beaulinia.

It was all a rush to another airfield and a push into a small, rickety-looking biplane, presumably carrying mail. Candy thought those sacks looked more like body bags. Eric thought, *all very humbling.* Later, he would refer to this adventure as "The Flight of the Humble Bs."

They arrived stiff and weary and humble to be met by Carlos and Charlotte, who transported them to the embassy. As they drove up to the front verandah, Fred and Jack dashed out the door attired in the Student Prince uniforms and stood at attention to salute the Bohners. On close inspection, Eric stopped and grinned. "Near and Far! My band-aides! Candy, look at these two! We're so glad to see you both," and shook hands, while Candy, laughing with pleasure, hugged both of them. They were home at last, Eric thought with relief.

"But how long will this home last? Those gung-ho planners in Washington will blow it to smithereens. Ah, but surely not an American Embassy. Now, how would these kamikaze crazies recognize it?" He happened to be staring at the embassy flag pole with its flag hanging limply in the breezeless air. "Flags, of course. However, that poor, limp rag of a flag makes a poor showing. We need something big and stiff."

Carlos and Charlotte said they would not stay now. Carlos would stop by in the morning to take Eric on a tour of the island's defenses, and Charlotte would telephone Candy.

Fred approached, "Mr. Ambassador, Jack says dinner is ready." They moved into the dining room on the left of the entrance hall. Fred held "the Madame's" chair for her. Eric noticed only two places were set. "Fred, you and Jack must join us as always. We want to hear what's been going on here. And Mrs. Bohner, I know, will want to tell you the whole horror story of the deathly Keene Valley days."

While dinner and lively conversation progressed at the American Embassy in Beaulinia, Secretary of State Mayday in Washington was talking on the telephone to Felix Wino at the Pentagon: "That's right, I said 'gone.' He's probably back in Beaulinia by now. (Pause) I know, I know, they were to depart Monday. Well, they changed their plans and actually sneaked out in a most unbecoming fashion. (Pause) Why, he even beat up a guy with his umbrella! (Pause) Where? On the flight to Martinique. (Pause) I don't know. They lost the trail from there. But where else would he be? (Pause) Never mind! What'd Carlos say to your friend's final offer? (Pause) He said, 'Come and get it'? (Pause) Now, now, before you push the button, give me time to reach Bohner. No need to move up your schedule yet. (Pause) Well, that Commander Groper you mentioned can go it alone, can't he? (Pause) I don't mean to tell you your business, but it seems to me that one aircraft carrier should do the job in a pinch. (Pause) Take it easy. I mean, Beaulinia is a very small island, with a volcano, you know . . . (Pause) You didn't know? (Pause) Well, don't be crude! I don't know if it's active. Look it up in an atlas. It's not classified information. (Pause) Hold on a minute, Felix. Oh, Miss Dickey, please bring me a map of the Caribbean. Felix? (Pause) Get one of your fly boys to pass over. (Pause) You're right. I guess it is a trifle late for reconnaissance, when you don't know what Carlo's secret weapon *is*. (Pause) Ask Bohner? He may be difficult to reach. But try your Army Map Service. (Pause) Oh, they can't all be 'elite pussycats.' There's the Library of Congress. (Pause) Oh, you mean you don't want Congress to know. However, we are overlooking the fact that this is Saturday evening. And isn't there a reception at the Pan Am Union Fellow told us to attend? See you there (Pause) Black tie, I think. Best to Gertie."

He hung up and called to his secretary, "Thank you, Miss Dickey. I shan't need the map after all. But put a call through to our ambassador in Beaulinia."

After ten minutes of trying, Miss Dickey gave up. "I'm sorry, sir, I let it ring until it went dead. There was no answer."

"We'll send a cable, then. Take this down. 'To Amb. Eric Bohner, etc., Tell Carlos we'll throw in Granita and Tarioca free and clear. That's our final offer.'"

"Excuse me, sir."

"Yes, Miss Dickey?"

"We don't own those islands, Granita and Tarioca."

"I'm sure they'd like to become territories of the United States, if necessary."

"Yes, sir, of course. But not necessarily of Beaulinia."

"We can work that out at the U.N. when the time comes. To continue—uh, where was I?"

"Throwing in Granita and Tarioca."

"Oh, yes, 'and with a generous finder's fee for you.' Sign it, 'SOS Mayday.' After you send that off, you may go home, Miss Dickey."

After his talk with Mayday, Felix Wino, Secretary of Aggressive Defense, placed a call to Dan Russki, Chief of Inter-Department Security. "Dan? Felix here. (Pause) You sound sleepy. (Pause) It's only six o'clock. (Pause) In the evening! (Pause) Well, get a grip on those nerves. I want you to advise the president before his weekly Sunday broadcast. (Pause) What do you mean, you told him not to broadcast? (Pause) That's a blackout, you blockhead. We want everything to continue in a normal way. (Pause) Hang your nerves! Take aspirin in bourbon. (Pause) I see. And then I woke you up. Aren't you on *Face The Press* tomorrow? (Pause) You can't say no. You already said yes. (Long pause) I realize you can't face anything at this point, but I can't substitute for you. I'm tied up with a crisis. (Pause) Now look, Dan, don't get personal. Send your deputy, Jean what's-her-name. (Pause) That's all right, Dan, no need to thank me. We're all the president's men and women. Go back to sleep—no, wait—after you've called Jean."

Two hours later, the President's limousine with police, secret service and news escorts, drove up to the entrance of the Pan American Union building. Fellow liked to arrive early to avoid the crush and be more visible and "fresh looking" for photographers. The Pan Am Band struck up his favorite tune, "For He's a Jolly Good Fellow" while the Dean of Ambassadors, Juan Gonzaga, stepped forward to greet his old friend in his customary jocular manner: "Hey, Fellow. Well met!" to which the President always jokingly responded, "Go Gonzaga!"

Gonzaga continued, "Allow me to escort you, my dear Fellow, as you requested, to the ambassadors from communist-free countries south of the border. First may I present to you, Mr. President, Ambassador Enrico Baccardi from Tarioca. Next is Consul and Mme. Jean Papillon from Ile-de-Diable. And now our newest member, Ambassador Georges Hatteras of Beaulinia." They all shook hands for a photo session, while Fellow was struggling to remember why the last mentioned country sounded familiar. "Please forgive my wife's lateness. She got tied up visiting a prison drug-rehabilitation center earlier today. All rather amusing; held as a hostage for a while, in fact. They were demanding a ransom. But you know my policy. No deals with terrorists. She was released an hour ago after the local police tossed in tear-gas bombs, which messed up her makeup and hair. She's having both redone now." He then excused himself to follow Gonzaga to the formal reception line.

SOS Mayday, who had just arrived, was horrified to see Fellow talking to Beaulinia's ambassador. Such a gaffe. And a news picture of that would be difficult to explain next week. Well, he must prevent the president from giving the Sunday broadcast he had planned. But how? Then he remembered that it was always recorded a day or two ahead. He'd get hold of Russki to substitute another tape, and went looking for him. He encountered Wino at the buffet who informed him that Russki probably wouldn't make it to the reception. "You can call him at home."

Ruski, still under the influence of aspirin and alcohol, was finally roused at midnight by a repeated ringing of the telephone. "Dan, this is Mayday. (Pause) I said Mayday, SOS! What's the matter with you? You sound drunk. (Pause) All right, all right! Just a bit slurry. (Pause) I said sleepy. Now listen." But the receiver dropped from Russki's hand while he leaned back on his pillow, fast asleep.

"Hello, hello," shouted Mayday.

Mrs. Russki picked up the receiver and said, "I'm sorry, Mr. Russki cannot be disturbed at present. At the sound of the tone, please leave your name and number and he will get back to you in the morning."

Mayday ground his teeth. Then he called Bat Cassidy, Chief of the Civil Intelligence Commission (CIC), to request him to send a man to break into the Round Office and swipe the radio tape. 'I believe it's labeled 'The Monroe-Fellow Doctrine.'" It wasn't any easier controlling a president than it was an ambassador, thought Mayday.

## Chapter 23

## Flag Day at the Embassy

Early Sunday in Beaulinia, Fred and Jack were up on the embassy roof with cans of red, white and green paint. Their orders were to paint flags to cover the front and the back of the sloping roof. "Gee, Jack, green? Couldn't you find any blue?"

"Not a drop."

"How do you make green into blue, then?"

"I dunno. Try mixing red."

"Wouldn't that make purple?"

"Look, Freddy, just do the best you can! It'll be covered with stars, anyway."

"Oh, yeah. How many stars? Gee, I can't draw a star, Jack."

"Make 'em round, Dumdum."

"How many stripes are you doing, Jack?"

"I think twelve. I'm running out of roof."

They spotted Carlos driving up the hill in his jeep. He jumped out and shouted up at them, "Is that a flag? Great idea. Paint one on your windmill too."

Eric stepped out on the verandah, looking trim and spruce in his crisp khaki shorts and open-collared tan shirt. He welcomed Carlos.

"Eric, my friend, you're looking very chipper and British this morning. All you need to complete the correct outfit is a swagger stick and monocle."

"Want me to get them, Carlos?"

"You won't need them where I'm taking you."

Eric glanced up at the roof, asking. "Like my idea?"

Carlos laughed. "It's brilliant, Eric. No red-blooded soldier or sailor will shoot at his own stars and stripes. But come along, my friend, I'm going to show you my defense preparations. Where's Candy this lovely morning?"

"She's on the telephone to let the family know we're safe. Not that they were worried, I'm sure. They all acknowledge Candy's survival ability. I am surprised that Washington hasn't called. They probably know by now where we are."

"Do you want to hear from them?"

"Not particularly, but Candy likes to know the children can reach her."

"Okay. We'll stop at the exchange and get the incoming wires hooked back up. I believe there's a cablegram for you too. Hop in and let's go."

"I say, Carlos, Fred has mentioned hearing occasional rumbles recently from the volcano. I thought it was extinct. It's not going to erupt, is it?"

"It might, Eric, with some assistance. That's what I'm going to show you."

"Up to your old tricks, Carlos?"

"You might say so." They were bouncing along merrily in the jeep. "First I want to tour the coast road and inspect all the windmills. Don said they were ready and rarin' to go."

"Go where?" asked Eric.

"You'll see. We must anticipate our enemy. Don and Captain Candiman—you know, your pilot of yesterday—have done a nice job with their little electronic diffusion sets. We know quite a lot about that floating electronic palace, the S.S. *Sinclair*. Only better spell that S-I-N-K-L-E-R, and you'll know what I have in mind." They wound their way in and out and around, frequently passing scores of men, women, and children pushing and hauling boulders up Mont Dieu Merci, that extinct? dormant? boiling? volcano.

"You see," explained Carlos, "since our air force consists of two jets and three dilapidated 'crates,' I am forced to depend on brain power."

"Do you really think President Fellow and followers will attack you?"

"They've threatened a take-over."

"Can't you complain to the U.N.?"

Carlos laughed. "That's really funny, Eric."

"I say, Carlos. I'm seeing a vast number of windmills, but no guns to speak of."

"This is electronic warfare, Eric. You zap your enemy with laser and infrared distractors, which the Pentagon spellers would call LAIDS, I'm sure." And he roared with laughter.

Eric, more straight-laced and linguistically accurate, said, "LAIRDS is the correct acronym."

"So be it. These innocent-looking windmills will produce smoke or fog, which laser cannot penetrate easily. And ignited boulders will make false targets for infrared seekers. But those are simply supplemental."

They had now reached the top of Mont Dieu Merci. Carlos said, "We'll get out here and take a look. It's beginning to get hazy, but you can still make out our sister island, Beaulieu, on the horizon to the south. And there's the peak of its extinct volcano, Mont Soufrière. Have you visited it, Eric? It too was once a French possession, but gained its independence." They were walking around the rim of the crater, now surrounded by huge boulders. A large group of men were milling about and shouting while they worked on what seemed to Eric to be enormous smudge pots.

"You see, Eric, my plan is to produce the effect of an erupting volcano. Look down in the crater."

Eric saw a jumble of strange equipment partially camouflaged and specially painted to look like molten lava. "So that's Fred's rumble machine down there."

"Yes. Some sticks of dynamite produce a realistic sound. And then we hurtle boulders down the mountainside to make it look real. With the smudge pots throwing off foul-smelling smoke, *voilà*, another Stromboli."

Eric was surprised. "Do you think this will work?"

"Want me to turn it on?"

"That won't be necessary," replied Eric, backing away. "I'll take your word for it. So this is your famous weapon that everyone is eager to acquire?"

"*Mais, non.* But that's what those miniminds will believe. They are hoping to see my BULL in action, although exposing themselves to it is either very courageous or foolhardy."

They started walking back to the jeep. "Now, let's have some lunch at the palace. You can see it from here. I'll have the boys paint a large red cross on the flat roof of the rear quarters, the medical school, and the hospital. I should have made the flag of Beaulinia a red cross, too, instead of a red poinsettia on green. Well, we can't think of everything. Charlotte designed it."

"By the way, how is Charlotte taking all this?"

"You'll see. After all, she paid for well over half of the island, and she intends to keep it."

A warning siren was suddenly heard, one short blast repeated every three seconds, which meant "reconnaissance plane sighted." Carlos shouted, "Set off the volcano!" Then to Eric, "Over here, inside the hut and out of sight. They're going to let her roll." And, "Level one, Joel, not too much."

Eric thought, *All this to impress one lone island-hopping chopper patrol! I must be on a movie set; Grade B one at that.*

Mont Dieu Merci turned into a Diablo. It rumbled and shook, while smudge pots smoked sulphur, fiery boulders bounced around the crater rim, and sparks and flames shot up in the air; all to put on a grand show for the lone helicopter that flew by once and then headed straight back to its mother ship out in the Atlantic.

After the infernal machine was turned off and the smoke and stench had blown away, Carlos's band of merry men came out from the underground, waving their caps and gleefully shouting, "Hurrah, hooray, it flew away!" Eric was amazed. He wasn't sure whether he'd been to Disneyland and back or was watching an operetta finale. He did know that Carlos was a great showman.

"Carlos, would you mind taking me right back to the embassy? I'm worried that Candy might be upset."

But not at all. Candy had been talking on the telephone to Charlotte, who was able to explain every roar, fire flare, and smudge smoke to the unbelieving Candy. Fred and Jack had hit the deck at the first sound of the siren. Literally. They had rolled themselves right off the roof, plunging to the sundeck in the rear, and dashed into the cow shed, the handiest cover in the woods. At the all-clear sound, Jack marched out with Fred trailing behind. He turned to see Fred limping and asked him. "Twist your ankle?"

"No, old Bessay did it again. Kicked me in the shin."

Jack rushed inside the house to look for the madam.

She was still sitting calmly by the phone, chatting and laughing. Jack turned to Fred in relief, "I need a rum punch."

Fred said, "Better make that beer. Here comes the old man." They turned back to the kitchen.

Eric raced in the front door, calling, "Candy, Candy, are you all right?"

"I'm on the phone in the library, Eric. I'll be right there." She hung up and stood up just as Eric rushed in, stumbled over the long telephone cord (it had been installed to make the phone more mobile), and grabbed the side of a bookcase to keep from crashing to the floor. Creaking slowly, the shelves opened to reveal the hidden closet. He had unwittingly sprung the lock.

"Eric," cried Candy, "what are you doing? You're tearing down the house!"

"Not quite! I have stumbled upon a secret room."

"Gracious, now how did that get there?" Candy stood rooted to the spot.

"Oh, come, Candace, it must have always been there. Your Mr. Snow installed it, evidently." He moved to enter it.

Candy shrieked, "Eric, don't go in. It's a trap. It might slam shut and I couldn't get you out and you'd end up a skeleton in a closet."

"Then just find a skeleton key," joked Eric. But he carefully examined the side of the shelves where the catch was before entering. "The cupboard looks bare, Mother Bohner."

Candy thought, *What has gotten into Eric? He must have struck a funny bone when he tripped; he's attempting humor.*

"Ah, this is perfect," Eric exclaimed. "Looks fireproof. Maybe bomb-proof, too." He turned on the light switch.

"We could take shelter here when the bombs fall."

"I'm afraid it would be a bit of a squeeze. No, this is perfect for my research papers and books. And we could move in the safe—if we can move that monster at all. I say, what's this?" He pointed to the dusty carton sitting innocently in the corner, then picked it up and sniffed it. "It's talcum powder, I think, unless it's an explosive. Get the 'band-aides,' Candy. Don't look that way! You know we call Fred and Jack that."

"Oh, yes. I thought you'd cut yourself." She went out the terrace door to scan the roof for a sight of the aides. No sign of them, but there was a puddle of red paint on a lawn chair. "Now that is not blood," Candy reassured herself; "Just a bloody mess, as Jenny would say." She found the young men relaxing with a beer on the kitchen sundeck. They jumped up politely as she approached. "Oh, there you are. Would you both come with me, please. The most extraordinary thing has appeared in the library."

They went around the house outside and suddenly found themselves confronted by Eric stepping through a secret outside door of the closet.

"How very clever," he muttered. "Candy, Fred, Jack, look at this, would you. Now with a path easily made down the hill through the poinsettia to the beach, this would have made a perfect smuggler's hideaway, or escape route for your Mr. Snow, Candy, if the Feds were after him."

"He is not 'my Mr. Snow.' He was Grandpa's, who midway through their partnership . . . And they were gendarmes then, not Feds."

"Well, it all looks very unsavoury."

Jack and Fred were relieved that the closet had been brought out into the open. Fred asked Eric, "Did you find anything, sir?"

"Oh, just a dusty box of talcum."

'Talcum!" exclaimed Jack, and decided not to mention their discovery of this two days earlier. "Let's see."

"You two help me find what makes this door open from the outside. And then I suggest we tap other walls inside. You know, I find this intriguing."

Candy left them to their sleuthing to arrange a simple lunch for the four of them, which they were soon enjoying on the terrace. Jack liked "the Bohners' style." "Oh, the Ambassador could rail and flail and get upset in private, but Mrs. Bohner would tell him, 'That's the way it is, Eric, so there's no sense in fussing.' In public they always seem bland and unruffled." Jack could picture them inviting invaders of the embassy to have some tea before ransacking the place.

Fred liked the way the ambassador, usually a silent, thoughtful person, would talk to him about his many experiences and discuss his collection of antique curios with such great pleasure. In contrast, she was so bubbly and chatty. An odd combination. "The Odd Couple." He smiled to himself.

"Now it's back to work, everybody," announced Candy. They all stood, picked up their snack trays and trooped across the front verandah to the rear sundeck. Candy paused. "Uh, oh, isn't that the Healey's Daimler crawling up the drive?" The men hastily disappeared around the corner, while Candy watched the big black car pull up to the front door.

Mrs. Healey was driving. Ambassador Healey hopped out, wearing a one-piece jumpsuit and parachute boots. "Halloo there, Candy! Glad to have you back. Emily here just had to know if you needed any help, so I'm giving her a driving lesson at the same time. It's a time for sacrifices!"

Emily extricated herself from behind the right-hand steering wheel and ran up the verandah steps to kiss Candy. Her outfit was delightful; a colorful floral chiffon tea dress and dirty old sneakers. She said, "We're preparing for the invasion, you see. My, it seems just like 1939!"

Eric returned and shook hands with his guests. "Healey, good of you to come," he heard himself say but winced at such an outright lie.

"My dear boy, we didn't expect you back. We're the only 'dips' remaining here. French, Swiss, German all decided it was time for their holidays and departed *en masse*. I noticed the flag painted on the roof. A minor point, but shouldn't it have thirteen stripes? Anyway, jolly good idea. Want to send your chaps down to do ours?"

Eric could picture Fred and Jack struggling with all those blue—no, it would have to be green—white- and red-crossed stripes. He told Healey they still had the windmill to paint. "Let me show you our defense measures," while forgetting the secret door was still wide open, and was the one thing he did not want to show Healey, who liked to "blab." However, to his surprise, Healey knew all about it.

"What, you only just discovered it, old boy? It's no secret here. 'Whitey' Snow had it installed, I was informed. Everybody on the island knew what he was up to and nobody cared. Helped the economy, you know. There's a trap door in the wine cellar, too, that old-timers told me led to an underground passage."

Eric, all excited, said, "Let's have a look."

Candy and Emily sat down on the shady verandah. The day had turned hot and muggy. "Now tell me all about the murders in Keene Valley," began Emily. "And that nice young man, Bill Riddle, we met here. Isn't it surprising that Jennifer Parody is your cousin! You know, I went to school with her mother. She was Ann Partridge then. We used to joke with each other about her coming from Pairtrie, while I, as Emily Swann, came from Swimmin. Of course I knew your cousin Peregrine, too, although he wasn't around much. Well, we knew you didn't shoot him and cut him up and stuff him in a freezer, although the *London Daily Post* suggested that."

Candy thought to herself, *Konrad never mentioned that one from gleaning those London papers in Lake Placid.*

Emily went on: "Well, my dear, how is Jennifer? The idea of arresting that poor girl! She certainly wouldn't shoot her father. She was well brought up, and it just isn't done."

Candy sat back and let her ramble on, throwing out bits of information. "You know, Peregrine popped up here, shortly after we arrived. I believe he stayed in this house, too, but I don't remember who the owner was then, just before it was bought by your government for an embassy. He wanted to rent a warehouse for a new business he was starting up. Then he unloaded his boat and took off without even saying goodbye. Called it, let me think. High Seas Unlimited. It's still down there by the docks rotting."

Candy sat up, alert. "I wonder if Jenny knows about it?"

"Her mother never mentioned it in her letters to me. Perhaps I should write her about it. Oh, I think she's gone to Washington, to be with Jenny."

"What's today? Sunday? Telephone rates are cheaper. I could call my brother there and find out."

Emily continued: "You know, if Carlos hadn't informed us of his air-raid warning system and Merci Dieu, or is it the other way around, erupting artificially, Austin and I would have been really upset, and I could never have undertaken a driving lesson today. I've been trying to learn for thirty years. What do you think will happen next?"

Candy was spared answering that as the two ambassadors approached, covered with dirt, looking like grubby little boys at play. "We've found an escape tunnel," announced Eric.

"Escape to where?" asked Candy.

"Not sure yet. But from the direction it was headed, I'd say the cow shed."

"Well, Bessay's a treasure, but hardly what . . ."

"A treasure! That's it, Bohner, we're on to something big."

So off they marched to Bessay's abode to muck about in search of the light or treasure at the end of the tunnel.

"My, I haven't seen Austin having this much fun in years."

"It's a very confusing case," resumed Candy.

"Treasure hunts are supposed to be."

"No, I mean the Parody, Riddle, Middleton, Dibble,

Wall Case. Five bodies. Then Dr. Cough keeled over with a heart attack, and my Aunt Nittie in her sleep. That's two more deaths, not to mention those overdosed rats in the barn."

"It seems to me you're safer down here. Oh, I forgot, we're on the verge of a war. But then Carlos says, 'not to worry.' Can we trust him? Think of him taking on the Americans! You and Eric, as representatives, are rather enemies or prisoners now, aren't you?"

"Diplomatic negotiators, I'd prefer," Candy remarked dryly.

"Yes, of course. Forgive me."

The treasure hunters returned for help. "We can't seem to budge Bessay."

"Get Jack," suggested Candy. "She likes him."

So the two naval consultants were called to remove the alien object disrupting the search party's advance. Jack soon persuaded Bessay to follow him out and behind the shed, where in the thick grass, she promptly fell through a well cover of rotted wood. Only it wasn't a well. "Ambassador, is this what you are looking for?"

Eric and Austin, holding a pitchfork and shovel apiece, came around behind the shed. "By jove, that's it. But what's the cow doing there?" asked Austin.

"Bessay put her foot in it, sir."

"Well, she's up to her udder now since we've been standing here."

"I agree, Austin," said Eric. "It is utter nonsense. She seems to be in a sinking hole."

Jack and Fred got a rope to tie around bellowing Bessay's neck. Then they heaved and hoed, while Healey prodded her behind. At last, freed from her frustrating predicament, Bessay lumbered off into the woods, mooing "mucho disgusto," as Fred remarked.

Fred then took Eric's shovel, jumped into the hole, and began digging, until he struck wood—another trap door. After removing more dirt all around, he was able to pry it open, only to find more loose dirt. He continued digging for a few minutes, wondering if he'd suddenly fall through, and thinking that he'd better have a rope tied around him. Then his shovel struck a hard object with a clunk. He pushed aside more dirt and pulled out a round, white object, a skull! Fred, scraping away, muttered, "What's this, a graveyard? Here's another one, and bones to go . . ."

"My word," said Healey. "You don't suppose those poor devils got trapped in the tunnel, do you?"

"Well, is it a tunnel?" asked Eric.

"Want me to keep digging, sir?"

"Guess you'd better, Fred. We'll sort out the bones."

A most distasteful proposition, Eric realized. "I believe I'll call Doctor Duval to give us his medical opinion, sober or otherwise." He retreated to the house to telephone, and passing Candy and Emily, informed them of their discovery.

"At least they aren't bodies," Candy said with relief. "Come on, Emily, let's take a look."

Eric reached the doctor, who sounded coherent. He said he'd be right over, in spite of there being patients beyond recall. Although it had been whispered about that Monsieur le Docteur, as Duval was called, had lost his license to practice in France, he was actually from Backwater Flats, Louisiana, where he learned Creole and thus understood the native speech of Beaulinia. Certainly his English showed no trace of a French accent, unless he so desired. It was not polite to investigate credentials or their lack in Beaulinia, where the living and duty-free drinks were cheap. He earned a small livelihood as the island's official coroner and treated the natives' ailments gratis. He was distinguished looking in a dissolute way, and entertaining company.

He soon appeared at the embassy and took charge of the growing number of scattered remains. "Let's put these two together on the sundeck over there," and began to puzzle out tibia to pelvis to ribcage to spine, as Fred and Jack brought up more bones.

Eric reminded the aides that the windmill still needed a flag painted on it. "And, Dr. Duval, we'll leave you to concentrate on your bare bones." He and Healey walked off.

"Ah, Jacques, perhaps you could find me some wire or cord to hold these jolly fellows together. And a *soupçon* of rum to keep me together too," requested the doctor. Jack obliged.

Eric and Healey returned to the terrace side of the house to locate the closing mechanism of the secret door. "My dear chap, just run your finger up the edge there, I believe. No? Perhaps then along the bottom. I recall now that it required a foot movement. Now let me think!"

While Healey was thinking "confoundedly slowly," Eric felt, he *was* pleased to have this secret, or not really secret, room. At least, it would be fun to surprise the children when they came to visit.

"Ah, Bohner, it's over here on the right. Kick that catch with your foot. Here it comes! Sorry to push you like that, but it snaps shut rather quickly." And he shoved Eric into the bushes. "Don't know my own strength these days. Let me give you a hand. I hope that isn't poison sumac there."

"Oh, Austin," called the lady-like Emily. "We'd best be going. Shall I drive, dear, or you?" Eric and Healey walked around to where the Daimler was parked. As he climbed in, his parting words to Eric were. "We must get together soon for battledore and shuttlecock."

Eric groaned, "And I was just beginning to like him!"

As they drove off with Emily at the wheel, Candy turned to Eric, remembering she had something to tell him. Now what was it? Oh, yes. The warehouse; Cousin Peregrine's High Seas Unlimited. That interested Eric. He suggested they stroll down to the dock area and look it over, "Strange that Carlos hadn't mentioned it. Perhaps he didn't know. Those fly-by-night companies come in and out pretty quickly."

"Why, Eric, that sounds like smuggling or illegal drug pushing."

"Charlotte would never permit that," scoffed Eric. "Now, where's my cane? I know, I know, Candy, as you say, in the hall closet."

He'd forgotten about Dr. Duval and his skeleton crew. So had the doctor, who was fast asleep in a deck chair, empty rum bottle still in hand. Eric looked out the back hall window and saw, seated on two chairs, the skeletons the doctor had wired together. They looked quite debonaire. He was certain that the doctor would stay for dinner and left him to his preprandial nap.

He returned to Candy, cane in hand, to find her talking to Jack and Fred, who still had buckets and brushes in hand. Eric told them there would be three guests for dinner, the doctor and his two anorexic patients. They saw what he meant when they reached the sundeck. They decided to surprise the Doc when he awoke. They pushed the two skeletal chairs up to the center table, which they proceeded to set with plates, napkins, glasses, and silverware. Some finishing touches to the diners followed: hats, neckties, gloves, even a pair of dark glasses to add to the surrealism.

The Bohners returned to an early and pleasant dinner. The Doc had come to by then and joined them. His bony friends dined alone outdoors. He had named them Tartuffe and Pantagruel, or Tuffy and Gruelly for short.

Candy had forgotten to call her brother in Washington which was just as well, since the Beaulinia Telephone Exchange shut down at six o'clock. At seven-thirty, the electricity went off. They were in for a blackout, indicating that something was afoot sooner than they had expected. Fred found a wheelbarrow to transport Doc Duval's Tuffy and Gruelly down the hill to his "surgery" for further study. No one thought to report it to the authorities.

It had been such a peaceful day. However, some time after midnight, "all hell broke loose" when Mont Dieu Merci began to rumble. Flares shot up, sulphurous smudge pots sent out evil-smelling smoke and "burning" stones rattled around, some rolling down to the sea. Carlos was aware of a ship lurking out there in the Atlantic darkness. At the embassy, it was useless to try to sleep any longer. They all groped their way down the stairs and out to the terrace, which faced the ocean. The binoculars were passed around, but to no avail. It was a pitch-black view over a moonless water. They could hear the whirring of the windmill vanes performing their defense duties. Since the smell of sulphur was none too pleasant, Candy brought out some scarves to cover their noses and mouths. They didn't help much with the odor, but did muffle the conversation.

Chapter 24

# A Benign Caper in a Pickle

Back in Washington at the break of dawn, President Fellow, dressed in brass-buttoned navy blue blazer, starched white cotton duck trousers, and white commodore's cap, entered the Round Room, temporarily designated The Intelligence Command Center, or Caper Room for short. As Commander-in-chief, he greeted his eager fighting team, Vice-President Jake Hand, Aggressive Defense Secretary Felix Wino, whom the press would later dub "Wi-not," and Secretary of State Willard Mayday.

"Good morning, gentlemen. As you know, this is my first war in office."

"Better call it War Game, Mr. President," interjected Wino.

"Benign Invasion is what we decided on, I thought," added Mayday.

"Whatever," continued Fellow. "As you know, our armed forces need the experience. The navy, especially, has been spending too much time lolling about in port."

"But, Mr. President, whined Felix, "The ships' computers suffer disjunction."

"You'll have to use plain language today, Felix," snapped Fellow.

"They keep breaking down."

"Now what about the press snooping around? Where's Barry?"

Barry Wheeler, White House spokesman, was called in to report on the status of media meddling.

"Well, Barry, have you blacked out?"

"Sir?"

"Have you blacked out all news from here?"

"Yes, sir. I informed the press that you were visiting Vice-President Hand at his vacation hide-away."

"I am? When?"

"Now, sir. This is his hide-away today, and he is listed as being on vacation."

"Very good, Barry. This is all so hasty since our original plans called for next Thursday as 'Be Kind Invasion Day.' "

"It's 'benign,' sir."

"That's fine, Barry. Now, Felix, how has your team managed the media?"

"We've already jumped the gun on them by moving up our 'be kind' invasion four days. Media persona—er, that's people—know the navy relaxes in August. Nothing ever happens then. Our sailors need leave, er, vacations, like everyone else. Media people take them, too. They call them the 'Dog Days of August.' "

"You better believe it, Felix. Have you seen any good

television shows lately? All reruns of sitcoms we didn't want to watch the first time. Why, even the news looks stale. I don't know how many times I've seen that hurricane! They do change the name, though, to fool you."

"I've heard that the programming brass take a three-month hiatus—that's another word for vacation, sir, in the summer. And no one takes the time to listen to your weekly radio chat, either, during this period."

"Oh, so that's what Dan Russki meant. I had such a strange call from him yesterday. He said something about scratching the tape. I thought he was drunk. That's why I told him to stay home today. Well, now, how are reports of the invasion to be handled?"

"I dunno," answered Spokesman Wheeler.

Wino answered, "One of our most reliable near-sighted servicemen has been trained as a reporter with the *Army Gazette*, and will be on hand to send back inspiring stories after the take-over."

"Splendid, Felix! The press services will be hopping mad not to have been included."

"They have only themselves to blame. They never look at the good side of an invasion, benign or 'be kind,' sir, as it may be. And they've proven themselves just too unreliable by making up disparaging innuendos—er, uh, blatant lies, that is."

"Then we'll just let the lying dogs of August sleep, eh, Felix? By the way, our regular Monday-morning prayer breakfast should be served soon. We want to go into that island, what's it called, on a wing and a prayer."

During this pleasant conversation by the dawn's early light, the secret communication center of blinking lights and bleeping sounds, playing softly in the background, suddenly erupted with a deep voice calling, "Do you read me, Cat? Do you read me?" "Cat" was Felix Wino's code name; "Big Boy" was the President's. Mayday didn't have one, since he was just a silent partner—very silent—in this undertaking, a.k.a. The Caper.

"Cat" Wino dashed over to the controls, and with Wheeler's fumbling assistance, managed to push the correct button for a two-way scrambled communication. "I read you. Cat scanning."

The deep but irritated voice continued: "This is Commander Groper, newly appointed to the bridge of the U.S.S. *Gary Cooper*. There seems to be an error in calculation. We are standing off the island of Beaulinia, whose extinct volcano is erupting. On a scale of one to ten, I'd give it a nine and a half. What to do? Can't seem to locate Captain Flemming on U.S.S. *John Wayne*. Await further orders."

Now Commander Groper was not in a good mood. He was in command of a new ship, untested and untried. A week ago, he had been ordered to sail her from the Norfolk Shipyard before all the new computers had been installed. This premature action had caused the replacement of many of the navy specialists by civilian R & L maintenance people, working frantically at sea now to "functionalize" the equipment. They did not like taking orders, either. Then it was discovered that in the haste of departure, Nukes instead of Nikes had been installed, which could hardly be called friendly persuaders. However, the last straw was when a computer confused the two islands of Beaulinia and Beaulieu and printed out "Beaulieuni." Utter baloney was what he was getting, he bellowed; plus an imminent mutiny by his civilian computer "consultants," who weren't going to permit their precious, billion-dollar equipment to be damaged by any volcanic action. Nor was his naval crew willing to fire off a nuclear warhead. He would wait for Capt. Jock Flemming, on his way from Puerto Rico, presumably. He wasn't sure, because there was some sort of jamming going on to prevent communication with the *John Wayne*.

"Well, stand off then for a while," ordered "Cat" Wino, after listening to Groper's long list of complaints. "I'll try to locate Flemming and get back to you." He signed off.

Then turning to the others asked, "Any of you guys know how to work this contraption?"

Jake Hand, standing by the window discussing with Mayday the sad state of the rose garden in this heat, offered "to take a crack at it." "I used to be a ham operator—uh, worked with a homemade shortwave radio, Mr. President." With much twiddling and punching of knobs and keys, he managed to raise first a Coast Guard frigate off the coast of Alaska; then, a Russian trawler off the tip of Florida. "Getting closer," he muttered. Ah, finally, a sleepy sailor on duty at a tiny listening post on the Virgin Islands picked up his signal.

"Yes, sir? You say you're looking for the *John Wayne?* She steamed past about O-two-hundred. Had a curious cargo. It looked like balloons."

"Ham" Hand turned to Wino. "You take over now. I don't think my hearing's too good. I think he mentioned balloons."

So, Felix Wino began: "This is Cat calling Virgin. Big Boy is in a pickle looking for the Caper fleet."

"This is not Virginia and there are no Big Boy capers or pickles here, sir."

"Now look here, you son of a-a-a seaman, that's a code word."

"Sorry, sir. Even if it's a hot word . . ."

Wino, growing excited shouted, "You jack-ass, I am Secretary of Aggressive Defense calling from the Caper Room. Big Boy wants to know if you can reach the *John Wayne.*"

"The old movie star? I think he died. And my name is not Jack Ass-i-am. Look, is this some kind of a joke? I'm not permitted to receive personal calls."

"This is official, you numbskull. I want to speak to Captain Flemming on the . . ."

"I'm sorry, sir, you must have the wrong number," the "Virgin" seaman stated with finality and hung up, or rather, unplugged his switchboard.

While this breakdown of communications at the Command Center was taking place, Captain Flemming did arrive at the scene of Groper's quandary. He too had noticed Beaulinia's volcano erupting in the face of all previous knowledge to the contrary and himself erupted from the bridge to the ship's communications center to read the computer printout. On finding the same misprint "Beaulieuni" that Groper had, he stormed out swearing, "Eternal Father, strong to save! Never can trust those electronic gimmicks. They can't even spell. They must mean Beaulieu. There it is over the horizon and looking mighty peaceful and quiet. No volcano acting up there." Then, "Full steam ahead," he ordered, and signalled the *Gary Cooper* to follow. By this time, the helicopter carrier, U.S.S. *Monroe Doctrine*, hove into sight and proceeded to follow the other two ships to Beaulieu.

It was full daylight in Beaulinia with Carlos on the alert at his command post on the front terrace of the Casa Blanca, peering through binoculars at the sight of a single ship standing silently by, but soon joined by a second and then a third, and feeling some trepidation, *i.e.*, quaking in his boots. What followed next was hard for him to believe, for the three ships slowly moved on and past his island without firing a shot. Of course, his volcano, Dieu Merci, was firing away with its timed eruptions. Not a single aircraft flew over for a close inspection. All he could do then was sit down, remove his quaking boots, and heave a sigh of relief.

The Bohners and their aides had also been following this extraordinary armada, when the Healeys joined them on the terrace.

"Do you think they will return?" Emily asked.

"Perhaps it's a feint," added Austin.

"Well, let's wait around and see," suggested Candy. "Meanwhile, perhaps Jack and Fred could produce some breakfast for all of us."

Eric had remained silent with wonder and relief. Now,

he suggested, "Let's turn on the radio for some news. Candy, where's the old short-wave set?"

"I think it's in the hall closet."

Eric disappeared indoors. He opened the closet door and peered into the darkness. "I don't see it, Candy."

"Turn on the light, Eric. Oh, no, you can't; no electricity. Well, not everything can be up front. Feel behind the tennis racquets."

Amidst the clatter of fallen objects could be heard, "Ah, here it is." Eric returned to the terrace, placed the radio on a table and turned the switch. Silence. Of course, no batteries. Candy proposed that they use the batteries from their flashlights which probably would have been the wrong size; but Fred now appeared to tell them the refrigerator had just gone back on, "So we've got electricity once more." They all rushed to the television set in the library.

However, it was not until afternoon they learned from a local broadcast what had happened concerning the "benign" invasion of Beaulieu, their closest island neighbor. Prime Minister Maurice Pincus of Beaulieu was interviewed by Tarioca TV. He said what a total surprise this had been to the citizens of Beaulieu, "*Et naturellement*," he had to order the police to "*abattre ces folles ballons*"—to shoot down those crazy balloons.

"*Par chance*, they were unmanned, what *les militaires* call '*les drones*.'"

Carlos came over to the embassy later with more information. "When the marines landed in an amphibious hexapod—it's a spiderish-looking, six-legged, erector-set-looking tank—Pincus didn't know whether to laugh or give up, or both. He surrendered. He said he'd sue for peace. And he'd sue for plenty more. By permitting the U.S. forces to do some damage, Pincus could bill them for repairs. In fact, he sounded jubilant over the telephone. '*Croyez, mon ami*,' what this will do for my bankrupt *economie*,' he crowed."

When the news from Washington appeared later, White House spokesman Barry Wheeler had a slightly different version. "Early this morning, President Fellow as Commander-in-Chief of the Armed Forces, with a maximum loss of three balloons and one hexapod, routed all Communist presence and influence from the island of Beaulieu. The world must realize that the Monroe-Fellow Doctrine, all in good fellowship, is being vigorously enforced and enforcing at all times. So as not to needlessly endanger the gallant men of our armed services, total secrecy was maintained before and during operations. Members of the press will be permitted on the island in rotation commencing tomorrow."

The next scene appearing on the screen took place in the Round Room. The president was congratulating Felix Wino for his "capable handling of a serious threat to our democracy" and thanking SOS Mayday for his "helpful presence in time of national need." The vice-president was not mentioned for his ham-handed contribution. After all, he was presumed to be on vacation.

Chapter 25

"Libation Day"

Beaulinia would have a Merci Dieu celebration; actually, a Merci Carlos. He threw a party for everyone on the island. All contributed to the food and fun; homemade creole dishes, milk and ice cream from the Bohners' cow,.

whiskey from the Healey's bottomless wine cellar, and from Charlotte, what else? Why, charlotte russe, of course. Jack and Fred helped string up colored lights in Bulim Square for music and dancing. It was Fiesta Day, Liberation Day, and for Doc Duval, Libation Day.

"The Edenrocs," an impromptu group, took over the old bandstand, requesting Fred to perform with them. Well-known in all the local bistros for his mellow baritone voice, he chose to sing *"Bésame Mucho"* with little feeling for the cow, but "mucho gusto" for *la bonne chance*. This was followed by "The Ordures," a popular band made up of garbage can lids, rattles, mandolin and marimba. Dancing began; Fred and Jack were the life of the party. They danced and pranced and stomped with all the maidens young and not so young.

At intermission, Madame Charlotte, feeling no pain nor hesitation, did her Carlotta Banana routine, costumed in a long, loose gown with a string of bananas around her ample waist, and a bowl of fruit perched on her lovely head. She wiggled and rolled her eyes as she sang:

"I'm Carlotta Banana and I mean to be
As a-round and a-firm as you ever will see.
I can bruise too easy, so you mustn't feel
You can take advantage of my sex-a-peel."

Next, Carlos was prevailed upon to recite *The Giant Gnatcatcher*:

"What feathered friend do we behold
Whose sorry lot, it must be told,
To sit in nest on egg to hatch her
One big baby gi-nat-catcher."

Carlos modestly declined to follow it with an encore. He went in search of Eric, who was attempting to perform some magic tricks for an assortment of children. He was pretty rusty and was relieved when Carlos took him aside for a quiet chat, Carlos began, "Now, old friend, it is time to take the bull by the horns and blow your own. I do not think that the benign invaders will return, but I shall continue to maintain alertness. And you can help." Eric couldn't imagine how, though. "You see, my omnipresent ambassador in Washington has passed on word that they botched the job. They mistook Beaulieu for Beaulinia. I wonder how that happened!" He laughed and looked knowingly at Eric. Eric laughed, too. "So you pulled the wool over their eyes, Carlos?"

"It was a lot of BULL!" and Carlos laughed again. "I too can perform feats of magic. But to be serious, they are still interested in gaining the secret weapon by hook or by crook. I am prepared to sell. But my price is astronomical, which I think they'll be willing to pay, after they've patched up Beaulieu."

But Eric was still intrigued by what Carlos had first touched on, and asked, "You mean to say that those batheads couldn't tell one island from another?"

"With a little confusion from me, yes. To them, it's a matter of 'when you've seen one, you've seen 'em all.'"

"I believe I'll be recalled now."

"I don't think so. Because, you see, you must get in touch with your chief at State and tell him that you have persuaded Carlos that in the name of the Pan American Union and the Monroe Doctrine, the paper and not the ship, we must all work together to wipe out any taint of Communism from the Caribbean Basin. I'm just throwing their words back at them! And that Carlos would be willing to negotiate with them on that premise. Simple as that. They'll be tied up for a couple of years calming down all the other islands and pouring money into Beaulieu as a token of their 'fellowship.' Meanwhile, you will discover that they will want you to remain here as ambassador, until you reach retirement age. At that time, Charlotte and I hope you and Candy will want to settle here."

"We may at that, Carlos. We've been very happy here. But I do miss the availability of a large library."

"That's no problem, Eric. I plan to build up this 'one-room university,' and medical school into a showplace you'd be proud to associate with. Your help would be welcome. After all, you're the first person to be awarded an honorary degree. You could start a department of Basque Literature to attract students away from the Costa del Sol to come bask—I mean—soak up sun and knowledge here.

"Carlos, you think of everything!"

"I try, Eric, I try. In the meantime we continue to grow bananas and poinsettia and rent warehouses."

"Oh, that's what I've been meaning to ask you; it's about the High Seas Unlimited down on Wharf Road. It seems that cousin of Candy's, Peregrine Parody, who got himself killed in Keene Valley, owned it. And it's piled high with bales of white stuff."

Carlos laughed. "Okay, Eric, you want me to look into it? Although strictly speaking, we don't make a habit of breaking into warehouses when they're paid up. They're a good source of income. And in this part of the world, one doesn't ask too many questions. But since this Parody is dead—Oh, any partners or heirs?"

"He has a daughter, who was arrested in Washington."

"For smuggling?"

"No, for murder."

"Your wife has some interesting relatives."

"Carlos, you wouldn't believe it!"

## Chapter 26

## Just Blew In

Candy telephoned Washington Tuesday afternoon when the Beaulinia Telephone Exchange resumed business. She thought her family would be "worried sick" about her and Eric. Not at all. Of course they had known nothing about the president's proposed caper to invade the island. She felt let down. But Pattee, who answered her call, had plenty of news to relate. "Horace phoned from Keene Valley to inform you—he was surprised you were not here and we were—anyway, he said that Miss Wall had been arrested, after Lieutenant Whistler found the grave of that young hippie in a blanket in her vegetable garden. Lettuce, or was it cabbage patch? You don't suppose she ate—or worse yet, served vegetables to others, do you? That would be like cannibalism! I'll never look at another Cabbage-patch doll!"

"Miss Wall?" asked Candy. "Nice Miss Wall, who took such good care of Aunt Nittie? Why would she do that?"

"I believe she's head of a drug ring in K.V. The stuff comes down from Canada, they say. And a congressman at the Ausable Club, Sam Brasher."

"Well, what about him?"

"Oh, he was arrested too."

"I didn't think congressmen could be arrested, can they?"

"Well, why not? They carted him off to the Elizabethtown jail."

"I thought they had some kind of immunity, like foreign diplomats and policemen."

"I never heard that. Anyway, they think he killed that tennis player Riddle. For cheating."

"For cheating at tennis? I never!"

"No, for cheating on a dope-dealing deal, I guess. It should be in tomorrow's paper. John and I are sticking around for that. The Washington newspaper should give out all the juicy details about him."

"By the way, what has happened to Jenny?"

"She's been pardoned—or is it exonerated? All charges dropped and her passport returned. Or rather, she had to go downtown to get it, which annoyed her. At least that nice Lieutenant Whistler called her to apologize, so that made her feel better."

"Would you ask her if she knows anything about a warehouse in Beaulinia belonging to her father? Hold on, Eric's shouting something." (Pause) "He says not to ask her. He's still suspicious."

"Her mother's arriving from England today. We're taking them out to dinner tonight, so we can meet the famous Partridge in Pairtrie."

"Oh, I must tell you what has been happening here. Wait a minute, Eric's shouting again." (Pause) "He says he won't pay for this long-distance call if I don't hang up in two seconds. Claudia and Konrad all right? I'll write. Good-bye."

"Candace!" Eric continued. "Keep quiet for now about happenings in Beaulinia. It's in the realm of diplomatic affairs, and that's my department. I'm forced into playing 'The Great Game.'"

"Oh, dear," sighed Candy, not knowing what he meant. Then shrugging her shoulders, "Oh, well, in three weeks, I'll be back in the States for the U.S. Tennis Open. That too is a Great Game."

"Candace, I don't know what you see in all that tennis. First Wimbledon and now Flushing Meadows. A waste of money buying those tickets."

"Well, you gave them to me for my birthday."

"I did? Oh, so I did."

"Besides, it gives me a chance to see the children."

"I know, I know. But just don't discuss Beaulinia at present."

Candy told Eric about the arrests of Sam Brasher and Miss Wall, and the hippie's body found in her vegetable garden.

"That's one funeral we did not have to attend," remarked Eric as he left the library to look for Fred.

Candy was still sitting by the telephone when it let out a ring. The call was for Eric. She called after him, "Eric, Carlos wants to speak to you." She left the room to go upstairs.

Eric returned and picked up the receiver. "Yes, Carlos." (Pause) "What the . . ." (Pause) "I see." (Pause) "Yes, of course, Carlos, right away." He hung up and called Fred, who by this time was at the door to tell him that he and Jack had spotted a balloon descending into the bay.

"That's just what Carlos said. And he thought since balloon and balloonist were wearing American flags, the American Ambassador had better greet the fellow. But Carlos will send someone right over."

They caught up with Jack, already clambering down the path to the water. By the time they reached the beach, the balloonist was trying to extricate himself from the basket bobbing in the waves, and disentangle the limp and soggy lines. He then introduced himself to the three amazed embassy people as Balloonist First Class, Evert Bunge, from the U.S.S. *John Wayne*. "I'm looking for the American Ambassador." Eric identified himself, while Jack and Fred helped tie up the remains of the balloon.

Bunge was thinking hard what next to say. Captain Flemming over at Beaulieu had ordered him on this "spy mission" to find out what was going on at Beaulinia. "Be wary, my lad. Don't let on that we sent you. And try to land near the building with that peculiar-looking American flag on it." Bunge had asked him, "But, sir, what excuse shall I give for dropping in so unexpectedly?" "Oh, you'll think of something, Bunge," was the captain's reply, adding, "And don't bungle it!"

So here now was Evert Bunge on the beach, hemming and hawing. "Er, sir, I uh beg your pardon for, uh, droppin' in this way. Uh, I was, er, wonderin', uh, if I could, uh, go to the head."

"Go the head of what?" asked Eric suspiciously.

"Uh, I, er . . ."

Fred spoke up. "He wants to use the lavatory, sir."

Eric, a trifle taken aback, said only, "Follow me."

They all followed him up to the house. Candy, hearing Eric pacing up and down the hallway while Jack and Fred escorted Bunge to the lavatory, called downstairs to him. "What's going on, Eric? Visitors?"

"In a manner of speaking. A balloonist just blew in, wanting to use the lavatory."

"How odd," exclaimed Candy. "Why couldn't he have, um, you know, um, er over the side or . . ."

"Candace, that's quite enough! Ah, I hear Carlos's men coming now," and he strode over to the front door.

Carlos's son, Don, arrived. "Any trouble, Ambassador?"

"I don't believe so, Don. But it is curious. A balloon landing on the beach, and the balloonist asking to use the lavatory."

"Enemy, sir?"

"Depends on whose. He's an American from the *John Wayne*. Ridiculous name for a ship. I thought he was a cowboy."

Just then Jack and Fred, wiping tears of laughter from their cheeks after hearing Bunge's story, escorted him out to the verandah, where the ambassador was waiting.

Don could tell from their faces that this was a laughing matter!

But maintaining seriousness, he said to Eric, "I expect you'll want to phone your chief of protocol concerning this, sir. So, if you don't need me, I'll report back to Pops."

"Ah yes. Quite. And thanks, Don. That's what I must do. Telephone." Eric regretted this ending to the past few "carefree" days. He mumbled, "So now it's back to bureaucratic nonsense and high-flying diplomacy. Hah! That's a good one. High-flying nonsense ballooned out of all proportion."

He returned to the library. He had no difficulty reaching his chief, James Appleby. Nor did he have any reluctance giving him a piece of his mind. What were they trying to do? Start World War III? Disgraceful action! And picking on tiny Beaulieu. Why, they might have blown up Beaulinia! And here is Carlos about ready to negotiate, if they would give him, their own ambassador, enough time and a free hand, without any rash and bullyboy interference from Washington, to manage in a proper and diplomatic manner for the benefit of all concerned. (Later in the State Department, this would be referred to as "Bohner's Coup," to distinguish it from his earlier difficulties simply called "Bohners."

Throughout this tirade, Eric was astonished to hear "Yes, sir," and "Very well, Ambassador," and "Whatever you think best." It was Eric's one brief, courageous, and sweet moment. When he hung up the receiver, he mused, "Perhaps this isn't such a bad job, after all." But he felt he had made an awful scene and noticed his hands were shaking. Leadership was a new and frightening role. But look at Candy! Bossing people never bothered her. However, he was certain he'd remain pretty much the same old Eric, although speaking up brought some wondrous results.

Candy brought him back to earth. "Do we invite First Class Balloonist Bunge to dinner?" she asked. "And when does our official staff return?"

"Yes, to the first question, and I hope never, to the second," answered Eric. "It's nice to have the place to ourselves, and in comfort. You have Jack to help in the kitchen and the little girl, Zina, from town to help him, while Fred carries the paper load."

"But the grass needs mowing, the bushes clipped, and the tennis court . . ."

"Let's ask this Bunge chap at dinner if he would like to stay on and take over the outdoor chores."

At dinner, Evert agreed wholeheartedly to stay, providing he could have time to repair his balloon. Since he was a farm boy from Iowa, the outdoor chores would pose no problem. The ambassador, though would have to get permission from his captain.

Eric did better. He called Appleby to tell him to notify the Pentagon in general and the navy in particular not to send any more spies by balloon or other craft. "It would be dangerous," he continued, "since Mont Dieu Merci could erupt at any time." (Pause) "No, the embassy was not hurt this time. However, we are short of staff, and request that Balloonist First Class Bunge remain with us indefinitely." (Pause) "Oh, cut the grass and underbrush." (Pause) "He will have plenty of time to repair his balloon, and will draw up a list of any parts needed." (Long pause) "No, I think a balloon will lend a nice touch to the embassy, and will supply us with additional means of transportation." Eric felt proud of himself, Appleby kept his thoughts to himself.

## Chapter 27

# The Cope and Dope Specialists

The following morning, Mr. Tucker, director of the "One-Day Antiterrorism Course" at the Diplomatic Heritage Institute, telephoned Eric. "Mr. Ambassador, Mr. Appleby informed me of your predicament on Beaulinia and suggested I enroll you, your family, and staff in our class on 'Coping with Violence,' a recurring problem these days."

"Absolutely not!" fumed Eric.

"Mr. Appleby believed that would be your reply, sir, and therefore has set up a contingency arrangement, whereby I am to arrive on the first possible Beaulinia flight to conduct the class at your embassy probably this weekend, unless, of course, there should be further volcanic action."

Eric was thinking of asking Carlos to turn on his inferno once a day, but controlling his temper replied, "I believe we are coping with violence quite well, Mr. Feeney."

"Oh, I am sure you are, Ambassador, but are your loved ones as fully protected as they should be?"

Eric thought about that. "Just what would this course cover?"

"We focus on a variety of threats facing Americans abroad: terrorists, criminals, natural disasters such as fires and, er, of course, volcanos."

"And you've thought of some solutions, Mr. Feeney?"

"Well, of course, Ambassador Bohner, common sense is our best tool."

"In other words, Mr. Feeney, you plan to conduct a course here on common sense. Is the State Department qualified to teach that?"

"This is the Diplomatic Heritage Institute, a separate organization. We frequently advise the Department of State as an outside consultant," Mr. Feeney huffily replied.

"Very well," agreed Eric, "we'll meet your plane, and in an armored car." Eric smiled at that idea. After hanging up, Eric thought, *Better still, I'll send Jack and Fred to meet him in those fancy plumed operatic uniforms; our first line of defense to stun the enemy.*

The next few days before the weekend arrived, the Bohners and staff were left in peace. Eric wrote, Fred typed, Candy weeded the flower garden, Jack was in the kitchen inventing a new sauce, which he'd get poor obliging little Zina to taste, while Evert, between bouts with lawnmower and bushwhacker, struggled to repair his balloon. He hoped one day soon to take the Bohners soaring silently over the volcano and nearby islands, avoiding Beaulieu, of course, where the U.S. Army was now in control. U.S. aircraft flew by every day to and from that island, one of them attempting to land on Beaulinia. "A nosey spy," Carlos called it and set off a few Fourth of July rockets to discourage it.

Saturday, the airport reopened. The port of Bulim had never been closed, and trading had never come to a halt, especially with Cuba. After all, Carlos liked a good "Havana" and he did have to get rid of those abundant banana and okra crops and the fine Beaulunseed oil made from the elu nut. So the Beaulinia "milk run" airline resumed its thrice-weekly flight to and from Miami.

Expected on the first incoming flight was Mr. Tuck Feeney, lecturer on antiterrorism. The Bohners referred to him as The Holy Terror. He did not appear. Fred suggested, "Maybe he got hijacked." He turned out to be absolutely correct. On that very Saturday, Tuck Feeney was sitting meekly in the Havana Airport along with fifty-six other passengers of the Washington-to-Miami flight. He had decided not to identify himself and concentrate on how he could explain all this to his superiors. Not unexpectedly, he was recognized by the press the next day, after his plane returned to Miami, and even appeared on television, which the Bohners watched with avid interest. They could thus not expect his arrival until the next flight on Tuesday. Eric said he would certainly tell him how to handle a hijacker, and a few more things, too. They agreed that Mr. Feeney wasn't looking forward now to his visit or presenting his lecture and answering their questions.

On the Tuesday flight, Feeney met Narcotics Agent Nathan Zimmer or Nat, as he preferred to be called, sitting next to him. They were a contrast. Feeney with his worried and pasty look and Zimmer with a square face and chunky build. They introduced themselves and discovered they shared a common purpose: to deal with the Bohners. Zimmer was on orders to investigate the High Seas Unlimited warehouse and was telling Feeney, "Surely if cocaine or heroin were stored there, it would not have remained untouched all this time. But the Parody, Riddle, Brasher connection must be checked out. That little detective from King (sic) Valley kept pestering us about 'puzzle pieces not fitting properly,' and although the DEA can hardly find the time or manpower to check out every small-town detective's hunch, this one did involve a congressman who seemed to be peddling 'coke.' My orders are to clear Brasher's 'good' name. He's a friend and supporter of the president."

They were met at the airport, Zimmer reported much later, "by two embassy staff members dressed in swashbuckling uniforms and plumed hats. Honestly, Chief, I expected 'em to burst into song. But you know, it was a beautiful drive we had to the embassy. The island is a paradise. We should have invaded it instead of Beaulieu."

Ambassador and Mrs. Bohner, awaiting Feeney's arrival, were surprised to discover he had a companion, and were rather shocked to learn he was a narcotics agent. It was decided then and there that Fred would drive Eric and Zimmer directly to the wharves. "But, first, take off those silly uniforms, you two," Eric ordered. Jack would remain to help Candy with Mr. Feeney.

Unknown to anyone at the embassy was the arrival of Jenny and her mother on the same flight, to be met by the Austin Healeys. Ann Partridge Parody had requested her friend, Emily, to invite them for a visit. When Candy called Emily to invite her to hear the Feeney Way to Cope, she was told the surprising news of their arrival. Now, what should she do? How to cope, indeed! She decided not to mention the upcoming lecture; *They'll have to learn to cope by themselves since Eric would never allow Jenny in the house.* Instead, she explained that she and Eric had high-level, hush-hush guests staying for a few days, but of course she'd be over to see Jenny and meet her mother as soon as she could possibly find a minute. A lame excuse, she thought, but it would pass for diplomacy.

"You know, Jenny would love a game of tennis," continued Emily.

Candy, who had just gotten Evert to weed the tennis court, must now tell him to put back the weeds, she told herself, as she said aloud, "As soon as we can remove those pesky weeds."

With two extra for dinner, Jack rounded up the local girl, Zina, to help him prepare a suitable meal for "the coper and doper." And Candy advised Mr. Feeney to make himself at home and feel free to look around on his own to check out "our weak points." Then she went off to answer a ringing telephone.

It was Fran calling with the usual greeting: "Can, this is Fran!" She was quite excited to be announcing her engagement to "Bud" Abel Smythe. She continued, "At our age it seems foolish to have a long engagement, and therefore the wedding will be the Sunday after Labor Day in the garden at Keene Valley, in front of the outdoor barbecue fireplace, oh, of course covered with potted plants and vases of flowers. Now, Can, I want you to be my matron of honor, and John will give me away. You do have something suitable to wear, I hope. Stylish would be nice and a new hairstyle would help."

Candy agreed to participate as stylishly as possible. She wasn't certain Eric could get away, she told Fran (remembering to herself Eric's vow never to return to K.V.), but that she planned to be in New York around that time for the U.S. Open Tennis, and getting to the wedding was no problem. Fran offered her the use of her house in Greenwich, so Candy didn't have to ask. Later, Candy looking at a calendar discovered the wedding would take place on the same day as the men's finals. She wanted to call Fran to ask her to change the date. Eric said, "Absolutely not. That's unthinkable, even if it is Fran!"

Candy had forgotten about Mr. Feeney, who, with clipboard in hand, had been taking copious notes of the shocking lack of security and fire prevention inside. Then turning his attention to the outside of the structure, checking doors and windows and feeling around in general, he tripped the outside lock of the secret closet and sprung open the invisible door. Blinking in surprise, he stepped into the cool and dark area, groping for a light. He touched the closing mechanism by accident, causing the door to slam shut. Thus Feeney found himself without flashlight, cigarette lighter, or matches, sealed up in a dark and unknown room. What to do! He fainted.

Dinner was ready at seven o'clock or shortly thereafter when Eric and Zimmer returned from the docks. But no Mr. Feeney was to be seen. Eric suggested having a drink in the library while waiting for him to appear. After handing Zimmer a whiskey sour, he remarked, "I say, we don't have mice, do we Fred? Hear that?" They all listened. "Sounds like books being gnawed." Eric went over to the bookcase to listen again. "Why, can mice speak? Sounds like a muffled, squeaky voice."

Fred suggested they open the bookcase, and pressed the switch. The shelves slowly swung open to show a very uncoping Mr. Feeney on his knees, suit rumpled, voice hoarse, and eyes glazed. "Why, Mr. Feeney," said Candy, "there you are. Dinner's ready anytime."

Fred hauled out the poor, trapped creature, sat him down and handed him a good, stiff drink, while Mr. Zimmer, all agog, and remembering this was the old Snow House with quite a reputation back in the old days, asked, "May I?" as he stepped in where Feeney had formerly trod.

"Ah, hah! What's this?" He grabbed the box of white powder, held it up, opened it and sniffed. "Yup, it's probably the real thing!" he exclaimed. "Now, Ambassador, perhaps you can explain this."

Candy suggested they sort it out over dinner, and "Please bring your drink along, Mr. Feeney."

## Chapter 28

## Awareness and a Warehouse

Since Mr. Feeney had not finished his survey of the embassy premises, he postponed his lecture to the following day after lunch. Fred accompanied him on his rounds to see that he stayed away from booby traps and hidden doors. The mail had arrived early and was waiting for the Bohners on the library desk. Eric proceeded to slit all envelopes, both his and hers, with a fine, antique brass opener, before sorting the pieces. The first one he looked at was a bill from Jenny's lawyer, Miles Pendleton. "Confound it!" he roared. "Will you look at this, Candace! Two thousand and sixty dollars and thirty cents for services and expenses by that paddy-wagon chaser of an attorney. He has the gall to send the bill to me! And what did he do?" Then in a slightly softer tone of voice, "By the way, what *did* he do? Where is that murdering cousin of yours?"

*Oh dear*, thought Candy. "Now Eric," she began, "she was released for insufficient evidence, I believe is the term. Lieutenant Whistler even . . ."

"Ah, ha! That Whistler's responsible, I see. And after I explained to him how she was guilty as all hell. You know, people who come into contact with your family do everything wrong. Well, where is she now?"

Candy hesitated. "Traveling, I believe. Now, Eric, there's no need to get upset. Why Jenny's one of the family. She's a very sweet and charming woman."

"So was Lizzie Borden."

Fred knocked on the door. "Sorry to interrupt, sir, but Mrs. Austin Healey with two guests has arrived and is waiting in the drawing room."

Candy was in a quandary. Those two guests were of course Cousin Jenny, the topic of this unpleasant conversation, and her mother. If she didn't warn Eric now, what would he do on unexpectedly encountering them? That would be a close encounter of the worst kind. "Tell them, Fred, I'll be right there, but please close the door here." Then whispering, "Now, Eric, you must keep your voice down and your temper under control. Those two guests of the Healeys are old friends of Emily's from England. You see, Emily went to school with the former Ann Partridge, who, er . . ."

"Get on with it, Candace."

" . . . who had the misfortune to marry Cousin Peregrine, you know. And happens to be their guest here."

"And the other one—the other guest?" Eric asked innocently.

"Well, it's her daughter, er, um, Jenny. Eric, don't say anything!"

"I am not going to have those evil women in my house!" hissed Eric.

"It's not exactly your house. It belongs to the government."

"We must protect government property, then. Mr. Feeney would agree."

"I'll tell you what. You go out the terrace door here and around in back to the firing range or down to the beach. Look for Mr. Feeney. Give me half an hour to be sociable to relatives and Britishers and get rid of them politely. Now, please go quietly."

For once, Eric obeyed and Candy crossed the hall to the drawing room to deal with her guests. Jenny introduced her mother, who asked to be called Cousin Ann. She was a handsome woman about Candy's age. Candy instantly recognized her as the "Mrs. Parradine" sitting next to her in the royal box at Wimbledon. This caused a flurry of comments, including inquiries about her obliging niece, Pamela Mallow. Candy then apologized for having to cut short their visit since she was required to attend a meeting on coping with disasters, sent down—that is, a Mr. Feeney from Diplomatic Heritage was sent down—to show them how to cope. Candy did not think this was the right time to mention the lawyer's bill Eric had just received. And, yes, they must get in a game of tennis soon, hoping the court would be weeded and fit for playing once again. She gently ushered them out the door, waving on the verandah until their motor car drove through the gate. Sighing with relief, she hurried back to the library to read her letters.

The first one she picked up was from Konrad. He was proud to announce that he had a job as an assistant economics adviser on the *Wall Street Upbeat*, a weekly financial publication, and was now working in New York and staying with Chester until he could find a place he could afford.

He and Lily had decided to get married "while you're up here, Mummy, to attend the tennis matches. We are planning to have the ceremony in Keene Valley, since that's where we met. Aunt Fran is getting married too. Think of that at her age! But of course we do not want a double wedding. Maybe we could have ours the day before at the church, if the Reverend Miss Gentle isn't still too tied up with local funerals. And Aunt Fran is going to sublet us part of her large house. I wanted to telephone you all this, but it was too difficult to get a call through. Did you see any of the action on Beaulieu? We'll make all the arrangements, if you wouldn't mind paying for the flowers, food, and incidentals for a small party afterwards, if not at the house, then I guess at the Spread Eagle. Lily's parents will be there."

Candy sighed. This wasn't her day. Now she'd have to miss the women's finals and men's semifinals. And what is worse, persuade Eric to go to Keene Valley. She wondered if Mr. Feeney really understood the meaning of "cope."

She next found a letter from Claudia. She was all excited at receiving a grant to photograph the flora of "B & B" (Beaulinia and Beaulieu). "And it wouldn't be expensive staying with you and Daddy. I'll be coming in October and November or next spring. Right now I am busy arranging a small exhibit of my most recent microphotography examples of uncommon flowers and insects." Candy thought how refreshing it would be to have Claudia here. And wouldn't that perk up their handsome naval staff! Then she read a P.S. "Klara and David showed up and are staying here a few days before returning to New Mexico. Both have lost weight. David has to use a cane, and Klara's in a neck brace. I called them 'the old couple' since they moved so slowly. We sat up all night talking." Candy hoped she'd learn from Klara a few details of her alpine adventure. At least they were all right!

Mr. Feeney and Eric returned to the library. Mr. Feeney was questioning Eric about his embassy staff and did not like the answers. "According to Commander Groper's report, Mr. Nearim and Mr. Farnon were rated 'ineffective subordinates.' That's two minuses for the embassy, wouldn't you say?"

"Look here, Feeney, I'll evaluate my own staff. I can't stand incompetence, which was all I got from the original bunch you people sent me. Fred and Jack are the two most intelligent, level-headed young men I've ever found working in an embassy. And if you even hint at having them removed, I'll . . ."

Candy interrupted hastily. "Mr. Feeney, please sit down. Eric I don't think it's too early to serve drinks, do you?"

Eric disliked drinking himself and couldn't see why anyone else needed "the damn stuff" either. But he was a polite host and quietly fixed a drink for Feeney.

Mr. Feeney decided it would be wiser to question Candy. "Mrs. Bohner, what have you in the way of domestic staff at present?"

"Down to practically nothing, Mr. Feeney. Because of the recent, er, surprising events here, Jack, that is, Mr. Farnon, has assumed the chef's role, and very creditably and effectively," she stressed. "Then there's the little Creole, Zina, who helps in the kitchen. Her mother comes several times a week to clean."

"Umm, this Zina is a native, I assume. Is she to be trusted?"

Candy was ready to choke, but forced herself to reply calmly, "She comes from a fine family. All very capable and honest. I'm giving her tennis lessons. I believe she'll become a good player some day."

Feeney thought it would be safe to tackle Bohner once again. "Now, Ambassador, that young man working on the balloon. An odd item, I might add, for an embassy. What's his story?"

"Oh, he blew in from Beaulieu, and since we were

short-handed, stayed on to tend the premises and milk the cow."

"Cow," squeaked Feeney. "I don't recall seeing a cow. How remiss of me."

'I don't believe she's any threat," Eric remarked dryly.

"No, of course not. But to return to the balloonist. Did you see his credentials? We must keep in mind that spies frequently seem so guileless and eventually become indispensable."

"I understand, Mr. Feeney," said Eric, whose voice began to rise, "that Captain Flemming, under whom Evert Bunge served (the young man you are accusing of being a spy), informed State that Bunge was 'a first-class bungler and should be rated a fifth-class balloonist.' We find that recommendation good enough."

Fred came to the library door to announce that lunch was ready. Zina's older sister, Zita, was serving, but went unnoticed by Mr. Feeney, who probably thought they all looked alike.

The long-anticipated lecture took place in the drawing room directly after lunch. A screen and movie projector had been set up, and six chairs were lined up for the Bohners, their staff of three sailors, and Mr. Zimmer, the narcotics agent who had expressed interest in attending. They all seated themselves. Mr. Feeney began.

"I am privileged today, as a member of the Diplomatic Heritage Institute, to conduct this overseas seminar in coping with violence and terrorism. A variety of threats face Americans abroad these days, be it from terrorists, criminals, or more natural disasters. The 'Coping with Violence' class includes fire protection, how to avoid burglary, how to handle the psychological problems of dealing with terrorism, lessons in hostage survival, recommendations on rapid evacuation of families, and methods of avoiding assassination or kidnapping attempts. Our first film is on home security. If Mr. Farnon would close the curtains and Mr.

Nearim, I believe, will run the projector. There, now, are we ready?"

They all watched quietly to the end of the reel. Mr. Feeney now continued: "This film has been presented to make you aware of the importance of inspecting your overseas dwelling and offices for weak spots both inside and out and around the premises. Just ask yourself: Are there bars on the window, bolts on the door, sprinklers on the ceiling, smoke alert on the wall, fire escape or emergency ladder and rope outside? Is the building concrete? Has it a bomb-proof cellar, where the safe is kept? And what about barbed wired around the property, twenty-four-hour guards at the gate, booby traps in the garden? The only answer I can give you for this embassy is a resounding NO! Yes, ladies and gentlemen, you should feel worried. You have failed all safety suggestions, if not yet regulations.

"Now, we'll present a film on the techniques of personnel and personal safety, highlighting safety on the roads: How to maintain enough distance between your car and the one behind you, presumably carrying terrorists, so that you will always have sufficient space for maneuvering; how to take a different route each day to work, or while shopping or jogging to avoid kidnappers. . . ."

Doc Duval strolled in, pulled up a chair, and began to listen. Mr. Feeney, taken aback by such a visible and viable lack of security, lost his train of thought.

"Oh, I beg your pardon, Mr. Feeney," said Eric jumping up, "this is our neighbor, Monsieur le Docteur Duval." And to the doctor, "Mr. Feeney is advising us on embassy security. Please continue, Mr. Feeney."

"As I was saying, different routes to work. This film also answers such questions as: Number one, how to talk to a terrorist—You carry a cane and speak softly. Number two, how to maintain physical fitness while a prisoner—You try aerobics without music. Number three, how to foil microwave surveillance—with foil, gold, that is. We have recently added a segment on how to handle spy-dust—

Wash frequently. It's all good common sense, you see. Of course, we have not omitted debugging. I am sure you remember the Great Seal in Moscow?"

Candy asked Eric, "Is that like the Great Whale in *Moby Dick?*"

Eric was shocked. "Keep quiet!" he hissed.

The film began. The room grew hot and stuffy, and in the soporific darkness, Doc Duval's snoring could soon be heard. Candy believed it must be the soothing ambiance of the embassy that put Dr. Duval to sleep at every visit. Actually it was Jack's rum collins.

At the end of the film, the curtains were opened to let in the daylight and the spectators applauded Mr. Feeney's valiant effort to train them in antiterrorism. They must remember not to let any one of the two dozen automobiles or five hundred bicycles and scooters on the island follow too closely. And, too, Fred had better alternate his jogging around the perimeter of the grounds from clockwise to counterclockwise. No advice concerning hijacking had been offered.

Nor did anyone think to mention the skeletons found in an old escape tunnel, which is what had triggered the Doc's present visit. Afterwards, sitting on the back deck, he told Jack between cooling sips of drink number two that they were pretty old bones and they gave his office a nice, professional appearance. Mr. Feeney departed the next morning on the Thursday flight to Miami and Washington. He was considering retirement. As Doc Duval put it, *"Monsieur Feeney, il est fini."*

But Zimmer still had a job to do. Carlos had agreed to send two gendarmes to officially unlock the warehouse Thursday morning. Eric and Zimmer were to be driven down there by Fred after breakfast. Eric was not in a good mood, though. He was still mulling over what Candy had told him the night before; that he must attend Konrad's forthcoming wedding in Keene Valley. He had vowed never to return. Too far, too dangerous, too many dead bodies. A living hell, in fact. Konrad would just have to get married in Washington or even New York. *No, not New York; Candy would want to drag me to watch the tennis at Flushing Meadows. What a name! Sounds like a sewage plant. How very suitable.*

Candy had explained the sentimental reason behind the choice of location. "Pretty macabre, I'd say!" Eric had remarked. She went on to say that it was the bride who made the wedding plans. "Well, tell him to find another bride," had been Eric's unreasonable reply. But obviously weakening, his next sentence was, "But, I'm not paying for any of it! It's going to cost plenty in transportation just to get there." Candy omitted mentioning the cost for flowers and refreshments to remind him: "Now, you've already paid for my ticket to New York. But if you would stop in Washington to file a hushhush report on negotiations with Carlos, your airfare would be reimbursed. Claudia could drive us the rest of the way."

"Well, I am still undecided and you are not to nag me, Candace!" Eric, though, continued to fret. "They may want an automobile for a wedding present. Ridiculous custom, dreadful expense. At least one doesn't have to buy a gift for a funeral."

However, all that was forgotten in the eerie-looking warehouse of High Seas Unlimited, which was really a small storefront with a big name. Bags and bags of "white stuff" were piled up in bins and spilling over on the floor.

"What do you think, Zimmer? Narcotics?"

"I don't know. A lot of it looks like that talcum stuff found in your closet. Sort of flakely too, though. Look, do you suppose there is a lab here to test this stuff?"

"Doctor Duval has a small one. But I suspect it is more for making bathtub gin."

"Let's first have a look at some of the bags in the middle, and at the stuff in the middle of a bag here and there and down at the bottom, too. We can't examine every one. We must be selective."

"I'll get Fred to help." Fred was waiting outside, polishing the fenders of the old Packard. He loved that antique; called it 'Auntie," of course. He went inside to help when called by Eric. But on seeing half a dozen dusty bags brought out, he didn't want them to soil her interior.

"Well then, Fred, put them in the trunk," suggested Eric.

"There isn't one. I'll go find a cloth or clean bag to hold them and be right back, sir."

They did manage to get the bags to Doc Duval's lab, but it was useless. So was the lab. They must wait for the Saturday flight to send them to the Narcotics Laboratory in Miami. If those bags contained nothing illegal, Zimmer would look like a fool.

Eric said, "Look here, you could call your office and ask for instructions for simple testing here. Have you tasted the stuff?"

That idea repelled Zimmer. The same for Eric. Zimmer said, "I know, I'll ask the Miami office to send someone down on the afternoon flight today."

They dashed back to the Packard parked outside Doc Duval's office, raced back to the embassy, and placed a hurried and urgent call to Miami. "We're short-staffed but will do our best," was the reply. They then relaxed and took a stroll down to the beach to watch Evert working on his balloon.

Chapter 29

# Up a Tree

Meanwhile in Elizabethtown Lieutenant Whistler was ready to hit the ceiling. He slammed down the telephone receiver, stood up, and began to pace back and forth in his tiny office overlooking the shady Courthouse Green. His mind was in a whirl.

"Those fools in Washington, letting that girl go free to leave the country. 'Well, Miss Parody was with her mother,' they said! What's that got to do with it? Had they checked the entry date in her passport, as he had requested? No, they were 'busy with more pressing work.' Now, why has she suddenly gone to Beaulinia? As a guest of Ambassador Bohner? No, not him. He'd never allow her in the house. But now, Mrs. Bohner, a lady who obviously must spend much time outwitting and outmaneuvering her husband, might have changed his mind. Better call him and find out."

It took an hour to get through. While waiting, he again wearily reviewed the case. Was it "a gingham-dog and calico-cat" situation, where they knocked the stuffing out of each other? *We're pretty certain Riddle killed Parody with Cough's gun, supplied by Wall and delivered by the hippie roomer, our Cabbage-patch "doll." Then Jane Wall got the hippie out of the way to keep her quiet. But why were Wall and Riddle compelled to kill the colonel? Did he have something they wanted, or wouldn't do something* they wanted? And Brasher with his airplane, is he the mastermind and supplier? Why were Ernest and Harold killed? Were they bribed by Riddle or innocent victims in the way? Their death weapons were so obviously unusual—and silent. Now, who would own a hunting bow and a stun gun? And who all was in the studio to leave that slip of paper with its odd riddle? Could Martha the cook be involved? I'd rather have a tooth pulled than question her again. I'll bet she knows a lot more than she's chosen to tell. I know, I'll send Sergeant Vitus to pay her a visit. She's a clever girl.

The telephone ring interrupted further musing, with the operator's, "Ready with your call to Beaulinia, sir."

"Ambassador Bohner?"

"Speaking."

"Lieutenant Whistler in Elizabethtown. How are you, sir?"

"I'm glad you called, Lieutenant. There have been some rather unusual happenings here."

"How's that, Ambassador?"

"A Drug Enforcement agent arrived from Miami to check out a warehouse rented by Colonel Parody, called High Seas Unlimited. It's full of bags of white stuff. And I found some in a secret closet in the library, too. It seems like talcum, but we're getting it tested as soon as possible. Lab facilities are not very good here. In fact, the one we thought to use, Doctor Duval's, has quite gone to the dogs."

"I'm sorry, Ambassador, but the connection isn't too good. You said you were going to use dogs? Good idea."

"Oh, I say, I hadn't thought of that. You see, Agent Zimmer and I are reluctant to do the taste test."

"It tasted what, sir?"

"No, tested. I'll inform you of the results in a day or so. Perhaps we shall see you in Keene Valley after Labor Day, when we arrive to attend two family weddings: our son's, and my wife's sister's to that Col. Abel Smythe. Thank you for calling."

"Ambassador, wait a minute, sir! Perhaps you can help me. Are you still there?"

"Why, yes, Lieutenant, as I said, I plan to be here until Labor Day."

"Uh, the purpose of my call to you was to ask if Miss Jennifer Parody and her mother were visiting you."

"Not on your life, Lieutenant!"

"Well, are they in Beaulinia?"

"Oh, yes, they are staying at the British Embassy. Mrs. Healey, the ambassador's wife, and Mrs. Parody are old friends."

"Do you know what the Parodys are doing there?"

"Absolutely not! I won't allow that woman or her mother in this house. Although my wife did mention arranging a tennis match soon. But they'll have to stay out of the house."

"Perhaps Mrs. Bohner would have more information."

"That's true, Lieutenant. She does have a habit of keeping things to herself for a while and then suddenly springing them on me."

"May I talk with her now?"

"I don't believe so. I think she's up in the balloon."

(*Now, am I hearing correctly?* wondered Whistler. *What does he mean? No, I don't want to know!*) Aloud he asked, "Would you mind asking her to call me if she knows anything of importance?"

"I say, Lieutenant, personal long-distance calls from here are frightfully expensive."

"Oh, I mean, call collect, of course. She can just ask for the Elizabethtown Sheriff's Office." (No sense in giving him the number, Whistler realized. He'd garble it.) "Well, thank you, Ambassador—oh, and if Miss Jenny were to suddenly depart, would you phone me immediately—collect, of course."

"Of course, Lieutenant. Anything we can do to help."

"Thank you, sir. Good-bye." Whistler thought, *I must have called him on one of his vague days!*

Then, "Sergeant Vitus! Ginny! Would you come in, please."

Yes, Candy was up in a balloon. Also up in a tree now with Evert. They'd had a beautiful flight hovering over the island until a fresh wind riffled and Evert became ruffled. They thus found themselves balanced precariously in a mahogany tree on the British Embassy grounds. Candy was thankful it wasn't French, Italian, or German. Ambassador Healey could handle this with aplomb. "So glad you could drop in," he jested, as he put up a ladder which the athletic Jenny managed to scramble up easily and help Candy descend to the garden.

"Coming, Evert?" she called.

"A captain never leaves his ship," replied the stalwart balloonist.

"Nor a hot-airman his gondola," added Healey. "But I'm sure you could pause for refreshment. Just toss down a rope and let's see if we can maneuver you out of the tree tops."

Evert and balloon eventually touched ground to enjoy an English "elevenses." The ladies made quite a pet of this "nice-looking, cornfed boy from Iowa." And all wanted to go ballooning.

In the course of a pleasant conversation, Candy announced her son's wedding date, to be followed the next day by her sister's; and lamented that she would miss watching the semifinals and finals at Flushing Meadows. "I've been looking forward to it so, and really feel it should take precedence over these love affairs. After all, tennis is a love match, too, for some of us." Then she regretted mentioning that when Jenny asked:

"Candy, how's the weeding going on your tennis court."

Evert piped up, "Oh, I finished doing that, Mrs. Bohner, but meant to ask you what you meant about replacing the weeds."

Candy tried to hide her embarrassment and subterfuge

with, "I guess I didn't make myself clear. Just fill in any holes and divots. It's difficult to keep a grass court smooth."

"Well, then," boomed Jenny heartily, "I challenge you to the Beaulinia Women's Finals today. I'll be over at two."

Candy reluctantly agreed. Then she commented on the nice tan Jenny was acquiring.

"I wanted to cover up the prison pallor before going home."

Candy winced, feeling guilty, although she told herself it was Eric who believed Jenny should still be in prison developing a pallor. *But good news for Eric: Jenny's mentioned going home,* she thought.

"When will that be?" she asked.

"Oh, not for a couple of weeks. It's just divine here," answered Jenny's mother. "And Emily is making it all so pleasant. It's such a tiny place and no traffic. One can walk everywhere. The beaches need improving, but I daresay, all in good time."

Candy felt she ought to be going since there were chores to do and Eric's lunch to prepare before their tennis match. She'd see them later, and on departing told Evert she'd send Jack and Fred to help him with the balloon.

Jenny arrived promptly at two. Candy, Eric, and Zimmer were just finishing lunch when they heard Emily's minicar chugging up the drive. Before Eric could say anything, Candy dashed out of the dining room, grabbing racquets and balls in the hall, on her way to greet Jenny and Emily before they could enter the house. She then whisked Jenny around outside to the tennis court, while Emily drove off. Candy explained that Eric was tied up with stuffy sessions—or rather sessions with stuffy people—and could not be disturbed.

They played for an hour or so until it grew too hot and humid. Jenny suggested a swim. She and "Mummers" had discovered a charming cove tucked away not far from the Healey's own shabby beach. Candy rushed into the house to find a swimsuit and towel. Jenny had brought hers.

They walked the short distance to the hidden cove and enjoyed a refreshing romp in the water, but not for long. Candy disliked being continually slapped by waves. While drying off on the rocks, Jenny casually asked, "Candy, I was wondering if you would do me a favor. Remember the jewelry Dadders left in your care for me? It's rather valuable and so is what Mummers foolishly brought with her. I'm worried about being picked up for questioning again when we return to the States. We aren't going near Washington, of course. But I have no safe place to keep them if we travel around."

"Oh, Jenny, I'm sure you're completely cleared. They returned your passport. Where would you be going?"

"Mummers wants to visit Miami and New York City. And that's where we could meet you—working out itineraries and such."

"Why not see some tennis, too? I do expect to attend a few matches before going to Keene Valley."

"That's a great idea. Now, I was wondering if you could take our jewelry with you, since you travel under diplomatic immunity, or diplomatic pouch and all that. It would be utterly safe, and such a relief to us."

"Well, I brought them once, although without knowing what I was carrying, so I guess I could do it again."

"You are a dear! Let me fetch them," and she quickly disappeared around a sand dune before Candy could say anything else. "It looks rather battered," laughed Jenny, returning and carrying a locked, metal box. "I'll just slip it in your towel bag here and no one will be the wiser. Security means a lot in life," she sighed.

Candy was surprised at the swiftness of unfolding events and soon returned home heavily laden. No one was around. Eric had gone to the airport with Mr. Zimmer. She went upstairs to change and relax.

## Chapter 30

## Going to the Dogs

Candy happened to glance out her bedroom window to notice two backpacked hikers trudging up the front drive. It gradually dawned on her that she was watching her own daughter Klara and son-in-law David. Excitedly she called to them out the window, then flew down the stairs and out the door to hug them both.

"I thought you were back home in New Mexico," she exclaimed.

Between hows, whats, and wheres, she learned that Carlos and Charlotte had offered them free transportation to Beaulinia as a surprise to their parents.

"Did you reach the top of whatever it was you climbed?" Candy asked eagerly.

"Of course! Or more accurately, in a way," replied Klara. "Didn't you get my postcards? After the mudslide knocked us out of further climbing, I was still determined to reach the top of something. It was David's idea to go over to Chamonix and ride the cable car up Mont Blanc."

"Isn't that stretching the truth a little as a climber?"

"In the snows of Mont Blanc, it's just a little white lie," replied David.

"Well, come in and let's find a room for you and get you settled."

Now Eric and Zimmer had been at the Beaulinia Airport to pick up the narcotics-testing equipment. Eric had been too distracted to notice the arrival of Klara and David at the same time. To his utter astonishment and Zimmer's, two dogs were delivered to them instead of an agent. "Are you sure?" Eric asked the freight attendant. "What would we do with them?"

Zimmer answered, "They're sniffers."

"They look like pinschers to me."

"That too, sir, but they can recognize the scent of illegal substances."

"I don't think my wife will be too keen about having two large dogs around."

"Oh, they're well trained. I've worked with dogs before. Let's see, this one's tagged Dopey. Excuse me, it's Dobey. And the other one is—Killis."

The dogs and carton of testing equipment were brought over to the Packard. Fred was horrified to learn that the beasts were to be chauffered in his immaculate vehicle. Eric told him they could ride in the trunk . . . , "Oh, no, I forget, there is no trunk."

Fred suggested that they run along behind. But they had already jumped in and sprawled on the back seat. Eric and Zimmer were forced to sit on the jump seats.

They drove swiftly to the High Seas Unlimited warehouse. No thought was given to calling the gendarmes to reopen it. Zimmer said he could easily pick the lock. Unknown to them, though, the lock had been replaced with a new tamper-proof "molasses" type to keep out the Parody ladies until a thorough search had been made.

Eric and Zimmer found themselves in a very sticky predicament. Zimmer's skeleton key was stuck in the oozing substance, while Zimmer had some difficulty removing his hands from the same. Standing by and holding the dogs at bay, Fred offered to unscrew the hinges. He dropped the dogs' leashes and went to the Packard tool box for a wrench and screwdriver. The dogs galloped off to the pier and sat down panting in the heat. After the door was unhinged, they had to be rounded up and dragged into the building to do their sniffing. They detected no illegal substances, but did manage to get covered with white dust which stuck nicely to their molasses-covered faces and paws.

After this discouraging result, the dogs were led out, the door rehinged, and all headed for the car. Fred managed to get there first to lock all doors and refuse admittance. He insisted that Dobey and Killis needed a long walk after their confining flight. Dog-handler Nat Zimmer wisely agreed. Fred did permit Eric to enter for the ride back to the embassy. They drove off, leaving Zimmer to the dogs.

Eric was delighted to find Klara and David at the house. On going out to the terrace, he congratulated her on receiving her Ph.D. recently and wanted to know more about her dissertation. They sat down while David went off for a stroll.

"It's sort of silly, Daddy. I took those nineteenth-century nicknames of evolutional origin and development of language and applied them to my archaeological knowledge and language of the Navaho."

"You mean the 'bow-wow' or imitation theory and the 'pooh-pooh' or natural-sound theory. Isn't there another one?"

"The 'yo-ho-ho,' gesture-speech one, you mean?"

"Ah, yes." (Pause) "Now, I should think that Navayo-ho-ho would . . ."

"Don't say it, Daddy!"

David now joined them to enjoy an ice-cold beer.

Klara went on, "David's finally found the time from teaching to start his dissertation. It's very interesting and should be highly controversial. It's a new translation and interpretation of *The Horsite Saga*. Tell him, David."

"Yes, I believe I have discovered the true cause of the Trojan War from my research. As you know *The Horsite Saga* is a pre-history tale of Chief Horsa, so called because of his ability to tame the wild horses on the steppes of Ararat, in eastern Turkey. Or it could be that the beast was named after him. Scholars still disagree. No matter. Moving ever westward while trading on his name and beast, he easily overcame Hittites, Aphrodites, Ankarites, and most important for our story, the Trogladites, ancestors of the Trojans; all by horsepower. There on the shores of the Aegean he established a mighty empire.

"Now in the reign of his son, Horsa II, who continued to hold a monopoly on horses, the ever-eager and avid Greeks, rising with the dawn of western civilization and learning of this unique animal, ventured forth in frail boats across the foaming Aegean to his capital at Troy, then called Trog, to see for themselves and place an order. Delivery by Horsites would be D.O.D., that is, drachmas on delivery, they agreed. However, en route many of the horses sickened and died during their swim across the Hellespont and the overland drive to Macedonia. On arrival, the Horsites demanded from the Greeks immediate payment for the full number of horses ordered, failing to mention that only half had survived. Being astute horsetraders they quickly left the area after receiving their money and before the Greeks had time to make an accurate count.

"The Greeks never forgot such treachery nor the lesson of good horse sense in trading. They thrived on it, growing horse-powerful themselves. Now Horsa's descendents down to King Priam continued to be the leading dealers in horses and related items such as reins and saddlebags; a monopoly so strategically located at the crossroads of the Aegean and the Bosphorus. When glib-talking salesman of a son, Paris, turned up in Menelaus's court and boldly carried off his wife, Helen, without even swapping a horse for her, this was too much for the Greeks. They were determined to beat the horshite out of the Trojans this time.

"As we all know, they got their full revenge so aptly by building a wooden horse to fill with warriors outside the walls of Troy. By such perfidy of their own, they sacked and destroyed the city down to the last man and boy, and carted away the women and horses, the latter being the more prized booty. To blot out all memory of the Horsites, they renamed the animal *hippos,* and thus became the first *hippos* generation."

Eric was astounded and could only offer David another beer.

Meawhile, Zimmer, left to his own devices, took the dogs and testing equipment to Doc Duval's lab to begin work. But the dogs were obviously hungry, so Zimmer asked the doctor to take them up to the embassy to be fed.

Doc was glad to have an excuse for dropping in to enjoy Jack's generous rum collins, so off he went, dragged by two galloping beasts straining at their leashes to arrive exhausted and thirsty at Jack's kitchen door.

"Where'd you get the dogs?" Jack asked in surprise.

"Zimmer sent them. They need feeding."

"Here? I haven't any dog food. Let 'em loose to catch rabbits."

Doc and Jack unleashed the two dobermans, who then galloped off, first to the cowshed, Jack knew from the sudden mooing Bessay let forth, and then, changing direction, charged around the house, past the terrace and into the woods.

David sat up with a start. "Did you see that?"

Eric turned in his chair. "See what?"

"Do you have deer here, Dr. Bohner?" He always called Eric that, knowing how hard earned that title was.

"Why, no, do we, Candy?" Candy had just come out of the house and sat down.

Yelping was now heard and thrashing in the underbrush. Jack and Doc were glimpsed fleetingly as they ran past the terrace, calling to the Bohners, "We'll catch 'em. They're just hungry. Here, Dobey, here, Killis."

"Ah, yes," remembered Eric. "They must be Zimmer's dogs. Arrived on the plane with the testing equipment."

"Why would Mr. Zimmer send for his dogs? Does he plan to stay long?" asked Candy, a trifle worried.

"No, the Drug Administration sent them. They're dope sniffers."

"You mean like glue sniffers?"

"They detect drugs by smell."

"Well, thank goodness they didn't discover any on us. They look awfully big. Now where are we going to put them?" Candy was growing nervous.

Jack had returned to the terrace and answered her question. "They're really outdoor critters. They can sleep in one of the outbuildings, if we can catch 'em. I'll have to feed them, Mrs. Bohner. What would you suggest?"

Candy thought for a moment. "Oh, I know. Give them last night's goulash; there's lots of that left over." She refrained from adding that no one had eaten much of it, laced as it was with an abundance of wine.

In time, the dogs gobbled it up and settled down to sleep off the effects.

Jack muttered to himself, "At least the dogs appreciate my gourmet cooking. They'll be whining for more when they wake up."

Later the Bohner family and a weary Mr. Zimmer went off to the Casa Blanca for dinner, where the conquerors of Mont Blanc were to be guests of honor. Halfway through the meal, Carlos, with a sly smile, mentioned that the Parody ladies must have tampered with the new warehouse molasses lock. Sheepishly, Eric explained that he and Agent Zimmer were the tamperers. He got more laughter than sympathy on giving them the sticky details and messy results. And for all their efforts, they would have to settle for just talcum being stored there.

David remarked, "It might be worth something if it is talcum. Jenny Parody could package it as 'Paradox Talcum— the wonder flea powder for dogs. A pinch of talc on your doberman will keep him away all day.'"

Carlos proposed a toast to Dobey and Killis, the Paradox Twins, and added the hope that the island was not also going to the dogs.

## Chapter 31

## Breeding, Instinct, and Training

By Monday, Candy remembered to tell Eric about the box of jewelry Jenny had given her. He was outraged and still angry over the lawyer's bill, though Candy had passed it on to Jenny. She had expected this reaction, so waited quietly until he calmed down and became curious. "It was all done so casually and quickly," Candy explained. "I didn't have time to refuse. Do you think we should open it?"

Eric gave the matter some thought. "Zimmer was looking for narcotics. The white stuff in the lab turned out to be talcum. Although why that Cousin Peregrine of yours was hoarding talcum . . . Cornering the talc market? As David suggested, putting out Paradox Talcum—he's very clever to give it that name—to relieve your dog of fleas. Dogs! That's it, Candy. We'll give it to the dogs—to sniff, I mean. They are bred for that.

"Now, Eric, why have them sniff jewelry?"

"Because the jewelry isn't jewelry, it's cocaine."

"Well there can't be much of it. The box isn't that large."

"Ah, but a box that size would sell for a billion dollars, or thereabout."

"But what if it is talcum? That doesn't cost a billion."

"They would hardly be interested in smuggling talcum, Candy."

They went to consult Zimmer in the drawing room. He woke up the dogs, who had remained sleepy all weekend under Jack's care and feeding. They sniffed once, lost interest, and went back to sleep.

"So much for that theory," Candy dryly remarked. "Couldn't we just open it? Mr. Zimmer could be our witness."

Mr. Zimmer obligingly picked the lock of the metal box. They discovered no billion-dollar cocaine, but at least a million dollars worth of loose diamonds, rubies, emeralds and sapphires along with some rings and necklaces. A spectacular emerald-and-sapphire bracelet in particular caught Candy's fancy. She even tried it on, "for size," she joked.

"Well, that's that," sighed Eric, very disappointed. "We'd better put them in the safe and not back in your wet-towel bag, although not a bad hiding place, Candy."

"However," he added after they crossed the hall to the library, "we should inform Lieutenant Whistler that everything we've tested is talcum. Perhaps he can make something out of this. Er, why don't you call him, Candy. I had difficulty making myself understood last time. And tell him all you know of that Queen of Diamonds Jenny, and what you have arranged with her. Oh, and call collect, the sheriff's house, I believe."

After Candy Bohner's call, Whistler felt limp. "Why is it that everything those people touch turns to dust!" At least he did learn that the Parody ladies, "the talcum heirs," he chuckled to himself, would be returning to the States, and he did request that they be invited to Keene Valley for the weddings. He had said, "Yes, I know, Mrs. Bohner, it would be difficult to persuade your husband, but naturally, he wouldn't want to stand in the way of a murder investigation, or subvert the wheels of justice from their true course." A clinching argument, he believed. He knew his Bohners. He also knew that Mrs. B. would be having a disagreeable time right now persuading the ambassador.

*Well, what is there left?* continued Whistler to himself. *The stun gun and the bow and arrow. Now who would have a stun gun? City police use them. But we don't. I wonder where one could be bought? And then the arrow. Who goes bow-hunting in this neck of the woods? As a matter of fact, it is becoming popular with the "fancy" hunters. The old cross-bow has become pretty sophisticated. Hardly Miss Wall's type. Or Elmer's. I must check out sports and gun shops. Let's see first what the telephone book has to offer.*

There was a knock on the door. Abel Smythe poked his head in. "Just thought while I was in the building I'd see how you were getting on with the Parody, Middleton, Dibble, and Wall case. Sounds like the name of a city law firm, doesn't it," he laughed.

"Ah, come in, Colonel. I was just mulling things over. You hunt, don't you? Where would I find a really complete hunting outfitter?"

"Hunting-season fever, Whistler?"

"You could say that. Only my game is usually two-legged."

"I must take you out in the woods on maneuvers this fall with my son's Commando Club. It can be rough, but invigorating."

"Not a bad idea, Smythe. I'm looking for something sophisticated."

"Well, there are a couple of excellent places in Lake Placid. Olympic Armory and S & S, that's for Shootin' and Security; both are on Main Street. There's a surprisingly good new one right here in E-town, called Split Rock Guns, and I believe a small one in Keene, the East Hill Firearms."

"By the way, Smythe, congratulations on your forthcoming marriage to Miss Fran Amber. My mother likes her column in that woman's magazine. Perhaps later, after she's married, she'll turn her attention to etiquette in the field or good manners in the stream. That's an amazing family you are marrying into."

"I know what you mean, Whistler," he said with a twinkle. "How fortunate that none of them live all year 'round in the area. But thanks." He marched off, leaving Whistler to continue his hunting through the Yellow Pages. Then the solution—or one of them—dawned on him. He never knew how, really. Just instinct, training, and the words "Commando Club," he guessed. He got up and left the office in a hurry.

## Chapter 32

## Torpedoed

Agent Zimmer departed on the Tuesday-morning flight with equipment and groggy dogs, who had spent a long, soporific, and hazy weekend sharing rum collinses with Jack and Doc.

Travel plans for the others were discussed endlessly. Klara and David did have to return to their jobs and decided on the Thursday flight. Candy would leave the following Saturday for New York. And Eric—the real cause of the endless discussion—Candy had told him he must get Carlos to provide him with all sorts of material to present in Washington.

"Now, Eric, remember your airfare gets paid for that way. After all, you can't miss your son's wedding."

"Well, I'm not staying overnight in Keene Valley."

Candy refrained from telling him that he would probably be spending several nights, unless he could produce a genie with a flying machine to whisk him in and out that Saturday. She thought it was a pity Evert's balloon couldn't help Eric. *But that's ridiculous. Anyway, it's Eric's problem, since he's so stubborn. I'm not going to think about it. At all!*

Of course she did, and arranged his flight for the week after hers, allowing him several days in Washington before being driven northwards by Claudia. That day had not been settled and Candy made no suggestion. But her departure went smoothly, until reaching Miami when she discovered she had forgotten her admission tickets to the U.S. Open. She phoned Eric to have him absolutely, positively and without fail, send them on the Tuesday flight. Meanwhile, she'd hop over to St. Petersburg to stay with her sisters, Honey and Peaches.

They were happy to have her and eager to hear all the news, as long as they were not involved. Candy had instructed Eric to call her early in St. Pete, the minute the tickets were put on board Tuesday's flight and before she'd return to Miami early afternoon. But he hadn't phoned before it was time for Honey to drive her to the St. Petersburg airport, She, therefore, gave Peaches lengthy instructions on what to tell Eric if he should call. Peaches looked up from her piano where she was preoccupied with revising one of her compositions and asked, "What shall I tell him if he doesn't call up?" Candy didn't feel that required an answer; after all, Peaches' remarks were priceless.

All went smoothly and enjoyably for Candy after that. The tennis matches were exciting and with plenty of upsets. All too soon, Claudia and Eric arrived in Greenwich, where she had been staying in Fran's house, to collect her for the drive to Keene Valley.

By the time they arrived late Friday afternoon, the rest of the family was already there. John and Pattee had come a few days earlier to help with preparations for both Konrad's and Fran's weddings. Chester, who was Konrad's best man, and Horace, this time without Mary and the children, but with his frisky retriever, Torpedo, had just arrived before the Bohners pulled up to the house. Pattee rushed up to the car, shouting excitedly, "Have you heard the news? We simply couldn't believe it. Fran's in shock and absolutely speechless."

"Well that *is* news," agreed Candy.

"No, no, I mean Bud Abel Smythe has been arrested for the murders of Elmer Dibble and Ernest Middleton."

Eric's immediate response was, "That's just too much! I'm returning to Washington—this instant. Candy, do you hear? Are you coming with me?"

"Now, Eric, let's first hear the details." She awkwardly pulled herself out of the small and crowded Volkswagen. "And have some coffee or something, too. Is Martha still reigning in the kitchen?"

"No, she's gone," replied Pattee, leading the way up the stone steps and into the house. "Nittie's will has provided for her in comfort. It's all right to talk. Fran is staying up at the studio. She'll survive. It's more humiliating to be stood up at the altar than anything else I imagine. Oh, and by the way, Lily and her parents and sister are staying in the Gate House. We haven't told them anything, at Konrad's request. And Konrad said to tell you he'd be back in time for supper."

Candy managed to greet everybody before being rushed to the fireplace to sit and listen to the tale of the errant, or rather incarcerated, groom.

Pattee continued, "Well that nice Lieutenant Whistler dropped by last night to bring us the shocking news. Fran had obviously heard earlier and instead of telling us, had gone out in a hurry—over to Elizabethtown, I suppose, to find out what to do. He didn't go into all the details, but that just a hunch made him check up on crossbows and stun guns, which led him to Bud's collection. It seems he had quite an armory. Funny, Fran never told us. But then we haven't been here since the murders. Was it only a month and a half ago?"

While Pattee paused for breath, John spoke up. "Has anyone notified Miss Gentle that she'll have only one marriage service to perform instead of two?"

"Oh, she's probably heard by now. Bad news gets around fast. Or would this be good news for Miss Gentle? I think she found us all a bit trying," remarked Pattee.

"Well, I'd better call her to assure her we'll all be at the church at noon for the Blessing-Bohner ceremony." John was more in charge than Eric.

"Oh, do you think Fran will attend?"

"Pattee, what difference does that make?" John was growing impatient. He felt the way Eric did about the Amber clan, with one difference. He had been born into it and had grown accustomed to it.

Konrad's and Lily's wedding the next day went smoothly. As Pattee remarked, "They got hitched without a hitch." Except for one small, nervous error on Konrad's part. When the service reached "I, Konrad, take thee, Lily Maria," he said, "I, Konrad, take thee, Lily Marlene." The family hoped Mr. and Mrs. Blessing had not noticed that slip, although the bridesmaid, Lily's sister, was trying to hold back the giggles. It was a pretty ceremony—white church, white flowers, white gown. Lily loved white.

The wedding reception was a buffet luncheon in the Amber garden. They had cancelled the one planned at the Spread Eagle Restaurant, to use up the food bought for Fran's party. Later, after Chester returned from driving the newlyweds on their honeymoon to Lake Placid, they discussed where to take the Blessings for dinner. Well, it would not be to the Spread Eagle now, where the Blessings might overhear the news of Bud Smythe's arrest. Someone suggested the Deer's Head Inn in Elizabethtown. "But that's across the street from the jail where Bud Smythe is being held," Chester pointed out. Perhaps they'd better prepare a light supper at home. Pattee and Candy went to the kitchen to do their best. John was soon called to drive down to Valley Grocery for a few items.

The Blessings were planning to leave early the following morning. They said their good-byes after supper, anxious to get out of the big house and back to their private quarters at the Gate House. "Strange, nervous family" was the Blessings' opinion. "But at least Konrad seemed normal." And they had given him their Blessing!

"All right, Pattee, tell me more," said Candy, returning to her chair around the fireplace after Lily's family left. "So Lieutenant Whistler had a hunch about Bud. But of course a man can have a collection of armaments. You should see Eric's spears, daggers, dueling pistols and . . ."

"Of course, but Whistler traced the purchase of the stun gun. Can you imagine Abel—well he's not so able now—disabled is more like it. Well, Bud bought the stun gun right here in K.V. at the gun store next to the Noonmark Diner."

"But what was his motive?"

"Let me think."

John answered, "It must have been to silence Ernest and Harold. Pretty nasty way to do that. He knew Brasher well too, who is out on bail. Nobody has cracked yet."

Candy was thinking aloud. "You know, I can't picture Abel as being involved. Now from what I heard about his macho, sky-diving son, Caine, who bought the old Taylor chicken farm, and his commando-dressed pals . . ."

Eric interrupted, "What about Riddle's murder?"

"We thought Bud was probably responsible for that. He could have easily gone to Washington at Brasher's request. But Whistler doesn't agree."

"Jenny did it," Eric stated firmly.

"Oh, Eric, you don't know."

John agreed with Eric. "I think Whistler agrees too, Candy. He mentioned as motive a double crime of passion. One, in revenge for her father's cold-blood murder, and two, as a spurned woman in love. She'd met Riddle on a cruise ship."

"Oh, my goodness! Remember, Pattee, her telling us about sharing a cabin with a Latin type of 'perfect gentleman'?"

John suddenly remembered something else. "Candy, Whistler was hoping you'd be bringing Jenny to the wedding."

"John," exclaimed Eric, "you can hardly expect us to transport an illicit criminal across state lines! Why, that would be white slavery, I believe!"

"The real reason," Candy said, "was that she and her mother never showed up in New York. I guess that's why I caught a glimpse of Whistler in the back of the church. He was looking for Jenny there."

Claudia asked John about the bags of cocaine in Aunt Nittie's Buick.

"At least the lieutenant has some proof. Fingerprints of Miss Wall and her brother were found on the bags. A hurried, sloppy job on their part. They must have been interrupted by Howard's unexpected arrival."

"All right then," persisted Claudia. "Who killed Elmer?"

"Now let me see," mused Pattee. "Oh, yes. Wasn't he back in the hospital hiding from Lieutenant Whistler? I guess he put himself into a plastic trash bag and fell asleep, drunk. Then someone tied up the bag and carted it to the dump, where Horace found him."

Claudia wasn't quite satisfied. "Maybe someone put him in the bag after he fell asleep."

"I'm sure Whistler considered that," John said. "Miss Wall had no compunction in disposing of the hippie in her cabbage patch."

They believed they could all relax now. Justice would take its course. Fran would stay in the studio for a few more days. Although "appalled" at Bud's treachery, she did find a lawyer for him, and must feel relieved that he was arrested before and not after their wedding. She really wasn't very successful in selecting husbands.

Then Candy remembered Jenny's jewelry. Eric snorted, "Probably stolen gems. They're a band of jewel thieves, I suspect. Probably are known to Interpol as the Parody Diamond Ring."

Pattee joined in with, "Aren't diamonds called 'ice'? That would make Cousin Peregrine 'the Ice King.'"

"And coming to a fitting end in the ice house, too," added Eric.

"Well, I have the jewels now," said Candy.

"Quite. And keep them in a safe place. By the way, where are you keeping them?"

"I had to rent a safe-deposit box in Greenwich, while staying at Fran's. I don't know why Jenny didn't pick them up."

"See that Jenny reimburses you for that expense," ordered Eric.

John remarked, "Perhaps she'll contact you in Washington."

Eric brightened. "That's brilliant, John. And then we can have her arrested."

John thought. "Candy should call Lieutenant Whistler now concerning this to alert Washington."

"Yes, but the jewelry is in Greenwich," Candy reminded them.

"Jenny doesn't know that. You'd better try to get hold of Whistler now, Candy. Try his home. Here, I'll give you the number."

Candy and John went to the phone on the stair landing. "John, you talk to him, please. I don't seem to make myself clear when I speak to him by phone."

After John finished with the call he told them Whistler was grateful.

Sunday morning they were all standing on the front steps surrounded by the Bohners' luggage, waiting for Claudia to bring up the car parked down by the barn. Eric was anxious to depart. Then Candy remembered how she had missed watching the women's finals on television yesterday. But today would be shown the men's finals. Surely they could postpone their departure until tomorrow, she suggested. Eric's reply was shockingly rude except for the latter part, "Here's the car now. Get in, Candace!"

Candy said her good-byes, wondering where Horace was, though, and whispered to Pattee. "Please send me all the news on the case and when the trial is to be."

Then Horace, who had taken Torpedo for a romp in the meadow, came running up from there to say good-bye, they thought. He was waving something in the air, while Torpedo jumped around and barked excitedly.

"Wait, wait!" called Horace, "Torpedo just found something. It's—it's a—a hand. A human hand!"

Pattee, unbelieving, joked, "Ah, the hand that bites him."

John corrected her, "That's 'feeds' him, dearie," but then blanched on examining it more closely.

Chester, who had finished loading the bags in the car now, wanted to know "who has had a hand in this" until he too looked at it closely.

Eric, pausing to look momentarily when Horace called, now stumbled quickly into the car and shouted, "Drive off, Claudia." As the Bohners sped around the driveway circle in a cloud of dust, Eric's voice could be heard in anger, "Damn that Torpedo! Full speed ahead!"